CHASING THE PUCK

SIN BIN STORIES BOOK 2

LYSSA LEMIRE

Copyright © 2024 by Lyssa Lemire

All rights reserved.

No part of this book may be reproduced in any form or by any electronic or mechanical means, including information storage and retrieval systems, without written permission from the author, except for the use of brief quotations in a book review.

Cover by Mayhem Cover Creations

❋ Created with Vellum

1
TUCK

One hundred and eleven days. That's how long it's been since the last time I had sex.

For some people, that might not be a long time. For me? It's a fucking eternity.

Tonight, breaking this dry spell would be as easy as snapping my fingers. The house where I live with four of my teammates is packed for a victory party. The place is buzzing, drinks are flowing, spirits are high, and beautiful women have been shamelessly ogling me all night.

I'm talking to one right now, a girl in a tight blue dress who would only be too eager to help me reset the clock on this one-hundred-and-eleven-day celibacy streak.

She's making that very clear with the way she's batting her long eye-lashes at me; with the way she lets out squeals of laughter whenever I make a lame joke that isn't funny at all; with the way she's been finding any excuse to touch my arm or my chest; and especially with the way she's blasting me with fuck-me eyes blatant enough to spot from outer space.

Hell, ending this dry spell would be *easier* than snapping my fingers.

But I'm not looking at the girl standing in front of me, the one whose body language is practically begging me to bring her up to my room.

No. I'm looking at someone else.

I'm looking at the girl across the room. The one with chestnut hair, sparkly green eyes, and a light dusting of pale freckles on the apples of her cheeks.

The girl I haven't been able to stop thinking about since I met her—one hundred and eleven days ago.

The girl who's fixed herself in my mind and who's kept my cock from as much as twitching for anyone else.

The girl who says she wants nothing to do with me. Olivia Lockley.

She's over there talking to Summer, her best friend and my teammate Hudson's girlfriend.

Her eyebrows bounce and her face becomes animated as she says something to Summer. There's gotta be something really wrong with me, because I'm a lot more interested in wondering what she's talking about than I am in the fact that the girl in front of me just mentioned how flexible she is.

Then Olivia's face scrunches up, and I see her throw her head back to let out a peal of laughter. My heart leaps in my chest. I strain my ears to try and catch a note of it.

Olivia's laughter—her real laughter, not the sarcastic, derisive kind she so often directs at me—is a sound like silver windchimes stirred by a gentle breeze. The kind of sound that grabs your heart.

But of course, I don't catch even a hint of the sound over the pounding music and the loud rumble of conversation from the party.

My lips tug downward in disappointment. I raise my red Solo cup to my lips and down the last of my beer. Needing a refill will give me an excuse to disengage from the conversation with the girl in front of me. I'm just not feeling it.

I don't want to be a dick, though. This girl—I'm pretty sure her name is Samantha—has been nice. Plus, she's a fucking knock-out. If I weren't in this weird hundred-plus-day funk, I'd be more than willing to give her exactly what she's looking for.

So, instead of leaving her high and dry and bereft of a hunky hockey player, I call out to one of my teammates I notice walking by.

"Hey, Jamie!" I wave my hand to get the freshman second-liner's attention.

He responds with a nod and walks over. I greet him with a clasp on the shoulder, and when my hand has a good hold of him, I do a little switcheroo, positioning him in front of Samantha while I step to the side.

"Samantha here was just telling me she's from Northern California, too," I say, an encouraging smile on my face as I glance between them. "Maybe you two have, uh, some acquaintances in common. Ya'll get to know each other while I refill my drink."

With that, I pull away from them and thread through the dense crowd towards the kitchen.

Okay, maybe that was pretty lame as far as introductions go. It's not like the whole of fucking North California is a small town where everyone knows everyone.

But I didn't want to dash Samantha's dreams of ending the night with a hockey player, and Jamie's so damn shy around girls that he needs an extra push sometimes. When I glance back and see that they both seem into the conversation with each other, I give myself a pat on the back.

Despite the best efforts of about a dozen scantily clad girls who try to snag my attention during the short walk through the crowd, I make it to the kitchen, where it's less crowded. I fill up my drink and take a long first drag of it while I prop my hip against the counter of our kitchen island and let my eyes fall back on Olivia.

I let out a sigh when I notice her face pinching in laughter again, and it prompts me to wonder—what the hell's gotten into me?

Why am I so hung up on the *one* girl at Brumehill College who isn't into me?

The answer most people might offer is that I'm so not used to rejection that my ego can't handle it. But that's not the case at all. Despite what most people assume, my ego isn't fragile.

If one girl doesn't want me, it's no skin off my back. There are hundreds, thousands even, of others swarming this campus willing and eager.

No, that's not it.

There's just *something* about her. Something I can't put my finger on.

Sure, it's easy to list things about her that are attractive.

She's drop-dead gorgeous for one. Funny. Witty. A good and loyal friend to Summer. And a talented as hell actress.

But all those reasons aren't why I can't get her out of my mind. There's just something ... *else* about her. Something I can't identify or name. Something that has her lodged so deeply in my head there's no way I can shake her out.

Since I can't name that *something*, the best I can do is feel it by being around her.

My gaze lingers on Olivia and Summer as I take another long sip of my drink.

She wears an oversized grey sweater, contrasting with

the tight pair of blue jeans that hug her shapely legs. Her light chestnut hair is tied back in a ponytail, showing off the smooth, creamy skin of her delicate neck.

Fuck, what I wouldn't do to grip the side of that neck, my fingers curling possessively around the back of it, my thumb brushing underneath her ear as I pull her towards me ...

Suddenly, their conversation is abruptly interrupted when a burly, tattooed goalie appears and dips down to scoop Summer up in his arms.

That would be my grumpy teammate Hudson, who's grown a hell of a lot less grumpy than he used to be since he fell for Summer, his bubbly violinist girlfriend.

Less grumpy, which isn't to say not at all. He still wears a scowl half the time and has a penchant for communicating in monosyllabic grunts. But that's just part of his charm.

It's not a scowl that Hudson's wearing right now, but rather a look of hunger. Giggles bubble from Summer as she calls something to Olivia while Hudson marches her to the stairs and no doubt up to his room.

Olivia blows Summer a kiss, shaking her head with a smile on her face as she watches her best friend and my teammate disappear upstairs.

Something tugs in my chest. I can't deny that I feel a twinge of envy at what Hudson and Summer have.

I don't dwell on it, though, because seeing Olivia standing alone hits me with a new feeling: the same sense of opportunity that rushes through me when I'm on the ice and see the perfect opening for a shot on goal.

I finish my drink with a big gulp and set the cup down on the counter before striding towards Olivia, puffed up with confidence I have no right to feel where she's concerned—except for the fact that Tuck McCoy is *always* confident.

"Olivia," I greet her with only her name, savoring the vibration of it on my lips.

She side-eyes me, not even granting me the courtesy of turning her body in my direction. "Oh, hi, Tuck. I was just wondering whether I was ready to go home, and you being right here suddenly makes that decision a lot easier."

A smile curls on my lips as she brushes past me. "But don't you want to hear my notes?"

She stops. Slowly turns towards me with a quirked eyebrow. "Notes?"

My smile curls higher. "About your latest performance. I have some ... constructive criticisms."

Her lips purse, defiance flashing in her eyes.

Olivia is a drama major, and one hell of an actress. Fact is, I couldn't find fault with any of her performances even if I wanted to.

Especially not the one she gave at the play she starred in last week. I was on my feet clapping and whistling like the rest of the crowd when she came out to take her final bow, and the reaction was totally genuine.

But that's not going to stop me from teasing her.

"Criticisms?" she repeats. The outrage is evident in her voice. She folds her arms over her chest. "What would *you* know about acting to critique *me*?"

I shrug. "I'm a quick study. Been thinking about picking up acting, actually. On the side. As a fallback option in case I get injured and can't play hockey in the future."

She pushes out a laugh. Not the sweet, genuine laugh I long to hear, but the dismissive kind I'm used to her directing at me.

Still, I'll take it.

"Right," she begins, her voice thick with sarcasm. "Actors have to work hard their whole lives to hone their art and become successful, but I'm sure you'll just *pick it up*. As a fallback."

"Glad you have as much confidence in me as I do."

"I have confidence you'll keep finding ways to prove yourself even more delusional and obnoxious than I already knew you were, that's for sure," she retorts.

"Just think," I say, lifting my gaze like I'm falling into a daydream, "we're both big movie stars and become a Hollywood power couple. Tuck and Olivia. They'd call us ... Tolivia. Or maybe Oluck."

She snorts. "You've got *no luck* if you're hoping for that to ever happen."

"We'll lead a romcom revival starring in a string of romantic movies together. The audiences won't be able to get enough of our chemistry. We'll be a pop cultural phenomenon. As big as Taylor Swift."

Another laugh pushes from her, still dismissive, but this time I don't think I'm imagining the slight twitch upward I catch at the edge of her pretty mouth.

"Why don't you go hit on Melissa instead?" she says, tilting her head towards someone over my shoulder. "She'd be happy with the attention, and she's more your type."

"She's not my type at all," I say, not turning my gaze from Olivia.

She narrows her eyes. "You didn't even look."

"Don't have to. She have chestnut hair? Deep green eyes? Light freckles on her cheeks? Freckles that stand out even more when she blushes when I pay her a compliment, even though she tries not to? If not, then she's not my type."

Normally, Olivia will hit me with a comeback without missing a beat. This time, there's about a beat and a half of silence between us.

"You do not make me blush, Tuck."

"I'll whip out my pocket mirror next time it happens and prove you wrong."

"Why do I actually believe you carry one?" she mutters, rolling her eyes. "Besides, lame pickup lines don't count as compliments."

"Lame?" I ask, making an offended face as I place my hand over my heart. "I spend a lot of time working on those pick-up lines."

"Instead of that, have you ever tried *asking*?"

Her question comes out pointed and catches me off guard. My brow furrows. "Huh?"

"Asking someone on a date. You know, like normal people who aren't full of themselves do. Instead of spewing lame pick-up lines and expecting the girl you're throwing them at to immediately jump into bed with you? You haven't tried *that*, have you?"

"Well, I ..." I never get tongue-tied when talking to a pretty girl, but the accusation she just threw at me has the ring of truth to it. I'm feeling uncharacteristically tripped up.

"Has the thought ever crossed your mind that maybe if you just *asked* me out, *maybe* if you even did it politely ..." she tilts her head, softening her voice to conclude, "I might actually say yes?"

Holy shit.

I never have flat-out asked her to go on a date with me, have I?

Is it possible that I wasted one hundred and eleven days waiting for this girl to succumb to the cocky playboy charm that's always worked on everyone else, when really I just needed a different approach?

Could I have really sealed the deal with Olivia months

ago by just ... asking her on a date? Like a *normal person* would have?

As I see her green eyes softening, her body language opening up to me as beats of silence tick between us ... fuck, I think the answer is yes.

I'll kick myself for the wasted time later. Right now, I'm just worried about making up for it.

I take a deep breath, puff out my chest, and do what I obviously should have done a long time ago.

"Olivia, could I take you on a date sometime?"

"No. Bye."

With that, she spins around and walks away.

My jaw falls when she turns her back to me. As my eyes track her striding through the crowd to the door, an impressed smile slowly tilts my open mouth.

This girl's already made me sexless, but now she's rendered me speechless, too. Two things I'm *very* not used to being.

Olivia Lockley puts me in a lot of states I'm not used to.

When she steps outside and disappears from my sight, she sure as shit doesn't disappear from my mind. I know for a fact she's not going to any time soon.

And you know what? As much as she might not want to admit it right now, I don't think I'm going to disappear from hers, either.

2

OLIVIA

"I'm spending entirely too much time around the hockey team because of you."

When my best friend Summer doesn't respond to my complaint, I turn my head to look at her. Her glazed-over eyes make it clear that it went in one ear and out the other.

I guess it's hard to blame her for being lost in a cloud of puppy love when I follow the direction of her gaze and see her boyfriend, goalie for the Brumehill Black Bears, Hudson Voss, wearing a flannel shirt tucked into a pair of jeans that hug his muscular thighs.

Summer and I just left our Art History class, the one class we're taking together this semester. We were on our way to Brumehill Brews, the on-campus café, for lunch, but first, she wanted to stop here to check out the hockey team's photoshoot.

The Black Bears coach volunteered the team to the art department for photography majors to use as practice for advertising-style photos. The photographers are having them dress up in all kinds of outfits and pose in front of various picturesque backdrop screens.

Summer says the guys think their Coach has a thing for one of the photography professors, and this is his way of scoring points with her.

The players don't seem at all inconvenienced, looking like they're having the time of their lives posing and soaking up the attention.

I'm far from surprised that a bunch of hockey boys would be total sluts for the camera.

Speaking of total sluts ...

One of the players I don't know steps aside, and suddenly my eyes are pointed at Tuck McCoy.

He's in the middle of laughing about something. Like he usually is.

His laughter makes the dimples on his cheeks carve even deeper than usual. The angle of his jaw as he laughs accentuates its razor-sharp outline, heightened by the dusting of rough stubble across it, a shade darker than his sandy-blonde hair.

Guess it's easy to laugh when you're someone like Tuck. When you're rich. When you play a sport that your entire college is obsessed with and everyone, faculty included, treats you like a celebrity for it.

I know that's a petty thought to slink into my head just at the sight of someone laughing. But those thoughts are like antibodies, keeping me from succumbing to his looks, his smooth charm, his honey-sweet southern drawl.

Antibodies I need considering he's been trying to get with me ever since we met.

But I can read him like a book.

He's everything I know I need to stay away from. Entitled. Cocky. A guy who grew up rich, privileged, and talented. A guy who internalized the message that everything he could ever want is his for the taking, that all he needs to do is reach out and grab it.

I can read him, because I know the type. I know the type intimately, sad to say.

Tuck McCoy is cut from the same cloth as my ex, Ryan. The guy I wasted too many years and way too many tears on.

Which makes the way certain parts of my body react to what he's wearing right now particularly inconvenient.

He's sporting a flannel shirt, too. I guess that's the theme of this part of the photoshoot. Unlike Hudson, he has his sleeves rolled up. Exposing his thick, muscular, veiny forearms.

Heaven help me. Tuck McCoy shouldn't be allowed to roll up his sleeves like that.

It should be against the law. Banned by international treaties, Geneva Convention style. It's a weapon that's simply too powerful. I can't stand the guy and the sight has even me imagining licking those forearms like they're popsicles.

Ugh. I quickly reprimand myself for that thought.

It doesn't matter how beefy his forearms are or how good those jeans make his thighs look or how that rugged flannel shirt tucked into them accentuates his wide shoulders and broad chest—Tuck McCoy doesn't *deserve* my lust.

"Can we go now?" I ask Summer. "I'm starving."

But just then, Hudson notices her and decides to stride over, framing her chin in his massive hand and pressing a kiss to her lips.

I have to admit, the way her eyes flutter closed when his lips capture hers, the way her body leans into him so effortlessly, so naturally, so *securely* ... well, sure, I'm a little envious.

Even though I'm not even close to ready to open my own heart to another person after the disaster of my relationship with Ryan—who also happened to be a hockey player.

Has that fact biased me against their kind? Yes, it has. Hudson's the rare exception, because I've seen how good he treats my best friend.

But as for the others? They're not getting any benefit of the doubt.

When Hudson pulls away from the kiss, he and Summer take several beats to stare lovingly into each other's eyes. Beats of time during which my stomach growls. I really *am* starving.

Speaking of hockey players who absolutely are not getting the benefit of recently mentioned doubt ...

"Don't those two lovebirds just make your heart sing, Lockley?" There's no mistaking the easy drawl rumbling next to me. Tuck McCoy's sauntered right over without me noticing.

And he's doing that thing where he calls me by my last name.

I guess he thinks it's supposed to be cute. It isn't.

"Uh. Sure," I deadpan. What else am I supposed to say?

"Hudson! Tuck!" Lane Larsen, the Black Bears' team captain, calls from where the rest of the team are still standing by the photographers. "Get back here! We're about to get changed for the beach scene!"

"Beach scene?" Summer asks, her voice thick with interest. Her eyes roam up and down Hudson's body. "Does that mean you're about to wear ... swim trunks?"

As Summer and Hudson shamelessly flirt, Tuck coughs, drawing my attention to him. "I'm about to be wearing swim trunks, too, Lockley. If that little tidbit of information is of interest to you." His eyebrows wiggle suggestively.

"It would take me *weeks* to think of a tidbit of information *less* interesting to me," I retort.

I absolutely could not care less that Tuck McCoy is about to be wearing swim trunks, his bare torso fully exposed, looking like a total surfer bro with his golden tanned skin, scruffy sandy-blonde hair, and bright blue eyes …

Alright, I think it's time to go.

"Summer, I'm going to starve to death if we don't leave now," I groan. My complaint syncs perfectly with Lane shouting at Hudson and Tuck to get back to the photoshoot once again. Mercifully, Hudson and Summer give each other a peck of a goodbye kiss.

"Catch you later, Lockley," Tuck drawls as Summer and I turn to leave.

I, of course, decline to dignify him with a response.

We walk from a heated room in the art building out to the freezing cold of Vermont in January.

The only saving grace is that there's no wind. Still, the temperature is hovering at the very bottom of the double digits, and coldness wraps around every one of my limbs even though I've zipped my cute, cream-colored puffer jacket straight up to the neck.

The cold might be biting, but it's still beautiful today. The sky is a smooth, bright blue without a cloud to be seen. The campus walkways are shoveled clear, but elsewhere the ground is still covered with last week's snowfall, and the way the sun reflects against the pure white snow is dazzling.

The bare skeletons of the trees are still trimmed with fresh white snow along their branches, the temperature staying too low for it to melt off. I take a deep breath and fill my lungs with the crisp, bracing chill of the air. Every season is beautiful up here, and the scene that surrounds us is lovely enough to make up for the cold.

When we step into Brumehill Brews, I'm still glad to be out of it, though. There's nothing quite like stepping out of the cold and into a warm, bustling café right in the frozen center of winter.

I order a bowl of vegetable soup and a hot green tea; Summer orders a sandwich and a coffee. When we take our seats, I dip down to breathe in the warm steam rising from my teacup, letting it suffuse through me and unthaw my chest.

Feeling warmed up, I shrug off my jacket and rub my hands together before taking my first blissful sip.

"Know what Hudson said the other day?" Summer asks.

I smirk. "Well, I know what Hudson said to you a couple nights ago, when he clearly didn't know I was walking past your door to the bathroom."

My smirk grows into a grin when Summer's cheeks flush red. I'm happy for Summer that she has an incredible sex life, and I'm also happy that, since we live together, it gives me plenty of ammunition to make her blush like this.

My best friend pushes past my comment. "He told me that he and Tuck went to the bookstore the other day, and Tuck was asking if he knew what your favorite books are."

I groan and roll my eyes. I slurp up a spoonful of my soup to counteract the sour taste that rises in my mouth from hearing Tuck's name.

"Just fishing for material to hit on me some more," I explain.

"You know," Summer says, drawing out the syllables like she's leading up to something she knows I'm going to dispute, "he's really not as much of a cocky playboy as he seems."

I narrow my eyes at her accusingly.

"Well, okay, he kind of is both of those things," she concedes. "But he actually really is a nice guy."

My lower lip curls. "Whose side are you on?"

"Yours. Always. I'm just saying. Tuck might be cocky, spoiled, a little obnoxious sometimes ... but he's not a bad guy."

"Hm," is all the answer I give, shifting my attention to slowly slurping my hot soup.

I can understand why Summer would want me and Tuck to get along better. Tuck and Hudson have strangely kind of become best friends—more on Tuck's initiative than Hudson's—and it would be more fun for everyone if I weren't at Tuck's throat whenever we're around each other.

A traitorous thought sprouts in my mind: is it possible that I'm being too hard on Tuck?

Is it possible that Summer's right, that he actually is a nice guy? That his interest in me is genuine?

Is it possible that ... that I've held this grudge against hockey players for too long? After all, Hudson is a hockey player and he's a total sweetheart to Summer. I couldn't ask for a better boyfriend for my best friend.

Maybe it's time for me to ...

But before I can finish that thought, my phone vibrates on the table. My eyes snag on the image displayed on the screen.

Those charitable thoughts evaporate from my mind, and it feels like there's suddenly a ten-pound lead ball sitting in my stomach.

My iPhone chose this moment to share a "memory" with

me—a picture that I thought I'd deleted, but somehow survived in the far reaches of my photos.

I'm in the picture. Smiling into the camera, my eyes bright and happy and enthusiastic. And I've got my arms wrapped around ... my ex. Ryan.

Tension tightens in my chest as my gaze settles on his image. It's the first time I've glanced at a picture of him in ... I don't know how long. Months. But not long enough.

The guy who was my whole world from junior year of high school until winter break during my freshman year of college.

The guy who was screwing around with other girls the entire time. The guy who had me so wrapped around his finger that I convinced myself not to notice, even though he barely even tried to hide it.

The guy who was entirely aware just how hard I'd fallen for him and used that fact to take advantage of me emotionally.

The guy who was rich, cocky, too hot for his own good, and treated life like a game where the only thing that mattered was his own satisfaction. The guy who expected the whole world to bow down to him just because he was a star player on our high school hockey team.

A guy that a certain someone who Summer and I were just discussing has way too much in common with.

I punch in my passcode, open my Photos app, and swiftly delete the image before placing my phone face-down on the table next to my cup of tea.

You know what? No—I don't think I'm being too hard on Tuck.

3

TUCK

"If you had to spend forty-eight hours in the world of the last movie you watched, how fucked would you be?"

"It would be *28 Days Later* for me," Jamie answers the question of my other teammate, Carter. We're just shooting the shit in the locker room before skating back onto the ice for the third period of a game we're dominating. "I'd be pretty fucked." He shudders. "I can't stand that zombie shit. I'm definitely not cut out for any post-apocalyptic scenarios."

"*Predator* for me," Kiran says. He's a big, strapping dude who plays on the fourth line, and he plays rough and physical. "I think I'd be good, actually. I'd make it to the very end, me and Arnold Schwarzenegger hunting down that alien bastard together."

"I think I'd rather spend forty-eight hours trying to survive in *28 Days Later* or *Predator* than spend four hours trying to get through watching those artsy snoozefest movies Sebastian always has on," I say, throwing a teasing glance at Sebastian Laurent, our center forward. "I saw him in the living room the other day watching this movie and I swear, the camera was pointed down this abandoned alley for, like, five minutes straight with literally nothing happening. In black and white, too."

"There was a very interesting philosophical monologue going on during that scene," Sebastian counters. "And the shot was great. It was framed brilliantly, and the lighting was ..."

"Blah, blah, blah," I cut him off. I love Sebastian, but sometimes I'm surprised he's a hockey player instead of an English professor or working at a museum or some shit. "Things are supposed to *happen* in movies."

"Just because there weren't explosions or shoot-outs or car chase scenes, doesn't mean nothing was happening," Sebastian says, patronizingly.

"Be careful about insulting those artsy movies, Tuck," Hudson says, before adding with a wink, "those are the kind of movies your crush likes, too."

"Crush?" Carter asks. "Tuck has a crush?"

"Olivia," Rhys answers.

"Oh," Carter reacts, nodding his head. "Summer's friend, right?" he asks Hudson.

Hudson nods.

"Yeah, the girl who keeps shooting him down," Sebastian says.

Dick.

"Come to think of it," Hudson says, a devious glint in his arctic blue eyes, "you and Olivia have a lot of that artsy stuff in common, Sebastian."

"Hmm," Sebastian muses, making a big show of cupping his chin and nodding thoughtfully. "You're right. Maybe we'd be a good match."

These guys couldn't be more blatantly trying to get a rise out of me. Which is why I shouldn't give them one.

Too bad my face doesn't get the message, as there's currently a scowl carved so deeply into it that I can feel myself practically snarling. It's more than enough to get the guys chuckling at my expense.

Luckily, Coach Torres' voice pulls all our attention towards him. "Alright, men! You all ready to go out there and finish this job?"

We all respond in the affirmative, instantly pumped up. We're heading into the third period up 4-1. A comfortable lead made even more comfortable by the fact that our opponent's offense is cooked.

The last couple weeks of the season have been amazing. This team is clicking like I've never felt a team click before. From defense to offense to goalie, everything is firing on all cylinders. Our chemistry on the ice is seamless, like we can read each other's minds.

Hell, we come into every game and play every game with so much confidence that we think nothing of wasting the time between periods dicking around and talking about what movies we'd be able to survive in. Everything is just flowing, and it feels great.

Back on the ice, we manage to bottle up our Birchwood U opponents so effectively that they don't even get a shot on goal. In the last two minutes, Carter manages to blast a one-timer off a pass from Sebastian and score another goal, giving us a final score of 5-1.

Spirits are high as we're getting changed in the locker room after the game. Every one of us can taste the Frozen Four win this year.

Competition might be stiff—the Hot Shots team down at Ridley University in Pennsylvania are having a killer season, too—but right now, with the roll we're on, I can feel in my bones that no one's stopping us from taking home the Championship.

It's a short bus ride from Birchwood back to Cedar Shade, the town where Brumehill College is located. Since we just threw a rager last weekend, we don't have anything crazy planned to celebrate this win when we get back.

Still, I'd like to do something low-key with some of the guys when we get back. I'm just buzzing with too much energy that's begging to get burned off.

"Hey, bestie," I say to Hudson, wrapping my arm around his shoulders while we're walking to the bus. Grumpy, closed-off Hudson used to always make sure to tell me we're not besties whenever I called him that, but lately he hasn't been protesting. "Up for grabbing a drink when we get back home?"

"Sorry," he says. "I'm meeting up with Summer."

If five months ago you told me this grumpy bastard would get a lovey-dovey, faraway look in his eyes whenever he talks about his girlfriend, I wouldn't have believed you. But my eyes aren't lying; that's exactly what's going on right now.

"How about you two?" I ask Rhys and Lane. "Round of drinks at Loser's?" I'm referring to Loser's Luck Tavern, our regular bar back in Cedar Shade.

"Sorry, I'm hanging out with Stephanie when we get back," Rhys says, talking about a girl on the cheerleading team I've seen him with a couple times.

"I actually have a first date with a girl from my Physics study session," Lane says.

"Can't wait for the wedding invitations," I joke, slapping Lane on the back. I put on a smile, but inside feel a twinge of disappointment.

It'd be nice to have a girl waiting for me back home. Even if it's just a date or a casual hookup.

But I'm in a total and utter rut, all because I only have eyes for the one single girl in Cedar Shade who doesn't want anything to do with me.

I see Sebastian step up onto the bus ahead of me, and I hurry past a couple other guys to hop on before someone else snags the seat next to him. I usually sit with Hudson on bus rides, but I'm sure my bestie won't mind my absence this time.

Maybe if I make an effort to show interest in the things Olivia's interested in—even the things that are, objectively, boring as shit—it'll show her that I'm not just some fuckboy.

"So, Sebastian," I say, sliding into the seat next to him. "Give me some boring artsy movie recommendations."

4
OLIVIA

I roll to a stop at a red light on my way back from an audition with the Champlain Theatre Company in Burlington.

Vermont's capital is about a half-hour's drive from Cedar Shade, and the Champlain Theatre Company is a thriving organization that stages the best plays in the region.

Sure, it's not Broadway or Off-Broadway by a long shot, but it's a great company to gain experience with, and drama majors from both Brumehill and the University of Vermont always turn out for auditions.

This time, I'm going for a starring role in a classic: Lady Macbeth.

Generally, I'm more interested in modern productions, but there's no way I'm going to pass up the opportunity to snag an iconic role in a classic staged by a reputable company. That's the kind of thing that could do wonders for my future career.

And it's not like acting opportunities grow on trees. Making it in stage acting isn't any easier than making it in movies or television, and I need every leg up I can get.

While I'm stopped at the red, my phone rings. Glancing at it face-up on the passenger seat, I see it's my dad.

We've been playing phone tag for a couple days now, me missing his calls and him missing my calls back. I decide to flip on my turn signal and pull into the shopping center on my right to take the call.

"Hi, Dad," I answer.

"Olivia!" His booming, boisterous voice blasts through my phone's speaker. "Finally! I feared we'd never speak again!"

I laugh at my dad's signature melodrama. He delivers those words with the overwrought inflection of a veteran stage actor—which is what he is.

We spend a minute catching up and checking in; then he springs the reason for his call.

"So, your summer schedule is clear, right?" he asks.

"Actually," I reply, "I have that internship with the firm in Burlington. Remember? The one I've mentioned about a dozen times?"

Along with being a Drama major, I'm an Accounting minor. Because, remember that thing I said about how hard it is to make it in acting? I wasn't lying. It's *hard* making it in acting.

Ask my parents, both of whom were drama majors and met in college. They've struggled to make ends meet their whole lives, pursuing their passions without having any solid fallback options.

I definitely want to live out my dream. I want to make acting my full-time career, and I'm willing to put in the work to make that happen.

But I'm not under any illusions. I could work hard, sacrifice, do my best, hone my talent, improve my craft—and still not make it. I don't want to end up in that position without something more practical to fall back on.

Hence, the Accounting minor. And hence the summer internship with the big Burlington-based accounting firm that I've already accepted.

"Reschedule it," Dad says. "I've got something much better for you to do this summer."

"I can't reschedule it. It's a summer internship."

"I've got a much better summer internship lined up for you."

I angle my mouth away from the phone so my dad can't hear my exasperated sigh. The instant Dad gets an idea that he likes, he immediately assumes everyone else will rearrange their whole lives to bring it to fruition.

"And what's that?" I ask.

"I've got a role for you."

While Mom's left her acting days behind her, Dad's still holding onto the dream. He's still actively searching for roles, traveling around the country for auditions and production runs.

He's talented, has starred in some successful productions, and has received good reviews for his skills, but his career has been the picture of instability. He often goes long periods of time without being cast—and therefore, long periods of time without making any money.

Mom's always been the main breadwinner in the family. She went back to school for a teaching certificate so she could teach Drama classes at middle and high schools. That's given her more regular paychecks than Dad, but unfortunately, when schools face budget cuts, the arts are always the first things to go. It hasn't been easy for her, either.

Since I was a kid, my mom's always stayed home where

we live in New Jersey, while Dad's search for theatre work often saw him moving around, living in different cities around the country for weeks or months at a time.

"A role, huh?" I'm less than enthused. Normally I'm up for any acting opportunity, but my internship has to be my priority this summer.

"Down here at the Pyramid Theatre in Charleston," he says. My dad's been living down there for a couple months now, working with one of the hotter theater companies in the country right now. It's the most steady work he's had in a while.

"Really, Dad, I need to complete this internship. It's ..."

"So you don't want to share a stage with Benedict Monroe?"

I pause. "Benedict Monroe?" He's one of the biggest names in stage acting right now, having just wrapped up a starring role in *Lily's Problem*, an Off-Broadway production that got rave reviews and lots of media attention.

"That's right. We've casted him in the starring role for *Last Bus Out*. It's running from July to mid-August. We're going to take in so much tourist money this summer we'll be drowning in it."

My eyebrows leap up my forehead. I'm impressed. This sounds incredible. But ...

"I really do need this internship, Dad." I'm only an Accounting minor, and I feel like I need an internship under my belt to make myself a serious candidate if I ever do have to step back from acting and get a regular job in the field.

"I've got the role of Jasmine with your name on it," Dad says. Jasmine is a minor supporting character in *Last Bus Out*, but she does have a couple scenes where she exchanges lines with the stars.

There's no doubt it would be a great opportunity. To

share a stage, to even share lines, with a big name like Benedict Monroe?

Imagining spending my summer like that certainly makes for an appealing contrast versus spending it in a Burlington office building where the air conditioning is way too cold, hunched over a desk all day.

If I were the type of person to say screw tomorrow and live for today, the type of person who snatches high-risk, high-reward opportunities with dreams of sure success in her head rather than anxiety over probable failure in her chest, I'd jump on it.

But ...

"Sorry, Dad," I say, feeling a twinge of disappointment because acting in *Last Bus Out* in front of a big audience really would be incredible. "You should find someone else for the role."

"How about this? I'll give you some time to think about it."

I open my mouth to tell him that I've already made up my mind, but only a sigh comes out. When Dad gets an idea in his head, it can be completely impossible to talk him out of it. You just have to wait a little while until his first wave of excitement fizzles out.

"Fine," I concede.

We say our goodbyes and I hang up, feeling more agitated than I was beforehand.

Of course, my dad not accepting my decision is agitating. But what's also agitating is this balancing game I have to play between chasing my dream of acting and trying to make practical decisions for my future.

I don't want to end up like my parents, without a marketable skill and struggling to find precarious jobs to make ends meet; I also don't want to give up on my dream just because it's hard, just because it requires sacrifices, just because success is unlikely.

I know I have the talent it takes to make it on stage—I also know that talent isn't enough. Luck counts for a lot.

Now that I've ended the call with my dad, slivers of doubt start to furrow into my mind. Maybe I *should* take him up on his offer.

Sharing a stage with one of the top stage actors in the country? That's an opportunity that very few college students have. And there's no doubt that one of the hottest actors staring in one of the hottest contemporary plays is going to attract the attention of critics—critics who will then come and see me, even if I only have a couple lines.

And if I can make the most out of those couple lines ...

But this internship is important. For one, I've already accepted it. Backing out now would reflect poorly on me. And I'll need the experience if I want this Accounting minor to actually make me competitive if and when I'm looking for a regular nine-to-five job.

Know what would be great? If I were a spoiled rich kid and I didn't have to worry about practical considerations. If I didn't have to worry about setting myself up to make a decent living, because that was just a given.

A lofty position that *certain* people I know find themselves in ...

Letting out a puff of self-pity, I switch off the ignition of my car and head into the convenience store I'm parked in front of. Summer and I are running low on some household supplies, and now's as good a time as any to pick some up. Maybe a tiny shopping trip will help clear my mind, anyway.

But when I get back to my car, sling the bags into the

passenger's seat, and insert the key to turn the ignition back on, my mind becomes anything but clear.

The car won't start.

I try again and again, to no avail. I let my head fall back against my seat, clenching my eyes tightly. This car's been giving me trouble for a while now, but of course I haven't had the money to get it looked at. This is the first time it hasn't started, though.

I hop out of my seat again and walk towards the front of the car, popping the hood. When I find myself gazing at the intricate jumble underneath, I wonder why the hell I even bothered. It's not like I have any freaking clue what I'm looking at.

For a couple moments I just stand there, frozen in frustration, staring blankly at gears, tubes, and auto parts I know literally nothing about.

It's not a mystery what I'm going to have to do. I'm going to have to get it towed. My stomach turns at the thought. Heaven knows how many hundreds of dollars that alone is going to cost.

And have it towed to where? An auto shop for repairs I can't afford?

Better to just have it towed in front of my house and let it sit out by the curb. It's not like I need a car in my day-to-day life in Cedar Shade, where everything is within walking distance. I mostly just drive back and forth between Burlington for auditions and to see plays, since it's so much easier than catching the irregularly schedule bus that connects the small college town to the big capital city.

"Nothing hotter than a woman who knows how to turn a wrench."

My back stiffens at the sound of that familiar, casual

drawl. Surely, at this time of all times, the universe wouldn't be so cruel as to ...

When I turn my head to the side, I find that the universe is indeed that cruel.

By some terrible twist of fate, none other than Tuck McCoy is standing next to me. Right in front of the black Mercedes that his rich family no doubt paid for.

I bet he's never had to deal with a single moment of car trouble in his life.

As usual, my frustration at seeing him contrasts with the boyish grin on his lips. Lips that are entirely too plush. It's just not fair.

Everything about Tuck McCoy's appearance is unfair. His dimples unfairly accentuate his high cheekbones and angular features. His jaw is unfairly sharp and broad. His bright blue eyes are downright unjust.

"Please tell me you're not stalking me, Tuck," I deadpan.

He chuckles. That low, rumbly timbre of his voice? Also unfair. "I was driving past and had to do a double take when I saw some girl standing over her engine, gawking at it like she was looking at an instruction manual written in Mandarin. Couldn't believe it was you. What are the odds?"

"Low, which says something about my bad luck."

Those words are laden with pain from the depths of my soul, but Tuck just laughs them off again. He steps to my side, looking down at the engine along with me.

"Car troubles?" he asks.

I turn my head slowly to him, leveling him with a nonplussed glare. "No, I just decided that driving out to a shopping center on the outskirts of Cedar Shade and standing in front of my engine in the freezing cold would be a good way to pass time between classes."

"Hm," Tuck hums, taking my answer at face value. "In that case, I'll join you."

Seconds tick past. Tuck is just standing silently next to me, hands slung into his jean pockets, eyes glued to my engine.

My brain is discombobulated from the downright absurdity of it. Just how long will Tuck stand here in the freezing cold with me in front of my propped-open hood? Does he love tormenting me *that* much?

"You can go now, Tuck," I finally say.

"No way. This is just starting to get good."

I was putting off the pain of calling for a tow, but the pain of spending any more time here next to Tuck McCoy is even greater.

"I'm just going to call a tow truck," I say, reaching into my pocket for my cell phone.

"Have you tried jumping it yet?" Tuck asks.

"Jumping?"

"Jump-starting it. You know, the battery?"

My lips are a flat line as I blink dumbly at Tuck.

He grins. "You don't even know what I'm talking about, do you?"

I narrow my eyes on him, feeling my jaw tighten in annoyance. "Care to enlighten me?" It's true, I officially know jack-shit about cars. Sue me.

"It's not every day I know something you don't, Lockley. Let me savor the moment."

He dips his head back and closes his eyes, taking in a deep breath like he's inhaling the freshest scent of flowers on a gorgeous spring day. Then he lets it out in a long, loud exhale that ends with a satisfied sigh.

I roll my eyes. "Has the moment been sufficiently savored yet?"

He holds up his index finger. After two more beats with his head flung back and his eyes closed, he finally opens them and nods. "Yeah. Sufficiently savored. Alright, let me get my cables."

He brings out two cables from his truck, pops his own hood, and then connects the cables between his car and mine.

"This is supposed to ... revive the battery?" I ask.

He chuckles again, earning him another glare. "Yeah, Lockely," he says, a patronizing tone in his voice like he's explaining something only an idiot wouldn't already know.

He goes back to his car and starts it. He revs the engine a couple times and then rolls down his window to say to me, "In a minute or two, try to start your car."

I sigh. "If you say so." Normally, I wouldn't trust Tuck about anything, but he actually seems to know what he's doing here.

Kind of surprising. I would have thought his family would have a full staff of chauffeurs to make sure none of them ever had to sully their hands with tasks like this.

After a bit, Tuck gives me a thumbs up, signaling that I should try to start my engine.

I do ... nothing happens.

"Try again," Tuck shouts from his car.

I do ... and nothing happens, again.

I try a couple more times. Each time, no luck.

"Shit," Tuck says, stepping out of his car at the same time I step out of mine. "It must be something worse than that."

"Thanks for trying," I say. "But you can go home now. I'll just call a tow truck like I said."

"Lemme check a couple things," he says, ignoring my words.

He unzips his jacket and flings it onto the roof of his car. My breath catches when he pulls up the sleeves of his grey sweater, revealing those thick, dense forearms again. My eyes linger on the articulated veins and the downy brushing of his brown hair over the tops of them.

He leans over my hood and reaches his left hand deep into the maze of car parts. Suddenly, it feels like there's something in my throat making it hard to swallow.

Maybe a bug flew in my mouth or something. Surely it's not the sight of Tuck with his sleeves rolled up, reaching deep into the gears of a car with rugged masculine confidence that's affecting my swallowing ability ...

"Hm, that's not it," he grouses. "What about ..." He pulls his left hand out then plunges his right deeper into another part of the engine. "Nope, not that, either."

He takes a step back, scrunching up his mouth and regarding my car thoughtfully. He raises his right hand to scratch the top of his head, the action making his bicep pop noticeably even through the bunched-up sleeve of his sweater.

He lets out a heavy breath. "Lemme try one more thing."

This time he reaches deeper into the car, bending over deep enough that his sweater rides up his back. I catch a sliver of his smooth, clear skin. A chill dances up my spine —thanks to a cold breeze that just rolled by, no doubt.

"Try starting it one more time," Tuck says, straightening up.

I slide into my driver's seat.

Again, nothing.

"Damn," Tuck says, sounding genuinely disappointed. "Yeah. Nothing to do but get it towed."

"Thanks for trying," I say. He did take a chunk of time

out of his day, stood in the freezing cold, and got his forearms all greasy when we're not even friends.

"Call the tow truck and tell them where your car is. Usually takes them a while to get around to making a tow. I'll drive you back into town."

I think about turning down his offer, but then I consider the alternatives, like walking the couple miles back home in this cold weather down a road that has zero space for pedestrians. So, I agree.

A couple minutes later, after calling a towing company, I find myself one place I never intended to be: in the passenger seat of Tuck McCoy's Mercedes.

5

OLIVIA

The universe may have unfairly blessed Tuck McCoy in many, many ways, but there's one talent it's clearly declined to bestow on him: singing ability.

After enduring Tuck singing along to two Taylor Swift songs in a row—very loudly, might I add—I'm surprised my ears aren't bleeding.

"Has anyone ever told you that you're an awful singer?" I ask once *The Other Side of the Door* comes to an end.

Tuck turns to me and flashes a wide smile, his teeth a pristine, dazzling white. "Yes. Many times."

"You're doing this just to torture me, aren't you?"

He balks. "You mean you're not a Taylor Swift fan?"

"She's fine, I like her, but ..."

"*Fine?*" Tuck exclaims like he can't believe his ears. "What do you mean *fine*? She's a genius!"

I'm taken aback by Tuck's enthusiasm. "Geez, I never would have taken you for such an ardent Taylor Swift supporter."

"We call ourselves *Swifties*, thank you very much."

"How did—"

"Oh! Hold on." He reaches for the volume knob on his stereo to turn up the volume. "After this song. It's one of my favorites."

For the next four minutes, I'm forced to endure Tuck singing along to Taylor Swift's *Speak Now*.

When the last off-tune note from Tuck's throat finally fades away into the air, he turns the volume back down. "What were you about to ask?"

"How did you learn how to work on cars?" But then another thought occurs to me. "Or were you just pretending to know what you were doing to screw with me?"

Tuck lets out a booming laugh, and I'm ashamed to admit how deep in my core I feel the vibration of it. "One of the businesses my dad owns is a car dealership. He used to make me work summers in the maintenance department. I picked up a thing or two."

"Hm," I hum, surprised; and impressed with Tuck's dad for not wanting his son to grow up idle just because he was born wealthy.

"Surprised I've got some blue-collar skills?" he asks.

"Yes," I answer, making no effort to sugarcoat it.

Tuck chuckles again. "Yeah, my dad's kind of a hard ass. All about making me learn the value of hard work. I'd say it halfway worked. I'm all good with working hard when it comes to something physical. Academics, on the other hand," he tilts his head, "that's another story."

For a couple minutes we continue to drive in silence, until Tuck asks, "You're into those artsy movies right?"

"Artsy movies?" I repeat, amused by the phrasing. "Sure, I guess I am."

"Yeah. My roommate Sebastian is, too. I watched this one he recommended the other day. Some Italian title." A low, thoughtful hum rumbles from him while he searches his mind. "*L'Avventura*, I think it was called?"

My brow leaps up my forehead in surprised. "*You* watched *L'Avventura*? Really?"

"Don't sound so surprised, Lockley," Tuck drawls. "I wanted to expand my horizons."

"Well? Did you like it?" I'm genuinely interested now.

"It was ..." Tuck peters off, like he's searching for the right word. "It definitely, um ..." Again a thoughtful pause, before he finally comes out with, "Alright, I admit it, I hated it. It was *so* fucking boring!"

"It was not boring!" I retort, defensive of a film I admire. "It was thoughtful, introspective, philosophical, innovative ..."

"You're just throwing out euphemisms for *boring*."

"Well, what's a good movie in your opinion, then?" I ask.

He shrugs. "I'm an 80's action movie and 2000's romcom guy. Maybe not the most sophisticated choices, but after giving sophisticated movies a try, I'm comfortable sticking to what I like."

"2000's romcoms?" I repeat, caught off guard again.

We're stopped at a light, so Tuck takes the opportunity to turn to me and flash another toothy grin. "I'm really surprising you today, aren't I?"

He kind of is.

"I won't lie. I assumed you'd be too much of a macho meathead to be open about liking Taylor Swift and romcoms."

"Not me. I am who I am and I'm comfortable enough with my masculinity to like what I like. When you've got biceps like these," he flexes one arm, drawing my eyes to the bulging muscle, "and certain, let's say, *other* masculine assets, you don't need to worry about what other people think of you to know that you're all man."

I've been so sure Tuck is cut from the same cloth as my ex, but that mindset is a million miles away from how Ryan looked at things.

He cared a lot about what other people thought about him, and especially cared about no one thinking he'd be into something *girly*.

When we'd hang out and watch Netflix together, every time I suggested we watch something like Gilmore Girls or Bridgerton, he'd look at me like I asked him to take a walk around the block naked with his underwear on his head.

"Wow, Tuck. That's a great way to approach life," I feel compelled to admit.

"I'm winning you over, aren't I?"

"Let's not get crazy," I reply without missing a beat, drawing another laugh from him.

After a couple beats of silence, Tuck asks, "By the way, is something on your mind? Something, I don't know, bothering you?"

I quirk my eyebrow and turn my head to him. "Why?"

He shrugs. "Just seems like something's troubling you."

"Like what?"

Another shrug. "You tell me."

"So on top of being a Swiftie and an auto mechanic, you're a mind-reader now, too?" I quip.

"I'm a man of many talents." He takes advantage of being backed up at a stop sign to turn to me and wiggle his eyebrows suggestively. "*Many* talents."

After rolling my eyes, I stew on his words for a minute. Of course, he's right. I do have something on my mind. But Tuck McCoy is the last person I should be opening up to.

As true as that is, the words still come to my mouth, almost involuntarily. "I have sort of a dilemma."

"Hmm," Tuck hums thoughtfully, encouraging me to say more.

"I mean, it's not really a dilemma. I have two options, and I already know which one I'm going to take. It just sucks turning the other opportunity down. My dad just called to offer me a solid role in a big production of a great play, *Last Bus Out*, running over the summer. It would be the best opportunity of my career so far. I'd be acting in front of my biggest audiences yet, major critics would come to showings, and I'd be sharing the stage with one of the best stage actors in the country. But I've already accepted an internship at an accounting firm for the summer."

"*Last Bus Out*," Tuck repeats, chewing on the words. "Sounds like some artsy play where the entire thing happens during one bus ride and it's nothing but the passengers talking to each other."

"That's ... exactly what it is, actually," I say, a bit astonished at his accurate guess.

"So, you're taking the role and you feel bad about letting your internship down," Tuck says, like it's obvious.

I furrow my brow. "No. I'm sticking with the internship."

"What?" Tuck asks, surprised. "But you said this play would be the biggest thing that's happened for your career so far."

"Acting isn't the only potential career I have to worry about. Making it in acting is always a long shot. I need to make sure I have fallback options in case it doesn't pan out, and this internship is important for that."

"Fuck that," Tuck replies, stridently. "You're too damn talented to pass up a big opportunity to make sure you have *fallback options*."

Disdain is thick in his voice when he says those last two words, and it makes annoyance rise in my chest.

"That's easy for you to say," I retort.

"What's that supposed to mean?"

I huff. "It's supposed to mean that you don't have to worry about what happens to you in life. You're going to be fine no matter what. More than fine. You can just play hockey and goof off about everything else, and the worst-case scenario is your dad gives you a high-paying job at one of his companies. Me, I have to work to set myself up with a life that can provide me economic stability. That requires making sacrifices."

"You think I don't make sacrifices?" His question comes with a bite. "You think I haven't had to work hard to make it to where I am in hockey?"

"I'm sure you've worked hard. But you don't understand that sometimes people can't throw every practical concern to the side to do what they really want to do. Sometimes they have to buckle down and make disappointing decisions for the benefit of their future, because their future isn't already determined."

"My future sure as hell isn't determined," Tuck says, mirroring my own combative tone now. "I want to play professionally. You think my family's money can buy that opportunity for me? No fucking way. I have to work hard, give it my all every single game, study footage, assess my own weaknesses, and practice nonstop, just for a *shot* at a real pro career."

"Exactly. You're able to give hockey everything you have, because you don't have to worry about what happens if it doesn't work out."

Tuck blows a raspberry. "Yeah, right, I don't have to worry

about not achieving the dream I've had since I was a kid. You know, just the thing I've been working my body to the bone for, dealing with aches and pains and injuries, the thing I sacrificed summer vacations and a social life for while I was growing up. Yep, no big deal if it turns out it was all for nothing. Since I'm some *rich boy*, that's all that matters, right?"

I feel a twinge of guilt in my chest—but that only makes me more frustrated, because I didn't say any of that. Tuck's putting words in my mouth.

"That's not what I mean," I say, folding my arms over my chest and looking out my window. If I look at Tuck right now, I'm only going to get angrier. How is he making *me* feel bad just for telling him that he's giving me advice from a privileged perspective?

"Well, here's what *I* mean. You only live once. People out there would kill for the natural talent you have on the stage. I don't know shit about acting and even I can see it when I've gone to your plays. You owe it to yourself to see how far you can go with it, and you need to take every opportunity available to you to make it happen."

Yeah, I've seen what happened to my parents who followed Tuck's advice. A life of struggle and stress because following your dreams isn't always guaranteed to pay the bills, no matter how talented you are.

"My street is on the left here," I say, side-stepping Tuck's last comment. I'm done with this conversation.

"I know," Tuck grouses, turning onto my narrow street and rolling to a stop in front of my house.

I take a deep breath and push past my frustration with Tuck to say, "Thanks for the ride. And trying to help with my car." The thanks seem necessary, but there's no warmth in the words.

"Sure." The same coldness of my voice is mirrored in Tuck's.

Maybe I slam the passenger side door a little too hard when I hop out of his car. And maybe I walk a little faster up my walkway than I usually do.

I definitely let out a heavy, ragged huff when I shut the door behind me.

The frustrated feeling in my chest lingers. I keep playing back my conversation with Tuck.

I don't know why it should bother me. Of course I had a bad experience with Tuck. Don't I always? He and I are utterly incompatible, even as acquaintances.

But ... before we had that spat, I was kind of, actually, sort of ... heaven help me for admitting this ... enjoying our conversation. For a brief moment.

I guess there's a lesson in that: nothing good can ever come of letting my guard down with Tuck McCoy.

6

TUCK

I'm an idiot.

For the first time since I laid eyes on her, Olivia and I were actually having a conversation. A real conversation, beyond me trying to pick her up and her telling me to get lost. We were joking around, getting to know each other. Fuck, it felt good.

Somehow it managed to turn into a stupid argument. Somehow, *I* managed to turn it into a stupid argument.

I've played the conversation back in my head enough times to realize I probably came off as insensitive.

At the same time, when people imply that I haven't worked hard for what I've accomplished, that everything's come automatically for me, even in hockey, just because I come from a wealthy family ... well, it pisses me off. It's something I've had thrown in my face a lot.

Sure, being annoyed that people underestimate you because you're rich is the quintessential *first-world problem*. Still, it stings when it happens over and over again.

I don't like having accomplishments I've worked hard for dismissed. Who would?

And now, thanks to me getting lost in my head, ruminating on all this shit for the fiftieth time today, Jamie's managed to skate deftly up and steal the puck from me.

"Shit," I grumble.

The rookie just made *me* look like a rookie, taking advantage of my inattentive puck handling.

That's not the first time I've cursed myself for screwing up during this practice session. Frankly, I'm playing like shit today. And everyone notices.

After we're dismissed from practice, anxiety crawls up my back while I'm getting changed, just waiting for Coach Torres to shout my name and call me into his office to give me the tongue-lashing I deserve for my performance.

"McCoy!" Coach's voice booms from outside the locker room entrance just as I tug on my jeans after coming from the shower. "My office!"

"Took him longer than I expected," Hudson mumbles, casting a wry look at me. That earns him a middle finger as I walk past him.

"Two things, McCoy," Coach Torres announces when I step into his office.

I purse my lips. "Only two?"

He narrows his gaze, making it clear he's not in the mood for joking around. "Take a seat," he nods towards the very uncomfortable metal folding chair on the opposite side of his desk.

I oblige.

"I'm sure you don't need me to tell you what a pathetic performance you turned in today," he says. Coach Torres never sugarcoats a message. One of the things I like about him. "You've had a hell of a season so far, so I'm going to assume it's a one-off thing. But if I see any traces of the carelessness I saw on the ice today during this Friday's game," he holds up a finger and injects some hardness into his voice to make sure I know he's not messing around, "the next conversation we have about it is going to be very different. Clear?"

"Yes, sir," I nod.

He leans back in his chair. "Second thing. I heard from Martinello."

My English professor. The course I'm taking this semester is especially writing intensive. The syllabus has us writing bi-weekly essays, composing eighty percent of our grade.

And I *hate* essays.

The funny thing is, I enjoy debating. I know how to make a point and defend my argument with my words. When I'm speaking them, at least. But when it comes to doing it on paper, I'm hopeless.

"Yeah?" I ask.

"Sixty-two percent. That's the grade of the first essay you submitted."

My neck stiffens, and I hold back an f-bomb that wants to spew out of my mouth. I worked hard on that damn essay, and I actually thought I did a good job.

"Not a failing grade," Coach says, "but way too close for comfort. We're firing on all cylinders right now, and one thing that is not going to happen under my watch, is one of my top players getting tripped up by academic eligibility when we're this close to the playoffs. We're gonna nip this in the bud early. You've got a tutoring appointment scheduled on Monday."

I cringe internally. I hate tutoring. It's never done anything for me. But I'm not about to tell Coach that.

"Two-thirty in the afternoon, right after your last class.

You know where the tutoring center is. Make sure you're there."

"Will do, Coach," I force myself to say. Not like I have any other options.

As I walk out of Coach's office, I force myself to look on the bright side. Maybe if my tutor is a girl, I'll be able to turn on the patented Tuck McCoy charm and get her to write all my essays for me.

Ethical? Probably not. But just think of the satisfaction she'd get out of it. It would practically be an act of charity.

I poke my head back into the locker room, but all the guys are gone. "Thanks for waiting up," I grumble to the empty room.

My phone vibrates. It's a message from Lane. They're all at Chiyoda Ramen, a Japanese restaurant in downtown Cedar Shade, for an after-practice lunch.

I find them sitting at our usual table, a big sectional booth near the front windows. I walk up to the proprietor, Kazu, and order myself a pork belly ramen. He doesn't even nod, just slightly turns his head to shout the order to the cooks back in the kitchen, before continuing to look straight ahead.

Kazu's a little … anti-social.

Lots of students who've come here to eat think he's a jerk. But that's not really true.

He's just super introverted and doesn't have any interest in basic pleasantries like saying hello to his customers. He and Hudson, two grumpy birds of a grumpy feather, actually get along pretty well.

I slide onto the end of the booth, joining my teammates. "Thanks for waiting up," I repeat now that they're present to hear the snark. My stomach rumbles as I look at them all digging into the food that they've already been served.

"Don't mention it," Rhys says, not even looking up from stuffing his face with his chicken tempura rice bowl.

My stomach only growls louder when I take a deep breath through my nose, and the smells from everyone's dishes mingle. Kazu might not know how to exchange niceties, but he sure as hell knows how to cook. Everything this place serves is incredible.

I decide to distract myself by turning my attention to Sebastian, who wields his chopsticks deftly as he wraps his thick Udon noodles around them.

"Did you grow up using chopsticks or something?" I ask. The rest of us can fumble our way through eating a meal with them, but Sebastian controls them like he's been using them his whole life.

"There was this sushi place that opened in the town where I grew up when I was in middle school. Me and my best friend went there all the time. I got the hang of them there."

"Sophisticated motherfucker," I jest.

Sebastian's a worldly guy, even though he's never actually traveled outside the country. Aside from being into artsy shit, he reads all the time, and is always learning about different cultures. Brainiac even speaks French.

Mercifully, I hear a hotel-style service bell ringing from the order counter. This isn't a table-service kind of place. Kazu takes your order, shouts it to his cooks, then rings a bell for you to pick it up when it's ready.

I give Kazu a friendly nod as I pick up my bowl. I don't *think* I'm imagining that he dips his own head about half a centimeter in response. But I might be.

The other guys may have had a head start on me, but I finish my food at the same time as them. I'm so starved that I inhale it like air.

I've just finished slurping down the last of the broth and letting out a satisfied sigh when Hudson, who's sitting next to me, nudges me in the side and nods towards the order counter. "Check it out, he whispers."

I turn my head to look towards Kazu's regular place behind the wooden counter to see he's got a visitor.

A very special visitor.

It's Cindy. The owner of Last Word, the three-story bookstore-slash-coffee shop in Cedar Shade.

Kazu and Cindy obviously have a thing for each other. They're always finding excuses to visit each other's shops. They talk to each other often, every time with this mix of eagerness and shyness that makes them seem like teenagers who have a crush on each other and don't quite know what to do about it.

It's like watching a romcom from a distance. Me, Hudson, and Summer are totally invested in this budding relationship.

I wish one of them would just hurry up and ask the other out already. I like a slow burn as much as the next guy, but it's not like these two are getting any younger.

I strain my ears to try and hear their conversation, at the same time not trying to be too obvious about what I'm doing. I can tell Hudson's doing the same thing.

It's hard to hear the whole conversation, but it sounds like Cindy's giving Kazu a book that they'd talked about in some previous conversation. Now my busybody instincts are itching to know what the book is.

I'll have to make a point to stop by here again in the next couple days to see if I can catch Kazu reading it behind the counter.

"Talk about opposites attract," I say to Hudson after Cindy leaves.

"Speaking of opposites, Summer mentioned that Olivia was asking about you the other day," Hudson says, casual as can be.

A jolt of excitement races up my spine. I sit up straighter, my brow leaping towards my hairline as I lean towards Hudson with interest. "Really?"

"No."

My chest deflates. I sink against the backrest, drilling Hudson with an irked glare as he chuckles.

"Asshole," I grumble.

I'm still down bad for that girl. The fight we had in my car sure as shit hasn't changed that.

Before we argued, I got a taste of what it would be like to hang out with Olivia without her hostility towards me dialed up.

A taste of what it would be like to just drive around with her in my passenger seat, talking about anything and everything and nothing.

It tasted sweet. And that's sure as hell not all that I want to taste when it comes to Olivia Lockley.

7
OLIVIA

"Thanks so much, Olivia. I think I've got this." Belinda, one of the students I tutor, speaks confidently, wearing a wide grin.

"I know you've got this," I reply, returning her smile. "Just remember, stick to the outline, and after each paragraph, glance at the outline again to make sure you're staying on track."

"Right," she nods, holding the two sheets of paper we used to compose her outline for the essay she has due in two weeks. "I'll protect this outline with my life."

I work part-time in the Brumehill Tutoring Center, specializing in helping students write essays.

A lot of our tutors are volunteers or here as a requirement for a course they're taking—common for education majors—but they keep a couple students who've proven themselves especially good at tutoring as paid staff.

Apparently, I'm especially good at teaching people how to write essays.

It's a great part-time job. The pay is good, it's right on campus, it's easy to schedule my tutoring hours around my classes, and I honestly really enjoy helping people with something that so many struggle with.

Once Belinda leaves the tutoring room and I'm alone with nothing to distract me, my mind decides to go somewhere it shouldn't; somewhere I've been trying and failing to keep it from going to for the last several days.

Tuck McCoy.

I shouldn't, but I keep thinking about that car ride home. How different he was from the version of him I'd held in my head since we first met. I was actually enjoying—no, let me be a little more cautious than that—*tolerating* his company.

At least, until the argument we had.

Even though it's been days, an acidic feeling rises in my chest as I remember how cavalierly he dismissed my reasons for not doing the play this summer.

Then, something else happens that's been happening often over these last couple of days: something *very* inconvenient and unwanted.

As soon as I feel mad at Tuck, images of him standing in front of my car, his sleeves rolled up, pop into my mind.

Images of him plunging his corded forearms into the engine with a rugged familiarity. Images of the way his bicep muscle popped when he flexed his arm.

Stupid brain, dredging up the most enticing images of Tuck at the exact moment I want to just be angry at him.

Not only is my brain betraying me, but my body decides to join in, too. Those images of Tuck—especially the one of him reaching underneath the hood of my car, forearm veins popping as he closes his grip around something deep inside the engine that I wouldn't even know the name of—send a chill rolling over me that makes my nipples pebble under my shirt.

Then I remember the way he wiggled his eyebrows at

me with a roguish grin on his lips when we were at that stop sign, and I feel a twinge deep in my core—the exact same place I felt the low vibration of his laughter when I was in his passenger seat.

With a force of will, I push thoughts of Tuck out of my head.

I crumple up and throw away some of the scrap paper I used during the tutoring session with Belinda, and then sling my backpack over my shoulder and start to head out.

Ugh, I've been wound so tightly ever since that day.

I know I'm making the right decision to stick with my internship. It's the smart thing to do, the responsible thing to do.

But no matter what, it would've been disappointing. No matter what, I'd feel the frustration of wondering if I'm missing out on a career-making opportunity. The disappointment of rejecting an opportunity I know I'd absolutely love if only I didn't *have* to worry about doing the smart, responsible thing.

The argument with Tuck only made all those feelings worse.

Of course, I have the broken-down car on top of it all. It's just sitting by the curb in front of my house. Getting it repaired is totally off the table. Paying for the tow was a big enough hit to my bank account.

Luckily, I don't need a car here in Cedar Shade. But without it, I can pretty much forget about landing that Macbeth role in Burlington. Getting back and forth from the next rounds of auditions, and then the rehearsals if I actually got the role, would be a nightmare. Besides, rehearsals and performances would go later than the bus between here and Burlington runs.

Another opportunity I have to forego. Because I'm not rich, like some people are. Like …

Nope, shutting down that chain of thought right now. Not even going to call his name into my mind.

As I walk towards the door to leave the tutoring center, I pass Dr. Galloway's office, the tutoring coordinator. As I do, he calls out to me.

"What's up, Dr. Galloway?" I ask, stepping into his office.

"I've got a special assignment for my number one English tutor," he says.

My cheeks warm as a smile rises on my lips. What can I say, it feels nice knowing that I'm good at helping people.

"You want me to find Derek and tell him to come see you, then?" I joke, referring to another English tutor here.

"Modesty doesn't become you, Miss Lockley," he replies, adding with a grin, "it's too forced."

I chuckle. "Alright, what's this special assignment?"

"We have a student-athlete coming in who needs help with his essay writing. You know how demanding these athletic departments are that they receive gold-plated service. Are you up for an extra session this Monday? Two-thirty in the afternoon?"

I don't have anywhere else to be at that time. "Sure," I answer. Extra money is always welcome. Not that it'll be enough to fix my car, not even close, but it'll make paying for groceries this week less stressful.

I head home, looking forward to a very low-key Friday night and weekend.

No partying or excitement for me. I'm in decompression mode. I just want to veg out on the couch, maybe watch some mindless reality TV with Salsa, Summer's boyfriend's cat who lives with us now, curled up on my lap. Maybe have a glass of wine here and there with Summer while we let our brains rot watching said mindless reality TV.

Earlier today, I finally told my dad that I'm going to have to pass on his offer to come down to Charleston to act in Last Bus Out. At least that's one thing off my mind. Thanks to the car situation, I'm going to have to forget about acting in Macbeth, too.

Looking on the bright side, at least that'll make my schedule less hectic. All I have to worry about is finishing this semester, acting in one or two more student productions, and getting ready for my summer internship.

Is that as exciting as starring in a classic Shakespeare production with a professional theatre company in Burlington while I look forward to spending the summer in Charleston and sharing a stage with the hottest stage actor in the country?

Maybe not. But all I can do is play the hand I'm dealt.

I can feel some of the disappointment that this week's piled on me start to tumble from my shoulders. Yep, after a low-key, reenergizing weekend, I'll be all good to start next week with a clean slate on Monday.

8

OLIVIA

The weekend was exactly what I needed.

Operation *drink wine and rot my brain on trash TV with my bestie* was a smashing success. After finishing the schoolwork I had to do late Friday afternoon, I had a perfect weekend of being supremely unproductive and doing nothing of value.

It was exactly what I needed to recharge my batteries from the week beforehand.

Monday's classes pass like a breeze, and my shoulders are feeling so light that I'm whistling an easy tune as I walk into the tutoring center for my *very important* two-thirty session with the student-athlete.

"He's waiting in room five for you, Olivia," Dr. Galloway calls as I pass his office.

I shoot him a thumbs up and nod in acknowledgment.

That's a good sign. Shows this one is taking things seriously.

So often, we have athletes sent to us on the orders of their coaches, and it's clear they want to be anywhere else in the world but here. They act like us trying to help them pass their classes—which, you know, is the whole reason they're supposed to be here, in *college*—is some horrible imposition on them.

But this student isn't just on time, he's early. Maybe it's just because of the mood I'm in now, but I have a good feeling about this one.

I push open the door of tutoring room five—and the carefree, optimistic mood that's been buoying me all day flies away in an instant, like a bird launching itself out of the way of an approaching car.

A heavy weight settles in my stomach.

My eyes are locked on the bright, baby-blue gaze of none other than Tuck McCoy.

For a beat of time, our gazes tether, Tuck's face blank just like mine as I silently pray for a meteor to strike the tutoring center.

"Oh no," I manage to lament. The words that escape my lips might be tiny, but they're charged with a truckload of dismay.

Then, he laughs.

Throws his head back so that his tussled mop of sandy blonde hair bobs, opens his sharp jaw that's covered with prickly-looking stubble, and lets out a series of fucking *guffaws*.

My stomach churns as I step into the room and close the door behind me. I suppress the urge to run to Dr. Galloway and demand that someone else take my place. I know he's got his hands full making the tutoring schedule work here, and I already agreed to take on this client.

Before I knew who it was.

All I can do is accept my fate. My pitiful fate.

"Why is the universe so cruel?" I'm gazing up at the ceiling as the question passes from my lips.

Tuck's finally finished with his guffawing. "Hey, don't act like you're the only one disappointed here."

I point my gaze at him and lower my brow. "Oh?"

"Yeah, I was hoping I'd get some girl who I could convince to write all my essays for me." He adds with a wry grin, "Something tells me that's not going to fly with you."

I press my lips together in distaste. "You wouldn't really try to get someone else to do your work and pass it off as your own, would you?" I can't say I have the highest opinion of Tuck, but I don't think I'd have suspected that of him.

He just shrugs. "Guess we'll never know."

I'm not willing to let it go that easily. "How would you feel if another team cheated in hockey?"

Lines furrow into his forehead. "Huh?"

"If another team paid off the referees. Or switched their opponent's equipment so their skates didn't fit right. How would you feel about that? Because that's the same thing as getting someone else to do your work for you, and getting a grade you didn't earn."

"That's totally different," he protests.

I fold my arms over my chest. "How's it different?"

Tuck opens his mouth, but words seem to fail him. He tilts his head to the side thoughtfully, his eyes bouncing around like he's ransacking his brain for an answer.

"Uh. Because I say so?" A dumb smile curls on his lips. I guess when you're Tuck McCoy, *that's* usually reason enough for anything.

I narrow my gaze on him. "In my opinion, attempted cheating should be punishable under the academic integrity code, just like attempted murder is a crime itself even if it doesn't succeed."

"Is it just me, Lockley, or did I notice a glimmer in your eyes when you said the word *murder* while looking at me?"

I feel the edge of my lips twitch, but I tighten my mouth to keep from smiling. I don't want to give Tuck the satisfaction. "Don't tempt me," I answer.

Tuck lets out a low whistle. "Getting with a girl who likes it rough is hot as it is. But getting with a girl who literally wants to *murder* you? Shit, that must be …"

I turn around and reach for the door handle. "Alright, if you just want to goof around, I guess you really don't need help with your essays that much."

"Wait!" he exclaims. The trace of urgency is enough to still my movement towards to door and turn back to face him. "I really do need help. And … I know I'm lucky getting you as a tutor. I've heard other athletes who've been sent to tutoring and assigned to you say that you're a miracle worker. Stay. I'll behave. Promise."

There's a strange fuzzy feeling in my stomach, reaching up to my chest where it grows warm. I try to search for any sarcasm in Tuck's words, any hint that he's pulling my leg, but there doesn't seem to be any. He seems genuine.

"Fine," I accept.

I pull out a chair next to him and try to think of him not as the obnoxious, cocky hockey star who's been trying to get in my pants for the last four months, but as just another tutoring client who needs help.

"So, first of all. In your opinion, what do you think your biggest problem is when it comes to essays?"

"Getting bad grades," he answers.

I clamp down on my instinct to say something snarky in response. That's what I'd do if I were still thinking of him as a hockey jerk. But I'm thinking of him as a tutee in need.

"Okay," I reply, evenly. "Why do you think you tend to get bad grades on your essays?"

I've found that this is an important question to get pupils

to understand. It's important for students to be able to accurately identify exactly what their difficulties and weaknesses are, so they can be effective in improving them.

"I wish I fucking knew," he says, his exasperation evident. "This last essay I turned in, I thought I did good. I thought I made a good argument, good points. Then it's a fucking sixty-two percent when I got it back!"

"Do you have the essay with you?" I ask.

"Yeah, it's right here." His book bag sits in between our two chairs, and when he angles his body to reach down and unzip it, his knee brushes against mine.

At the tiny contact, sparks erupt and dance up my leg, settling between my thighs where they awaken a warm, buzzing feeling. My core goes taut. I take a deep, steadying breath through my nose, trying not to let my thighs clench.

"Here it is," he says, pulling out his essay. He lays it on the desk in front of us. "And look at how helpful my professor's comments are."

He points at the red ink underneath the grade of sixty-two sitting at the top of the front page: *Totally disorganized*, is all it says.

I'm not surprised by that when I look at the heading Tuck typed to the upper-right and see that his professor is Martinello.

"Yeah," I sigh. "That's definitely some Martinello-style feedback." Some college professors want to do all they can to help their students succeed; some think that college is supposed to be a more independent experience than that and take a sink-or-swim approach to their students. Martinello falls squarely in the latter category.

"Let me skim through it," I say. I'm not doing a deep reading, trying to look for every possible stylistic error or minor weakness in any of his arguments. First, I just want to get a sense of the general outline and organization of the essay.

Once I've skimmed through it, I can only come to one conclusion. "Okay. Martinello's comment wasn't helpful, but it wasn't wrong, either."

"What do you mean?" he asks.

"This essay is all over the place. Look, you first bring up this point in the second paragraph," I point to it, "then you totally forget about it and ramble about three different ideas for the next two paragraphs. Then you finally come back to your first point later in the essay, before coming back to, like, half the points you made between then and now and fleshing them out more."

"But the arguments were good, right?" he asks.

"Actually, they are," I say, a bit caught off guard by the realization as I flip between pages. "But you need to make one point at a time. And you don't really have a conclusion … actually, your conclusion seems to be in the third to last paragraph. Your last two paragraphs are just elaborating on other minor points you made earlier in the essay."

"But isn't it the argument that counts? The logic? If I make a relevant point and defend it well, isn't that what's important?"

"That is important, but it's not everything. Without proper organization, it can be hard or even impossible to follow what you're trying to say. It's like, imagine you're writing a letter to someone, but your handwriting is so bad literally no one can read it. It doesn't really matter what the letter says, does it? How you present your ideas is important, too."

"Hmm," Tuck hums, actually sounding thoughtful.

"What did you do before you started to actually write this essay?" I ask.

Tuck turns to me with a quizzical look. "You mean, what did I do that day? Well, I went to the gym. Beat Lane in a bench press competition," at that, he throws up both his arms and flexes them, making his dense, round biceps bulge. I feel like Tuck really enjoys flexing. "Then we went to the bar and ..."

"I don't mean that," I say, rolling my eyes at Tuck narrating an entire day of his life. "I mean what did you do to prepare for the essay? Did you make an outline?"

"Outline?" The word falls from his lips like he doesn't even know the meaning.

"Did you do any planning at all? Or did you just open up a Word document and start typing away?"

Tuck nods his head slowly. "Yeah. The last one."

I click my tongue. "That would be your problem, then."

"So you're telling me when I write an essay, not only do I have to write the essay itself, I have to write, like ... a *pre-essay*?"

"It's not that onerous to ..."

"*Onerous*," Tuck repeats the word, his brow leaping sarcastically. "That's a word of the day for you."

"It's not that *difficult* to make an outline," I rephrase with a slight bite to my words. I run down some basic outlining strategies with Tuck, and then give him an assignment: I want him to read through the essay he just scored a sixty-two on, identify all the specific points and arguments he made, and then create an outline for how he should have organized them to be more coherent.

He ruffles through his book bag. "Shit. You have a pencil or something?" he asks.

I fish one out of my own book bag and hold it out to him. When he grabs it, our fingers brush together, and an electric thrill travels from the point of contact, racing up my arm and expanding in my chest. I curse my traitorous nipples for tightening into hard nubs under my shirt.

To Tuck's credit, he really puts effort into what I ask him to do. He hunches over the paper in front of him, the posture accentuating how big and broad his back is as his thick slab of muscles strain against the shirt.

As he glances between his outline and the pages of his essay, the tip of his tongue peeks out from the crease of his lips.

A chill dances up my spine as my eyes latch onto it. My nipples tighten again, so much they ache this time, as the very unwelcome thought of Tuck's pink, wet tongue swirling around them intrudes into my mind.

An involuntary shiver rattles through me, noticeable enough to draw Tuck's gaze.

"So cold in here," I quickly say to cover it up, drawing my arms against my chest. "They really need to turn the heat up."

Tuck shrugs, pulling his attention back to his outline. "Seems hot in here to me."

I can't tell if he's making a casual observation or messing with me. I decide to give him the benefit of the doubt. First time for everything, I guess.

When he finishes the outline, he slides it over the table to me. I look it over.

I'm impressed. I review it with him and provide some advice for how he could improve it, what kind of details he should add so that the task of writing the essay could be halfway done before he even types the first sentence.

"Damn, Lockley," he muses, "there really might be something to this outline idea."

A small chuckle vibrates in my throat. "Glad I could convince you. You have another essay due soon?"

"Yeah. Middle of next week."

"Alright. We have another session on Thursday. How about you come to that one with a preliminary outline already made. Then we'll look it over, tweak it if needed, and then after that session you'll be ready to start writing it."

"Yeah," he agrees. "Sounds good."

When we're getting up to leave, he catches me off guard by saying, "Sorry, by the way."

"Hm?" I ask.

"About that argument we had. When I was driving you home last week." His features twist, like the memory is actually weighing on him. "I was insensitive. And a jerk. I don't have any right to judge your decisions like I did."

I feel numb with surprise. Tuck sounds … sincere? Like this is something that's been genuinely bothering him, something that's been on his mind since it happened.

I nod. "Apology accepted."

I don't think much of the words, but when I say them, a broad, beaming smile splits on Tuck's face. The expression lights up the luminous blue orbs of his eyes. "See you Thursday?"

"See you Thursday," I reply, turning towards the door.

As I step out of the tutoring room with Tuck right behind me, I'm not dreading Thursday nearly as much as I expected I would be half an hour ago.

9

OLIVIA

That night, I'm lying in bed, reading a book on my phone's Kindle app.

It's not my normal reading material. Usually, I like to read the classics. Heavier stuff. But after my low-key weekend of indulging in junk-food TV did me so much good, I felt like maybe a light, fluffy read is what I need, too.

Summer's a big fan of romance novels, so I asked her for a recommendation. Something on the short side, low-angst and cute. She recommended me a book called *Roommate Rebound*.

It's about a girl who hooks up with some guy while she's spending a weekend at the beach after a nasty breakup with her ex. When she gets back home, she moves to a new apartment, only to find out that the guy she hooked up with is her new roommate—*and* her boss at her new job.

I'm enjoying it a lot. It's funny, fast-paced, and I really like the FMC.

Plus, the spice is *hot*, and the author doesn't skimp on it. I'm twenty-five percent into the book, and after bumping into each other in their apartment in the middle of the night wearing next to nothing, the main characters are hooking up for the second time.

There's just one problem.

Whenever there's a spicy scene, I can't help but picture Tuck in the role of the MMC.

That's a big problem, because these scenes are long and really well-written. Frankly, they're turning me on. And I don't want to be turned on while imaging *Tuck* doing the things this book is describing the MMC doing.

I can't help it, though.

When the author writes about the girl spearing her hands into the guy's thick head of hair as he falls to his knees and kisses between her thighs, I think about the way Tuck's sandy-blonde tuft of hair bounced luxuriously as he threw his head back to laugh.

I think about how my fingers would feel lacing into that hair. I think about how good it would feel to tighten my grip, turning my hands into fists, how the pang of satisfaction knowing I'd be making his scalp burn would heighten the sensation of his lips dropping hot kisses on my thighs …

My stomach flips and my pulse skitters. I let that fantasy play out way too long.

Suddenly I'm aware of the liquid heat pooling deep in my core, aware that I'm rubbing my thighs together, feebly trying to alleviate the ache that's throbbing between them.

I keep reading, trying to push out any thoughts of Tuck. Trying to remind myself that the character in the book is written as having short black hair instead of thick sandy-blonde hair, that he's written as having dark hazel eyes instead of bright blue eyes.

I try.

But as my eyes follow the words on my phone's screen, I

realize my hand has crawled up my shirt and my middle finger is drawing lazy circles around my taut nipple.

I realize the images in my head of the scene I'm reading are giving way to memories of Tuck's pink tongue darting from behind his lips while he worked on his outline ...

I should pull my hand away from my breast, put my phone down, get out of bed, get a cold glass of water, anything to keep myself from continuing to think about Tuck like this ...

But it's like I'm in quicksand. I can't do anything to pull myself out.

Instead of taking my hand away from my breast, I curl my thumb and pinch my nipple lightly between my thumb and middle finger, the sharp pressure sending a jolt of pleasure straight to the apex of my thighs.

I let out a soft ghost of a moan. I drag my tongue around my lips, and once I imagine Tuck's mouth crushing against them, I know I'm a goner.

I draw my hand away from my breast, pulling it lower, letting my fingertips drag against the sensitive areas of my stomach as they crawl to the waist of my shorts underneath the covers.

I let myself sink underneath the quicksand of my fantasies. I don't fight it. I plunge my hand into my shorts and run my finger down my slit, feeling my heat and my wetness.

Pleasure detonates deep inside me when I brush my throbbing clit with the pad of my finger. I put my phone down as my eyelids flutter closed, eyes rolling back behind them.

Images of Tuck's bicep bulging, so hard and defined and sharp, like it was carved out of granite, blare in my mind as I graze my clit again. A wave of pleasure rolls through me and makes my back arch.

Maybe I'll regret this after I come down from the orgasm I can already feel building inside me. Maybe I'll regret letting my mind run wild, coming with images of the one guy I can't stand, the last guy in the world I should be thinking about this way, in my head.

But I'll just have to regret it, then; because right now, there's no way I can stop.

I imagine the razor-sharp definition of Tuck's ab muscles, of his wide chest, as he pulls his shirt over his head. My chest vibrates with another moan, the pleasure growing hotter as it snakes through me.

When I think about Tuck's head between my legs, imagining it's his tongue touching my clit instead of my fingers, I buck my hips forward, arousal humming through my blood. I can feel a ball of pressure expanding low in my core as an intense sensation tingles up my spine, a sure sign that I'm on the precipice of climax already.

My breaths grow shorter as I rub my clit harder, my other hand cupping my sensitive tit.

Images flash through my head of Tuck, looming over me and settling his trim hips between my thighs, his hardness pressing into me; me digging my fingernails into the dense, corded muscle of his back, or into his tight, firm ass cheeks as he thrusts ...

I suck in a sharp breath as my orgasm unfurls inside me. Pleasure pulses through my body. My eyes clench so tightly that splotches of light burst behind my eyelids, and all the while I'm bucking my hips, imagining that with each thrust upward, I'm being met by Tuck plunging down into me.

My body tingles all over as the aftershocks of my climax

surge through me. My head feels light and blissful, the residual bursts of pleasure cradling me like a warm blanket.

For a while, I'm floating on a puffy cloud of relief—but when the endorphins dissipate, I'm proven right. I do regret it.

My cheeks burn with embarrassment even though there's not a soul other than myself who could possibly know I just came thinking about the guy I've been trying to avoid for four months.

In three days, I'll have to share an enclosed space with him again, sitting right next to him knowing that I moaned in ecstasy imagining his head between my legs.

What would he say if he knew?

Has he ever done what I just did? Fisted his cock while thinking about running his hands over my body, thinking about thrusting between my thighs?

Embers of arousal still smoldering inside me start to glow again, but this time I'm in control of myself enough to push those thoughts from my mind.

I don't need to be thinking of Tuck tonight any more than I already have.

What I do need, is a cold shower.

10

TUCK

I groan in relief as hot streams of water flow over my tight muscles, relieving them after the punishing workout.

Rhys and I just finished a weightlifting session. It got a little bit competitive. Honestly, most of my weightlifting sessions get competitive. Most of everything I do gets competitive. What can I say? I'm competitive by nature.

I should've known better than to try and go toe-to-toe with Rhys when it comes to back and shoulder lifts, though. Rhys is a defenseman of the grittier variety. He doesn't need to be as fast and nimble on the ice as I need to be, so he can afford to carry more muscle.

Me, I've got plenty of muscle, but I prefer to stay leaner than guys like Rhys or Hudson, both because it suits my style of play better, and because I think it makes me look better naked.

And how I look naked is *very* important to me.

Still, I pushed myself as far as I could go with the weights, and I'm feeling the repercussions.

I moan in discomfort as I try to rotate my shoulder, the

tight and sore muscle restricting my range of motion. I turn my hips to put my shoulder directly into the stream of hot water, sighing in comfort as it eases the ache.

I close my eyes and let my mind wander as I take a deep breath of the steamy air.

Of course, my mind immediately goes to the same place it's been going to whenever I've closed my eyes since yesterday: to sitting next to Olivia in that tutoring room.

I can almost smell the strawberry and vanilla scent that wafted from her hair right now.

I dip my head under the stream of water, looking down so that my hair gets soaked. My eyes are still closed, thinking about that tutoring session ...

When our hands brushed when she handed me that pencil? Fuck, the arousal that ripped through me from that tiny speck of contact was more intense than anything I felt the last time I had sex.

Which was ... I've lost count of how many days. But it's been *months*.

When I finally open my eyes, I'm staring down at my cock, rock hard and bobbing up and down as it throbs with want.

I look side to side. The showers here at Brumehill are individual stalls, and Rhys is gone now. I'm alone.

When I remember the sparks that erupted when my knee glanced against Olivia's yesterday, my arousal only ratchets up. My balls are tight and aching, begging for release.

"Fuck it," I murmur as I wrap my fist around my cock.

A growl rumbles in my chest while I slowly pump up and down my length, keeping my grip light for now.

Rivulets of hot water cascade down my chest, trickling down the ridges and valleys of my defined physique as I increase the speed of my hand. A tight ball of pleasure coils deep in my core, sending tendrils of heat spearing through me until my muscles are taut and my grip is tighter.

When my fist glides over my swollen mushroom head, I graze the pad of my thumb over the opening of my dick, imagining it's the tip of Olivia's pretty pink tongue doing so instead.

My teeth grit at the sensation that rolls through me, a curse dropping from my mouth.

What I wouldn't give to have those sassy lips wrapped around my cock. I've always prided myself on lasting a long time in the bedroom, but she'd probably make me come in less than a minute.

The first time, that is. After that, I'd treat her to an orgasm or two of her own with my mouth or my fingers. Or both. Once I was ready for round two, *then* I'd show her all about the patented Tuck McCoy stamina.

I wonder if she's ever done this, made herself come while thinking about me.

I bet she has. Her words might be cutting, but she doesn't have as good a poker face as she thinks she does. I've seen the way her eyes bulge when she catches a glimpse of my muscles. The way her cheeks darken to a crimson hue when I make an innuendo. The way her gaze dips to my lips just before she looks away from me.

The thought of her cute face flushed with pleasure with me on her mind is enough to push me past the point of no return.

The hot pressure at the base of my spine tells me I'm just a couple pumps away from spilling my cum onto the tiled floor, and the tightness in my balls tells me it's going to be one big fucking load that I bust.

My hips rock forward with the motion of my hand, and

with every thrust, I wish my hips were slapping against Olivia's soft, round ass. My jaw muscles pop and my breaths become jagged gasps as my orgasm grips me.

"Fuuuck," I roar. My body convulses with savage pleasure while thick ropes of hot cum gush from my cock.

I'm so spent that I have to grip the edge of the shower stall. I'm sucking in air, trying to catch my breath as my semi-hard dick hangs limp. The swollen head is so sensitive that I wince when a stream of water grazes it.

Once my knees stop shaking, I quickly soap up, wash my hair, turn off the shower, and dry off.

As I'm getting dressed, I catch myself whistling, feeling light as a feather and totally unwound, high on endorphins from the workout and the most mind-blowing orgasm I've had in ... I can't even remember.

On top of all that, one thing boosts my mood even higher: I'm looking forward to seeing Olivia again on Thursday.

11

TUCK

"You're in a bad mood." Those are the first words out of my mouth when Olivia steps into our tutoring room.

"No, I'm not," she replies instinctively, before furrowing her brow and arching an eyebrow. "What makes you think so?"

"I can tell. You're grumpy."

"That's just because I have to spend the next forty-five minutes in your company," she shoots back. But there's no bite to her words. They're lighter than they usually are when she throws a verbal jab at me. Almost playful.

I try not to smile when I pick up on it.

"Nope," I reply, shaking my head. "It's not that. You have a specific kind of scowl when you're in a bad mood *because of me*."

A huff whooshes out of her—but, again, it's not a sharp huff. It's almost like she tried to disguise a laugh.

"What are you," she asks, "a scowl expert now?"

I just nod. "As a matter of fact, I am. Now that I'm besties with Hudson, I've become a master scowl interpreter. Just like how an expert bird watcher can look at two different birds that seem identical to the untrained observer, yet know that they're in fact totally different species."

"You're ridiculous," she says, but this time there's no way she can hide the half smile on her lips. My chest squeezes at the sight of it.

"But I'm right. Come on, spill the grumpy beans. We can't have a productive tutoring session while you're preoccupied like this."

She blows out a breath that she wants me to think is of exasperation, but I know it's really just supposed to mask a laugh. "I'm just a little ... hangry, is all."

"Hangry?" I repeat, making myself sound mortified. I push my chair back from the table and stand up. "We have to get you food. You can't get through a forty-five-minute tutoring session while you're hangry."

"Sure I can," she says, rolling her eyes. "Besides, I'm hangry for a very specific snack that I've had a weird hankering for all day, and it wasn't in stock at the convenience store when I stopped by on the way."

"What is it?" I ask.

"Those Pretzel M&M's." She lets out a laugh. "Stupid, right?"

I shake my head, a grave expression on my face. "There's nothing stupid about being hangry over a very specific snack craving. This is a deadly serious situation, Lockley. We have to get you those Pretzel M&M's." With that, I'm striding towards the door, like I'm The Terminator and nothing in the world can keep me from carrying out my mission.

"We can't waste a tutoring session traipsing around town looking for Pretzel M&M's," Olivia objects. "Your next essay is due next week, and we need to review your outline." She crooks an eyebrow at me. "You *did* make the outline, right?"

"Of course I did," I answer. "And you'll be very impressed with it. Trust me, I'm not going to have an issue finishing this essay. Your advice from Monday helped a ton. We're already five minutes early, so we have fifty minutes. We'll take my car, it's in the parking lot right next to the building. We'll be back with time to spare."

Olivia looks to the side, drawing her bottom lip between her teeth. I can tell I'm tempting her.

I *really* like the idea of tempting Olivia Lockley, even when it's over something as silly as this.

"Fine," she folds, her hangry-ness winning out.

I pump my fist in triumph. "Let's go."

About a minute later, I'm in the driver's seat of my Mercedes with Olivia Lockley right next to me in the passenger seat. I've already accepted I'm down bad for this girl, but it's almost a little concerning just *how* good something as simple as having her in my car feels.

Fuck, imagine how good it would feel to *really* have her in this car—in the back seat ...

I pump the breaks on that thought.

We're on a mission: satisfying Olivia's hangry-ness. I'll let myself indulge in thoughts of backseat shenanigans with Olivia later tonight.

"Let's try the gas station on the other side of town," I suggest as I start the engine. "They're always filled to the brim with snacks."

"Good idea," Olivia answers as she snaps on her seatbelt. Then she turns to me with a worried expression on her face. "Please don't tell anyone I said *good idea* to you. Especially not Summer. I'll never live it down."

I wiggle my eyebrows. "We're keeping secrets from our friends now? That's kinda hot."

She rolls her eyes and arcs her head away from me. "You're ridiculous."

That's the second time today she's called me ridiculous. Is it weird that I like it?

"Mhm." Before pulling out of my parking space, I sync my phone with the radio. "Alright, you get to pick the first Taylor Swift song. What's your favorite?"

"I don't have a favorite," she answers.

I turn my head to her, drilling her with a knowing glare. "Bullshit. Everyone has a favorite Taylor Swift song."

She shrugs. "Not me."

I know she's full of shit. So, I just keep looking at her. I can tell that my gaze is slowly burning through her defenses. "I can't start driving before I queue up the first Taylor Swift song of the ride, and it has to be your favorite. Because I know you have one."

Her cheeks color lightly with embarrassment, which makes my lips tilt upward. Olivia is so guarded, to the point where she holds back even from something like sharing a favorite song.

She's just the type who likes to keep things close to her chest. Which is funny, because she's able to pour out the most emotional performances on stage, with a packed audience's attention riveted to her.

"Alright," she admits defeat after a couple beats of my gaze burning on her expectantly. "*Mr. Perfectly Fine.*"

I hoot. "Knew you had a favorite T. Swift song." I turn on the song and turn up the volume, belting out the lyrics as we pull out of the parking lot and onto the road.

We get through *Mr. Perfectly Fine* and one more song before pulling into the gas station parking lot.

"Alright," I begin as I roll to a stop, using the same voice I do when I'm drawing up hockey plays with my team. "We have to be efficient. When we get in there, you check out the snacks they have displayed by the register. I'll check the candy aisle."

This time she can't hide a smile and a tiny laugh that bubbles from her curled lips. The sound makes my chest pang. I could very quickly grow addicted to hearing Olivia Lockley's laugh.

"Yes, sir," she says. Her words are sarcastic, but her calling me *sir* ... fuck, it does something to me. I clamp down on my desire so that I'm not walking through this gas station with a tent pitched in my pants.

We follow the game plan when we're inside. She heads towards the registers while I make a beeline to the candy aisle. And when I get there ... I spot them.

A display case full of Pretzel M&M packets, right on the shelf in front of me.

I open my mouth to call out to Olivia—but then I stop.

We've got plenty of time left. And I'm enjoying this silly little adventure with her way too much.

We can afford one more stop and still get back to the tutoring center with plenty of time to spare. I genuinely think my outline is really good, and there won't be much for us to go over today, anyway.

The big grocery store on the other side of town will definitely have some in stock, too. Then Olivia and I will have more time hanging out together in my car. And we'll get to wander around a grocery store together ...

Man, what's with me? Why does the thought of *wandering around a grocery store* with this girl make my heart sing like a hummingbird?

It does, though. And now that the thought's been planted in my mind, it only grows more appealing.

"You find any?" Olivia asks as I walk out of the candy aisle towards her, empty-handed.

I should feel bad when I lie to her, "Nope. All out here, too."

But I don't.

At the end of the day, she's still going to get her Pretzel M&M's, just ten minutes later than she would have otherwise. And I'll get to spend more time with her. Win-win.

"Darn it," Olivia grumbles. "Now I'm even *more* in the mood for them."

"Let's go to Wambley's," I say. It's the big grocery store on the other side of town. "They're definitely going to have some in stock."

She purses her lips thoughtfully for a beat. "I should say no so we can get back to our tutoring session. But I really want those M&M's now ..." Indecisiveness flashes across her face for a moment, but it doesn't take long for her cravings to win out. "Alright, let's go."

The slight twinge of guilt I feel about my little white lie washes away when I'm back in my car next to her. There's nothing wrong with a lie for the greater good, right? Because even though she won't admit it, I know that Olivia is enjoying this little adventure, too.

SHIT. How can they be out of Pretzel M&M's here?

Wambley's has a reputation for stocking everything. For as long as I've lived in Cedar Shade, I've literally never had something I was in the mood to eat, and *not* found it when I came here.

Until now.

Guilt pricks at the nape of my neck. Now it's my fault that Olivia's Pretzel M&M craving isn't going to be satisfied.

Olivia lets out a disappointed sigh as we stand right in front of the display case where every flavor of M&M's are stocked to the brim, *except* the pretzel kind.

"Oh, well," she shrugs. "We tried our best."

I offer to buy her as many of the other flavors as she wants, but she declines, saying that her craving is very specifically for the pretzel flavor, and she's not in the mood for anything else.

My chest sinks as I sling my hands into my pockets. We walk disappointed back down the aisle. "How the hell did they have every other flavor in stock, but zero pretzel ones?"

But then, as we turn towards the front of the store where all the registers are, I spot the answer to my question.

One guy is holding a single shopping basket, which is piled high with bags of Pretzel M&Ms.

I nudge Olivia and direct her attention to him. "I'm not seeing things, right?"

"Holy shit!" she whisper-shouts. "Who needs that many Pretzel M&M's?"

"For real. I know I shouldn't judge, but I'm judging."

Olivia shrugs. "Early bird catches the worm, I guess."

Nah. I'm not ready to accept defeat that easily. I walk towards the guy, Olivia following behind me tentatively.

"Hey, buddy," I greet him when I'm by his side. "Looks like you got all the Pretzel M&M's. You mind sparing a pack or two for us? We came all the way here just for 'em."

He turns his head. His eyes elevator me with an icy, distinctly unfriendly glare. "I'm not your buddy. And no. They're mine."

Then he turns his head forward again and takes a step

forward as his line moves up, brushing me off like I was nothing more than a mosquito he's shoeing away.

Unlucky for him, I'm not ready to accept defeat *that* easily, either.

Time to bring out the big guns. Tug on his heartstrings. I know Olivia's not going to like the strategy I have in mind, but it's for the greater good. For *her* greater good.

"Please, sir. My girlfriend," I tilt my head back in Olivia's direction, "she's pregnant." I have to fight a smirk as I hear Olivia suck in a dismayed gasp behind me. "She's not showing yet, but the weird cravings are already hitting her hard. And she needs some Pretzel M&M's. You know how it is."

The same unfriendly eyes drill into me. This time, his expression is accompanied by a haughty scowl.

"Girlfriend?" he utters the world disdainfully. "Back in my day, people got married first. Maybe if you were able to plan your life better, you wouldn't have a knocked-up girlfriend, *and* you'd have the food you needed without having to beg people standing in line."

Okay, fuck this guy.

Initially, my next plan was to offer him money to give me a pack of those M&M's if the pregnant girlfriend strategy didn't work. Now that I know what a shit-head this guy is, though, I have zero scruples playing dirty.

"Holy shit!" I jump half a step back, bulging my eyes like I've just seen something shocking, pointing across the store.

The ploy works. The Pretzel M&M hoarder instinctively whips his head in the direction of my jutted-out finger. While he's looking away, I quickly and deftly snatch a handful of M&M packets out of his bag, immediately passing them behind me to Olivia.

To her credit, she picks up what I'm laying down immediately, grabbing them from me and holding them behind her back, angling her body behind mine for extra secrecy. All this is accomplished in half a second, before the guy turns his head back to me, his eyebrows drawn low and his annoyed scowl carved even deeper.

"Huh," I say, tilting my head. "Thought I saw something over there. Guess not."

With that, I quickly turn away, careful to keep my body between Olivia and the guy's line of sight so he doesn't have a chance to see the bounty she's holding, rightfully pilfered from him.

We hurry to the self-checkout section.

"*Four* bags!" Olivia whispers in excitement, her eyes wide as she glances at me. She's looking at me like she's impressed. I have to admit, I like it. I like it a lot.

With our surplus of Pretzel M&M's, I grab a bag for myself and open it once I'm seated in my car. I pop one in my mouth, and I don't know why, but it's just about the best thing I've ever tasted when I bite down on it.

"Damn, these *are* good," I say.

"Mhm," she mumbles appreciatively. "Nothing like satisfying a craving."

I bet. There's one craving I have when it comes to Olivia Lockley that I bet would feel *otherworldly* to satisfy.

But you know what? As true as that is, right now, I don't even dwell on it.

Just sitting next to her in my car, singing Taylor Swift songs while I shove junk food in my mouth as we drive back to the tutoring center—this feels pretty damn otherworldly, too.

12

OLIVIA

My Dad isn't good at taking no for an answer.

When I told him last week that I was going to have to pass on his offer to come down to Charleston and act in *Last Bus Out*, I was surprised how easily he accepted my decision.

I should have realized he'd accepted it *too* easily.

It turns out, he hasn't really accepted it at all. Instead, it's more like he made a temporary retreat.

Over the last couple days, he's launched a counter-assault on my better judgment, texting me and calling me constantly, trying to convince me that this is just too good of an opportunity to turn down.

It's frustrating. I know it's a good opportunity. I'm not happy about turning it down. But this is my future we're talking about, and I know for my future, going through with this internship is the best decision.

It sucks to make a disappointing decision that you know is the smart thing to do, even if it's the boring thing to do. Having people try to talk you out of it only makes it worse.

I'm currently taking a deep breath as I hold my phone to my ear, enduring more of my dad's persuasion.

"Daddy," I say, a bite to the word after he finishes his spiel. Normally I call him *Dad*, but I've developed the habit of going back to *Daddy* when he annoys me. I think it butters him up and makes him less eager to argue with what I'm saying. "I know you wanted me down there to act with you. I wish I could do it, too. But I've already committed to this internship. It would be a really, really bad look if I backed out. It could hurt my professional reputation."

Static hisses from my phone. "What was that, dear?" my dad's voice comes out sounding choppy. "I think I'm breaking up. I'm ..."

The call drops.

I let out a sigh of relief.

I don't know what happened to his signal, but as long as it isn't a life-threatening disaster, which I doubt, I'm thankful to it for cutting our conversation short.

That was like talking to a brick wall. A brick wall that just repeats the same argument over and over, each time with more stress on the words, but without altering the logic one iota.

My stomach churns in annoyance as I feel my phone vibrate again. I guess my dad's signal is back.

Without even looking at the screen, I slide open the call.

"Yes, Daddy?" I answer.

But there's just silence on the other end.

Until, after about two beats, I hear a sharp breath.

Even though it's just a breath, it doesn't sound like my dad.

"Hello?" I ask into the phone.

There's a cough on the other end. This time, I pick up a hint of the voice, and my chest catches as I seem to recognize it. Dread pools in my stomach, thinking that surely it can't be …

"Sorry. I just … I need a minute."

My stomach drops. There's no mistaking the voice. No mistaking who I'm on the phone with.

I just called Tuck McCoy *daddy*.

He takes another deep breath and lets it out in a long, drawn-out sigh. "Still need a minute here. To recover. I just didn't think … I didn't think we were at that point in our relationship yet."

I roll my eyes and groan. "Tuck, I …"

"No, no," he interrupts. "Don't get me wrong. I'm not complaining. I'm *really* not complaining."

"I didn't know it was you on the phone."

There's another beat of silence. When he finally speaks again, his voice is low, rough and gravelly, with a sharp edge to it. "Who else are you calling *daddy*?"

There's an unmistakable undercurrent of jealousy in his voice—*real* jealousy. For some reason I'd rather not examine, it makes me feel a tingle low in my center.

"Uh, my actual father," I answer.

"Oh. I guess that's acceptable."

"That's a relief," I snark. "You know me, always desperate for your approval."

"Are you desperate for my *praise*, too?" Tuck asks, his voice throaty and suggestive.

There's that stupid tingle again.

"How did you get my number anyway?" The question suddenly occurs to me, and asking it is a great excuse to get us off the unfortunate track this conversation is currently on.

"Summer gave it to me," he answers.

I gasp. "The little traitor …"

He chuckles, a smooth and rumbly sound. If it were anyone else's chuckle, I'd probably reflect on how good it sounds, how its vibration is like a massage to my ears ...

"Don't blame her. I begged for it because I need to reschedule Monday's tutoring session. We're throwing a surprise birthday party for Kiran, one of my teammates."

I roll my lips. "Are you sure you're not putting it off because you won't have the first draft of your essay done in time?"

"No way. I finished it already. And it's by far the best essay I've ever written. I'm really proud of it. Seriously, you've been a lifesaver showing me how to outline and organize my thoughts and shit."

It's maybe not the most eloquent compliment I've ever received, but it is a compliment, and it sounds genuine. There's a bright, happy feeling in my chest, and I even feel an involuntary smile tilting on my lips.

"Alright. We can reschedule. How's Tuesday, same time?"

"Perfect. I'll do an extra shot in your honor at Kiran's party as a thank you."

I laugh. "That's really not necessary."

There's another pause on his end. "Hey, Lockley?"

"Yeah?"

"I just made you laugh."

For some reason, that makes me laugh again. "Wow, aren't you observant?"

"You didn't even try to hide it. I think this is a milestone in our relationship."

"See you Tuesday, Tuck," I say, rolling my eyes.

"You sure will." He disconnects the call.

Tuck is just too much. Too ridiculous. Too obnoxious.

Why did talking with him just put me in a better mood?

13

TUCK

This is our bye week. With a hockey-free weekend, the guys and I decided to take advantage of it by hitting up Starlite on Friday night, the hottest new club in Cedar Shade. Not that it has a ton of competition in the small college town.

It just opened last semester, taking over and renovating an old warehouse. It's got a hip, upscale vibe, and it's the kind of place that girls go all out for. This place is a sea of girls in tight dresses, wearing makeup that must've taken hours to apply. It's like a Paris fashion show in here.

The rest of the guys on the team—other than Hudson, of course, who's very happily spoken for—are taking advantage of it, mingling with gorgeous girls dressed to the nines.

That's what I should be doing, too.

But it's the same sad story for me. When I sweep my gaze over the room of dolled-up knockouts, not a single one of them stirs any desire in me.

I swear, I'm feeling so little below the belt in front of such beautiful women, that I'd worry I've got a medical condition—if not for the fact that just days ago, when I saw

Olivia, my cock was hard as steel, throbbing in rhythm to my heartbeat when I was doing no more than sitting next to her in our tutoring room.

Suddenly, as I'm sipping on an outrageously overpriced cocktail and letting my gaze wander across the room, I feel a twitch of life below my waist.

Because I spot Olivia.

When I do, the sight hits me like a sledgehammer to the chest. She's fucking *stunning*.

Her hair is tied in a tight knot, glistening under the soft lights. Her lips are bright red, her lashes long and dark. I don't know if it's the lighting, or some kind of makeup she has on, but her freckles stand out more than usual.

She's breathtaking. Literally. I realize it's been a couple beats since I've inhaled, and when I do, I feel a hitch in my chest.

My dick wants to rip out of my pants when she takes a step forward, and I catch of glimpse of what she's wearing through the crowded dancefloor.

Her dark blue dress is plastered to her body. Strapless, tight, with the hem ending just above her mid-thigh. The swell of her breasts and the curve of her hips are highlighted to perfection.

As she walks to the bar, laughing about something with Summer and a couple of their other friends, I notice two guys close to them turn and feast their eyes on her.

My jaw muscles pop, teeth grinding as my grip curls tight around my glass.

I can't expect guys *not* to look at Olivia with lust in their eyes when she's dressed like that, but that doesn't mean I have to fucking like it. Because I don't.

I try to calm my irritation by lifting my glass and draining the rest of the drink. It might be expensive as hell, but at least it's strong. A stiff drink is what I need if I'm going to spend the next couple hours in this place knowing Olivia's here, dressed like *that*.

Hudson's next to me, talking about something with Sebastian, but I notice him suddenly trail off mid-speech, leaving his words hanging in the middle of an unfinished sentence. I glance to my side and see his eyes riveted to Summer.

His jaw hangs slack, his eyes hazy with a drugged look. Our grumpy goalie is so smitten it isn't even funny.

Okay, actually it is.

Summer turns around from the bar with a drink in her hand, and their gazes lock from across the room. The expression on Summer's face changes, the amused grin she had from her conversation with her friends turning into a dreamier smile, an intoxicated look lacing into her eyes even though she hasn't yet taken a sip of her drink.

Hudson sets his drink down and marches over to her.

"Who would've guessed Hudson would become the biggest lovebird out of all of us?" Sebastian says, a chuckle in his voice. He's not feeling at all spurned by Hudson walking away from their conversation the second he saw Summer. He knows, like we all do, that Hudson's so in love that it's like he's under a spell.

A twang of envy pulses in my chest when Hudson steps to Summer, grabs her firmly by the waist, and pulls her close to him and into a kiss.

My gaze flits to the left, to Olivia, and when it lands on her, she's looking at me, too.

My blood thickens. Her long lashes and the dark outline around her eyes make her green irises pop with even more luminosity than usual. My breath catches in my chest as the rest of the room becomes hazy except for her.

"Definitely Tuck." Hearing my name pulls me out of the daze. I break eye contact with Olivia to turn to the side, where Carter's looking at me.

"Huh?" I question.

"We're talking about who's gonna be the last of us to settle down," Sebastian says.

Lane nods. "Tuck. For sure."

I narrow my eyes, feeling a strange prickling of annoyance on the back of my neck. "What makes you say that?"

There's a defensive edge to my voice. Which is weird, because if you asked me four or five months ago who among the Black Bears would be the last to settle down, I'd have said myself, too.

Shit, I'd probably have insisted it.

But when my gaze slices to Olivia again, who's now talking with her other friends and Summer, who Hudson has his arm slung possessively over, there's an unpleasant, regretful burbling in my stomach.

Maybe it's exactly that reputation that explains why Olivia won't give me the time of day.

"Maybe the fact that you've literally said you never want to settle down," Lane answers my question.

I guess he's got a point there. I chew on my inner cheek, having no response.

For some reason, this bothers me. The idea that everyone thinks I'm just naturally averse to settling down, to having a real relationship.

Yeah, my own actions and statements have earned me that reputation. It's something I've been conscious of and never bothered by before. But now there's a knot in my stomach as I ponder it.

I *could* be a relationship guy, damn it. I want—

I make a sharp turn mentally away from finishing that

thought, like a car veering suddenly off course when a deer jumps on the road and into its path.

Is that what I want? I've never wanted it before. I've never thought about it before. But ...

My gaze alights on Olivia again. She's turned towards one of her friends, and I'm afforded a view of her profile: the soft outline of her chin, the gentle swell of her breasts, the creamy smoothness of her bare arm ...

When I first met Olivia, when Summer took her out to the bar to celebrate with the team after a victory, what I wanted from her wasn't complicated. I can't deny it. It was lust at first sight.

But over time I became infatuated with more than her looks. I started to like her attitude, her wit, the way she challenges me. When I first saw her on stage, I was blown away by her talent.

She's interested in things I'm not, like those artsy movies; some might think that two people having different interests makes them less compatible, but for me it just makes Olivia more intriguing.

There's just something I feel when I'm with her that I've never felt with anyone else.

Yeah, what I wanted from Olivia was simple at first. But the tension I'm feeling from this conversation tells me that, somewhere along the way, what I want from her became a lot less simple.

That's obvious from the fantasies I have about her.

Don't get me wrong, I still fantasize about getting her alone in my bedroom. The things I'd do to her body. The noises she'd make for me. Shit, I fantasize about it multiple times a day. But ...

I think about other things, too. I think about having

more days with her like that one where we drove around Cedar Shade looking for Pretzel M&M's.

I fantasize about things as mundane as going to a coffee shop with her and sitting at a table doing our schoolwork, silently but together.

Things like spending a rainy night with her on the couch, bored to tears as she makes me watch one of her long, boring artsy movies—but still enjoying it, because I'm doing it with her.

Things like us trying to cook dinner together, me making a fool of myself because I'm totally hopeless in the kitchen, and us both laughing as we find the end result is so bad that we have to order delivery.

Things like me sneaking up behind her on campus as she leaves her class, surprising her with a present I bought her just because I can.

I realize I've got a goofy smile plastered to my face just thinking about these things. Man, I'm beyond down bad.

Down bad for a girl who herself has no interest in doing any of these things with me ...

At least, that's sure as hell what she wants me to think.

I know I'm cocky to the point of overconfidence. But I don't think I'm imagining the cracks I've noticed forming in Olivia's *I Hate Tuck McCoy* façade.

It hits me that I've been lost in this daydream for some time. When my gaze searches out Olivia again, she's not where she was. My eyes bounce around the room until I finally find her—talking to some guy.

My ab muscles tighten. An acidic feeling rolls through my chest, rising up my throat and filling my mouth with a bitter taste.

That fucker's standing way too close to her, using the loud music as an excuse to lean close to her ear.

I bet his nostrils are filled with the same strawberry and vanilla scent from her hair that I've grown to savor while sitting next to her during our tutoring sessions. The thought makes a downright irrational jolt of jealousy surge through me.

My gaze locks on her face, and I feel a measure of relief when I don't notice any interest in her expression. In fact, she looks like she's trying to disengage.

But the asshole talking to her clearly isn't getting the hint.

When she says something to him and steps away, he steps right along with her, bending down again—way too fucking close for my liking—and saying something else into her ear. That's when I notice Olivia roll her eyes.

A protective instinct pulses in my chest. I push into the crowd, heading in their direction. If Olivia needs rescuing from some oaf who can't take a hint, I'll be more than happy to assist.

Are my motives for walking over to her *entirely* altruistic? Maybe not.

But nobody's perfect. Sure as hell not me.

"There you are, Buttercup," I say, pasting a big, obnoxious grin on my lips as I step towards the two, angling my body to jut in between her and the guy, making him take a step back.

Olivia's brows start to pinch together, but when I shoot her a wink, she picks up on the message. "Yes. Hello ... dear."

Her expression twists in pain at having to offer up that pet name for me. My lips can't help but twitch.

As one song comes to an end on the speakers, another starts. I don't even recognize it, but I say to Olivia, "Oh! It's our song. Come on, let's dance."

I hold my hand out to her. For a beat, she eyes it questioningly, but then she recognizes it as a rope to pull her out of an interaction she's even less into.

She drops her hand in mine. Sparks explode all over me as I gently curl my grip around it. Fuck, her hand feels good. Soft, smooth, delicate. Already I feel my cock thickening.

She flashes a tight, mock-apologetic smile at the asshole who was clearly trying to pick her up, and then follows me as I walk backward. We melt into the dense mass of bodies on the dancefloor.

When I pull her close to me, she doesn't resist. Excitement hums through my blood as I savor the warmth of her pressed against my front.

I curl my arm around her waist and beam a roguish grin. "Our first dance."

14

OLIVIA

"First of all—*Buttercup*?"

Pressed against Tuck, I feel the vibration of his laughter in his chest. The sensation elicits a fuzzy warmth deep in my center.

"You didn't like it?" he asks coyly.

I kind of did. "Of course not."

He lets out a playful sigh. "We'll just have to think of another pet name, then."

"Or not," I protest. But there's no bite to the words. No firmness. They're weak.

I've been getting way too weak around Tuck lately. What should really worry me is the fact that, even as I realize this, I feel no resolution to reinforce the walls I've built up when it comes to him.

Tuck and I sway back and forth lazily as a slower, more mellow tune pumps from the speakers.

This would be the perfect time to thank Tuck for rescuing me from the guy who kept spewing lame pick-up lines at me, and then just step away. The perfect time to find Summer and the other girls and spend the rest of the night on the other side of the bar, studiously avoiding his gaze.

But I don't. I stay here, letting him lead me in our languid motions, feeling the heat of his body against me, the firm pressure of his arm wrapped around my back, the delicious definition of his muscles where his arm presses close to my side.

Another couple bumps into us, and I lose my footing. I stumble briefly, and it makes me grind close against Tuck, my waist pressing into a semi-hard length below Tuck's belt.

Sparks of arousal spread all over my surface. A tight, needy feeling twinges at the apex of my thighs. Involuntarily, a throaty groan escapes my lips.

I look up to see Tuck looking down at me, his eyes hooded and simmering with heat.

"I heard that," he says, the words a raspy and knowing tease.

The cocky, suggestive twang of his voice makes that tight feeling between my legs even worse.

Now's *really* the time I should step away. I feel like I did that night I was reading the romance book Summer recommended me, when I first started touching myself with Tuck on my mind.

I feel like I'm right at the precipice of a steep fall; like I still have time to step away, but if I wait any longer, I might find myself tipping over the edge ...

For the last couple weeks, I've been feeling down about making smart but disappointing decisions. Choosing to do what I *should* do, what I need to do, instead of what I'd like to do.

How nice would it be, just once, to do something I know I shouldn't? Just because I want to, just because it would feel good?

I don't step away.

Instead, I tilt my hips. I grind into him again, harder this time. Now the outline underneath his belt isn't semi-hard, it's rock hard. And it's huge. My stomach flips as I feel the indentation of it right above my mound.

"Fuck," the curse falls from Tuck's lips like a hoarse groan.

Tuck matches my boldness by crooking his hip so that his leg nudges between my thighs. My dress rides up on my hips, the front of Tuck's leg pushing the hem. The feeling of him between my thighs, the knowledge that the thin scrap of my panties is just about an inch away from his leg, makes a wave of heat unfurl over my skin.

Despite the heat I feel, my nipples pebble into tight nubs underneath my dress, as if this sweltering dance floor were as cold as the winter night outside.

Just then, the slower song that was playing ends, and it's replaced with a more rhythmic, kinetic track, better suited for the raunchy atmosphere of a nightclub. The pounding baseline heightens the way my heavy pulse is making my body throb. It makes me want to move my hips.

I do. I cant my hips forward, pressing myself against the flat of Tuck's leg. A whimper escapes my lips as way more pleasure than I expected erupts inside me, snaking through my body and making my heart slam against my chest.

"Holy fuck," Tuck groans, pulling me tighter against him with his muscular arm. He splays his other hand on the curve of my hip, his strong fingertips pressing into my skin over my dress.

My blood flow pounds in my ears. I'm doing something I know I shouldn't, and I like how it feels.

But there's still only so far I'm willing to go. I'm not going to take this all the way and sleep with Tuck tonight. That's a line I'm not willing to cross, not even with this newfound boldness coursing through me.

There are still too many ways that could go wrong.

Even though lately Tuck's shown me he's not the person I initially assumed he was, I still don't trust him. I don't trust that he won't change the way he acts toward me if we sleep together.

I remember how Ryan changed after the first time we had sex. If Tuck acts similarly after getting what he wants, I won't be able to keep from hating him. Really hating him. Which, considering he's Hudson's teammate and best friend, could make things awkward for Summer's relationship. I don't want to risk doing that to her.

I also don't want to risk how hurt I know I'll be if that does happen.

No, I'm not willing to be that reckless, but I'm still willing to be *pretty* reckless ...

Tuck presses his fingertips deeper into the softness of my hip, moving his big, powerful thumb to graze the outline of my hip bone. His touch makes me thrum with desire.

I tilt my hips again. I press myself hard against his leg this time, the friction between my thighs sending a wave of pleasure rolling through me. My stomach feels like it's upside down.

I can feel how wet I am. The peak of my thighs is buzzing, my clit tight, my pussy throbbing with liquid heat. I bet I'm so wet that the front of Tuck's pant leg is damp with the evidence of my arousal.

The thought only turns me on more. I grind into him again, swiveling my hips to the rhythm of the music. I let my forehead drop against Tuck's chest as a moan rips from me, and from his chest, I feel the vibration of his own.

His hand on my hip grips me harder, so hard that I'll

probably see five marks attesting to the presence of his fingertips on my skin when I take this dress off tonight.

"Let's get out of here," he rasps into my ear. His voice is always a cool, easy drawl, but now it's thick and hot with desire.

"No," I answer.

A noise that's a mix between a laugh and a pained groan escapes his throat. "You're just doing this to torture me, then?"

"Maybe I am," I tease. It feels like an out-of-body experience as the words float from my mouth.

Tuck angles his hips so his leg presses against my pussy again. I draw in a gasp. I can feel how soaked my panties are.

His leg still pressed against me, Tuck tips his hips just slightly, giving my tight clit the friction it craves. Ecstasy spears through me, my eyes rolling back as my lashes flutter.

"Fuck, Olivia," Tuck growls. "I can feel how wet you are. You're soaking my leg. You need to come, don't you?"

"Yes," I breathe, my eyes still closed.

"Then let's go—"

"No," I interrupt. "Here."

I can't believe I just said that.

I open my eyes to see Tuck staring down at me, his gaze burning with desire, his jaw muscles flexing with intensity.

"I think I know what you want," he says with gravel in his voice. "You want my fingers, don't you?"

A sharp ache throbs between my thighs. "Yes."

"Shit," Tuck groans. "When did you become such a dirty girl?"

I wish I knew.

He glances behind him. "Come on," he says, his voice low and conspiratorial. He takes me by the hand and leads me through the thick throng of gyrating bodies.

I don't know where he's taking me. All I know is I'm going to follow him anywhere right now. I'm missing him between my thighs, missing the friction of him brushing against my clit so much that a fierce ache is hammering between my legs.

My spine tingles with anticipation. Being brought to climax by the deft fingers of the guy I've been trying to stay away from, at a popular club on a Friday night—something I shouldn't even be considering.

It sure as hell feels good to do something I shouldn't for once. Something irresponsible. Something *indecent*.

We arrive at two stanchions and a velvet rope blocking off access to a dark hallway at the edge of the dancefloor. Tuck throws another glance over his shoulder before stepping over it. I do the same as he tugs me with him.

"They have private rooms you can book for events back here, but they're not using them tonight," Tuck explains. He tries two of the door handles, but they're locked.

He shrugs, then grips my waist and pulls me close to him, flush against his chest. Through my dress and his shirt, I can feel the stark outlines of his defined, rippling physique.

"Think this is privacy enough?" he asks. In the shadows I can just barely make out his plush lips curling into a dark, devious grin.

I turn around. We're shrouded in darkness down this hallway. None of the overhead lights are illuminated. We can still see into the main room, but no one out there could spot us. Even if someone stood right behind the rope and peered down, they'd only be able to barely make out the vague shapes of two people. They'd never be able to tell what we're doing.

"Yeah," I answer. "I think so."

"Good," he growls, the word a savage rasp.

He wraps his arm around me, the thickness of his corded forearm tight against my tummy. He pulls my back against his chest. My breath hitches as I feel enveloped in him. Here in this hallway, away from other people, his scent hits me. It's like sandalwood with hints of cinnamon, and a musky, masculine edge. Deep and overwhelming.

His smell combined with his touch makes me lightheaded. I get a lot more lightheaded, so much that my knees wobble, when I feel his right hand hot on my exposed thigh, torturously crawling up until he passes the hem of my dress.

"This is a one-time thing," I say, my head swimming as my thighs tense with anticipation, yearning for his touch.

"Fine," he breathes.

I suck in a gasp as the tip of his middle finger grazes the very peak of my thigh, right next to my pussy. The pressure of his finger is so tantalizingly close that my body goes taut. My clit throbs, and the whimper I release is so desperate it's almost a sob.

"You're fucking dying for it, aren't you?" Tuck taunts. He drags his other hand up my body and squeezes my breast through my dress.

I let my head fall back against his chest. "Yes," I admit. I'm a quivering mess, and I've lost all ability to be coy, all ability to engage in any push-and-pull with him. "Please," I whisper.

My eyes snap open when his finger grazes over my panties, up the length of my slit. I buck my hips forward as he ghosts his thumb over my clit. He teases me like this for what feels like ages, light touches and grazes of pressure exactly where I want it, but not nearly firm enough to satisfy the throbbing ache.

The low rumble of his laugh is warm on the shell of my

ear. I'm bucking my hips forward, trying to get more contact, more friction than he's giving me, and he's clearly loving the way he's playing my body like an instrument.

"You're so wet. Even through your panties," he says, the thickness in his voice making it clear that he loves that fact. "You're fucking *soaked*."

"I want your fingers inside me," I plead.

Tuck makes a deep, satisfied sound. Finally, he gives me what I want. He pulls my panties to the side and traces a firm circle around my clit.

My pussy clenches, white-hot pleasure rippling through me. I can't believe how good it feels. If Tuck weren't holding me against him, I'm sure that my legs would give out and I'd fall to the floor.

This time when I buck my hips, he supplies the pressure I crave. His thumb keeps circling my clit while his middle finger drags through my folds. My head is spinning. I bite my bottom lip to keep my soft moans from turning into loud cries, cries that could give us away.

Because if someone discovers us here, if Tuck has to stop before I get the release my body is screaming for, I genuinely think I might die.

Finally, Tuck slides a finger inside me.

I gasp. My opening clenches around his big, strong finger. My head swims with bliss. The base of my spine feels tight, and pressure swells deep and low inside me as my entire body burns in the most delicious way.

His other hand kneads into my breast, ratcheting the sensation higher. I find myself wishing my dress were off, wishing we were really alone, wishing I could feel Tuck's hand against my naked tit, the rough pad of his finger scraping the taut nub of my nipple.

But that can't happen. This has to be it. This has to be good enough, just this one time.

Tuck's finger crooks inside me, hitting the perfect spot, and it's enough to send me hurtling to climax. The walls of my pussy clench around him, every other muscle in my body going tight along with it as I'm rocked by the most incredible release I can remember.

Wave after wave of pleasure crashes over me. My eyes are shut tight, pinpricks of light flashing behind them like tiny fireworks against a jet-black sky.

My chest is heaving when my climax subsides. I feel so loose, so light. It's the most relaxed and unwound I've felt in … I can't remember when. It's only after it's been lifted from me that I realize how much tension I was carrying in my body.

"Fucking hell, Lockley," Tuck says. "That was the hottest thing I've ever experienced." He chuckles. "I can't believe I made you come on my fingers when we haven't even kissed."

He turns me around. In the dim light, I can see him bring his hand up to his lips, the same hand that just got me off. One by one, he plunges his fingers into his mouth, slowly licking off my juices.

Even in the dimness, I see his bright blue eyes flash with appreciation as he tastes me. I draw in a sharp breath, my core clenching at how erotic the sight is.

"Let's change that." He places his hand firmly on the back of my neck and pulls me into a kiss.

Our mouths crush together. When he rolls his lips, the taste of my own arousal bursts on my tongue. He angles his mouth to deepen the kiss, and it only fills my mouth with more of my own flavor.

I like it.

I kiss him back harder, wanting more. He slides his

tongue across the crease of my lips, and I part them, granting him access. His tongue spears into me and slants against my own, exploring the inside of my mouth with assertiveness.

Then—I pull back.

His eyes are hooded and hazy. His plush lips are swollen from our kiss. His cheeks are flushed. His chest heaving.

"One-time thing," I remind him. My voice is weak and thin. There's no missing the disappointed lilt in it, either.

He nods. "That's what you said."

"I mean it. I needed this tonight. But this can't be anything more than it was."

Tuck's brow pinches. His swollen lips draw into a straight, tight line on his face. But it only lasts a moment before his features return to their normal relaxed state. "Got it," he says. "Loud and clear."

As we walk back into the main room of the club, what's troubling me isn't whether I believe Tuck.

It's whether I believe myself.

15

TUCK

When I see Olivia on campus, I rush over to her, wrap my arms around her, and lift her off her feet, spinning her around so fast her legs fly back behind her.

I got a *ninety-four* on my latest essay in Martinello's class—all thanks to her.

"Tuck! What are you doing?" she asks through a bubble of surprised laughter.

"Ninety-four, Olivia," I say, still whirling her around, creating a scene in the middle of campus that students are stopping to gawk at. "A ninety-fucking-four!"

She gasps in my arms. "Your essay?"

"Damn right," I reply, beaming. "All thanks to you."

"It's not *all* thanks to me," she protests as I set her down. "I wasn't the one who wrote it." Then she adds, with a grin, "Despite your best efforts."

For just a second, looking at her standing in front of me, my brain short-circuits. I'm thrust back to last weekend, when I held her tight against me and fucked her with my finger. My mouth tingles with the memory of her taste, when I sucked off her juices.

My chest squeezes, desire igniting in my blood. My cock twitches as I remember how stiff I was when I got home that night.

Never in my life was my dick as rock-hard as it was when I got to my bedroom and immediately pulled down my pants, fisting it with the same hand that reached up Olivia's dress and into her panties.

But I clamp down on the desire, and it subsides.

We didn't see each other until our tutoring session the following Monday. When she walked into the room, I was already sitting there, waiting for her. Our eyes locked, and she said, in a firm tone, "We act like nothing happened. No one else knows."

I shrugged and answered, "You got it."

Since then, that's what we've been doing. Acting like nothing happened. We're back to normal.

Not our old normal, where Olivia can barely stand me. But our more recent normal, where she acts like she only tolerates me, but I know she's actually enjoying my company. The new normal where she only halfway tries to hide it when I make her laugh.

Of course, we might be acting like nothing happened, but we both know something did happen. I sure as hell don't forget that fact for even a single moment of the day.

I know Olivia can't forget it, either. The way I felt her shudder in my arms as I made her come, I'm pretty damn confident I gave her an orgasm that *no* woman could simply forget.

Still, we're doing a pretty good job of pretending. Even though there are times when our eyes meet, and a charged silence passes between us.

With this solid A on an essay from a notoriously difficult grader, Coach has already relieved me of needing to continue the tutoring session. Both Olivia and I have busy schedules as it is, and those sessions were only meant to be temporary until I turned my performance around enough that Coach is no longer worried about me getting dinged with an academic eligibility issue.

My chest falls as I think about no longer spending those forty-five minutes together with Olivia twice a week. Without that, I wonder if we're going to default back to our *old* normal, where she avoids me at all costs and we can't even have a conversation with each other, can't even joke around a little bit …

Damn. The thought feels like a pinch to the heart.

Olivia's walking to the arts building for her next class, so I join her on the brief walk.

Today is pretty nice. The temperature is low, but there's no wind, and the sun shines down on campus, tempering the chill. It's almost mild when you're standing right under it.

Olivia's wearing a pale purple knit beanie on her head, her light chestnut hair billowing out from underneath. Her cream-colored puffer jacket is zipped up, and her legs are encased in a pair of tight black jeans. The outfit might be pretty basic, but there's nothing basic about how adorable she looks in it.

As the excitement of my unprecedented ninety-four-percent grade wears off, and we're still chatting as we walk towards the art building, I can tell that something's bothering her.

I seem to be pretty good at sniffing out when Olivia's in a bad mood. When she's feeling off about something.

"Something wrong?" I ask.

"No. Nothing." Her answer is far from convincing.

The possibility occurs to me that she might be regretting what we did at Starlite on Friday. The thought makes my chest ache. I need to be assured that's not it, so I keep pushing.

"Olivia," I say, a sing-song tease in my voice. "You know you can't hide your emotions from me. If I can tell when a craving for Pretzel M&M's is making you grumpy, then you *know* that no secret is safe."

She blows out a laugh, rolling her eyes. There aren't many sights I enjoy seeing more than when Olivia can't help but let her lips form a reluctant smile at something I say.

"Fine. I am in a bad mood. It's …"

"Yes?" I prod, leaning towards her.

"It's this play I tried out for in Burlington. It's a production of MacBeth happening in the spring. I went to the first round of auditions, and yesterday they called me back to tell me I made it to the second round."

"And?" I know that she has to give up a great acting opportunity over the summer because of an internship that's important to her, but I don't see why a spring performance should be an issue.

"My car," she says, a mournful grumble in her voice. "It's still shot. There's no way I'm going to be able to make it back and forth from here and Burlington for all the auditions and rehearsals relying on the bus."

"I'll drive you, then," I say. I say it like it's an instinct, a reflex, the same way you kick your foot forward when the doctor bangs you on the knee with that rubber mallet.

She side-eyes me. There's a trace of wariness in her eyes, an expression that says she still wants to hold me at arm's length. "No, Tuck."

"Why not? I don't mind."

"You don't even know what the schedule would be. I don't even know. It might interfere with your games, or your practices, or your classes."

"I'd make it work." Again, it's an instinctive reply. Even though she's right. There's every possibility that I *couldn't* make it work, as much as I'd want to. There's no way I'd be able to rearrange my hockey schedule around driving Olivia back and forth to Burlington.

But I still can't stop myself from offering. The prospect of having Olivia alone in my car for the half-hour drive each way is something I'm pouncing on, like spotting the puck unattended on the ice during a hockey game.

"So, what? You're just going to pass on this opportunity?" I ask.

She shoots me a look of reproach. I feel a pinprick of guilt as I realize there was a word unspoken in what question, but which still had to ring loudly in her ears: I really asked her, *You're just going to pass on* another *opportunity*?

"I can't ask you to take time out of your day shuttling me back and forth between here and Burlington, not to mention how long the rehearsals there are actually going to be."

"You didn't ask. I offered."

"And you don't even know whether it's going to conflict with your hockey schedule, which it probably will. The worst thing I could do is agree to take the role, and then end up having to miss rehearsals or even performances because you have a game or a practice you can't get out of and leave them high and dry after I've already committed."

I draw in my bottom lip and gnaw on it. She's right.

It sucks, though. For two reasons. One, I'd *really* like having her in my car twice a day, multiple times a week. And two, it sucks that she has to miss out on another opportunity just because she's not as fortunate as some people and can't afford to have her car repaired.

Then, a thought occurs to me. A flash of inspiration that has a zap of excitement racing up my back. My lips want to carve upward in a smile, but I keep them straight—because I don't want to give away to Olivia what I have in mind.

I want this to be a surprise.

I shrug, feigning nonchalance. "Alright."

She tilts her head back a little, leveling me with a skeptical glare. She's not used to me giving up this easily. But she finally nods with acceptance. "Anyway, here's my building."

"Enjoy your fingerpainting class," I joke.

That gets me another huff-slash-laugh-slash-eyeroll combination. It's quickly becoming my favorite thing. "It's Art History," she says.

"Uh-huh. Well, if you're such an art historian, answer me this. Who invented fingerpainting?" I cross my arms over my chest, arching an eyebrow in challenge.

"You're ridiculous, Tuck," she says on a laugh that she doesn't even try to hold back this time.

"It's been said before, it'll be said again," I drawl.

"Bye," she says, her brow bouncing in amusement.

She turns around to walk up the stairs of the art building, and I find myself wishing very badly that the hem of her jacket was higher, so I'd get a glimpse of that heart-shaped ass I love so much. No such luck, though.

But I've still got a grin on my face as I walk away, because Olivia's about to find her problem of how to get back and forth to Burlington unexpectedly solved.

16

OLIVIA

I turn onto my street as I walk home from a short day of classes. I'm looking forward to brewing myself a hot cup of tea when I get one and jumping back into the book I'm reading. It's another romance book that Summer recommended.

I'm on a full-fledged romance kick. I don't know why it took me so long to get into these books. I'm strongly considering upgrading from reading on my phone to buying a real Kindle.

But after taking a couple steps down my block, an unexpected sight makes my brows draw together and sends a suspicious, uneasy feeling spiraling in my stomach.

My car's sitting where it's been since the day I got it towed, right at the curb in front of our house.

But its hood is open, and parked in front of it is a utility van. A hand reaches from behind the hood, gripping the top of it and pushing it down. A stocky man wearing a work jacket stands at the front of my car, brushing his hands against the front of his dark blue khaki pants.

Suspicion and concern gnaw at me as I hurry my steps towards him.

"Excuse me," I call. "What are you doing?"

"Just finishing up the job," he answers, gathering tools lying on the pavement in front of my car.

"But this is my car. I didn't order any job," I protest. I'm worried that somehow wires got crossed. I ordered the tow truck from an auto repair place, but I didn't order any repairs, because I can't afford them. Did they somehow automatically schedule a repair appointment? If they did, there's no way I'm paying.

"Someone did," the man shrugs. "Paid for it, too. Paid extra for a house call so the car wouldn't need to be brought into the shop. Everything's in order now, car shouldn't be giving you any more trouble."

He reaches into the pocket of his jacket and holds out my own car keys to me. "Here you go," he says.

My jaw goes slack. "How did you get these?"

"Your boyfriend gave them to me," he says. "Maybe he ordered these repairs as a surprise. Well, surprise."

"Boyfriend?" My brow furrows. "I don't have a boyfriend."

The mechanic grins and lets out an amused chuckle. "Maybe tell him that."

I hold out my hand and let him drop my keys onto it. He waves goodbye as he hauls his tool tote into the utility van and drives off. Once the initial surprise starts to wash away, it becomes clear who that *him* must be.

I pull out my phone and send a text. To Tuck.

> What did you do?

The bubbles indicating that he's typing bounce for a

while. When the message finally comes through, I expect a full explanation, but …

> **TUCK**
>
> What did I do today? A bunch of things. Took a shower. Argued with Hudson about whether UFOs are real. Ate a cheeseburger for lunch. Made fun of Sebastian for watching a documentary about the history of philosophy in the living room. Leg day at the gym. Argued with Hudson about whether time travel is possible. Totally is, by the way. Do you want to hear more about the shower?

My lips remain a tight, flat line on my face, my eyebrows tugging together with annoyance as I read his message. With a twitch of my nose, I call him.

"Hey," he answers, his voice bright and cheery. "I take it you *do* want to hear more about the shower? Or maybe more about leg day. I worked my glutes hard today, so they're firm and round and …"

"This isn't funny, Tuck," I cut him off. My voice is cold and harsh.

He's silent for a beat. "Wait. Are you mad?" He sounds perplexed.

"Yes, I'm mad."

"About the car?" Confusion is still obvious in his voice.

"Yes, Tuck. About the car."

There's another beat of silence, followed by a couple strained sounds where he tries to say something, but clearly has trouble finding the words.

"Why?" he finally asks, obliviously.

"Because I don't need you or anyone else coming to my rescue. I can take care of myself." Frustration rises in my throat.

My family's always struggled financially, and though it's been hard, it's built up in me an independent streak. It's something I'm proud of, honestly. I'm proud that I've made it without the help that a lot of people my age have.

Tuck swooping in with his family's money and taking care of this for me … it doesn't sit well with me. At all.

I know he was just trying to help, and part of me recognizes I should appreciate that; but right now, a much larger part feels offended. Like he's trying to play the rich big shot and treating me like a charity case.

"But you did need someone to help you with the car," he protests. He's saying the words like he's making a simple, uncomplicated statement, no different than reading a shopping list. "And I could help you. So, I did. Now you can go to the next round of auditions in Burlington and knock 'em fucking dead like I know you will. What's there to be upset about?"

"You don't get it," I bite back.

He huffs. "You're right about that."

"How did you get my keys, anyway? Are you breaking into my house now?"

"No," he replies, before following up with, "not really. I tagged along with Hudson yesterday when he dropped by to visit Salsa when you weren't there." Salsa's Hudson's cat who lives in Summer's room now. "I found your keys by the door and swiped them. Figured you wouldn't even notice they were gone since you're not using the car. Or at least you *weren't*," he says, adding emphasis. "You can now."

Underneath the annoyance at Tuck for overstepping boundaries, the frustration that he doesn't understand why I'm upset, and the sting of insecurity I feel at the idea of Tuck seeing me as someone who needs his charity, an ember of excitement glows.

Excitement that I actually might be able to get that Macbeth role now.

For some reason, that only ratchets up the negative feelings swirling inside me. I feel a pinch of shame that this opportunity is only available to me now because some rich guy took pity on me.

"I don't get what the big deal is," Tuck continues. "I was in a position to help you, so I helped you. That's what friends do, right?"

"Oh, is that what we are? Friends?" My sarcasm comes out harsher than I intended.

"Whatever, Olivia," Tuck says after a beat of silence on his end. "Talk to you later."

Then, he ends the call.

I'm stewing in a bad mood and conflicting emotions. The rotten cherry on top is the feeling of guilt that laces through everything. Tuck overstepped his bounds, and I'm not in the wrong to feel peeved about it. But I can't stop thinking of the hurt tone in his voice right before he ended the call, after I clearly implied we're not friends.

But we're not friends, right?

Does a *friend* finger you at a nightclub and then suck off your juices?

A shudder rolls through me at the memory. Now there's a tight heat at the peak of my thighs, and that sure as hell isn't making the cocktail of emotions I'm feeling right now any less vexing.

A gust of cold air blows up the street, reminding me that I'm still standing outside. I march up our walkway and into the house.

Instead of that cup of tea I was planning on, I think I need a big glass of wine.

17

TUCK

I kick the wall of the barricade with my skate when I plop down on the bench after a shift change.

"Shit," I curse myself. If there's one word to describe how I've been playing tonight, that's the one.

I've had the puck stolen from me, I've blown passes, I've skated sloppy, I've missed on shots that I had no excuse not to make.

I'm totally out of sorts thanks to another dumb fight with Olivia. I can't focus on what's going on around me on the ice, even though hockey's supposed to be the one thing in my life that I give one hundred percent of myself to.

Even when I'm skating past defenders with the puck on the blade of my stick, trying to avoid bodychecks, in the back of my mind I'm still replaying the conversation we had on the phone the other day. Trying to understand *why* me doing something nice for her made her mad.

I wasn't wrong for getting her car fixed for her, was I?

Of course I wasn't! Without her car, she'd have to pass up another acting opportunity that she deserves to take advantage of.

And it meant nothing for me to do it. Compared to the money my parents make available for me to spend, paying for her car repairs was no bigger a deal than buying your buddy a drink at the bar when you're hanging out.

Maybe that sounds arrogant, but I'm not bragging. It doesn't make me feel like a big shot or anything. It's just a statement of fact.

Players from the other lines finish up the second third of the game for us. Rhys isn't playing his best tonight, either. Not as badly as I am, but he's still below his normal standard.

Might have something to do with how Lane mentioned that his little sister, Maddie, has a date tonight. Second date in a week with the same guy, someone she met in her Biology class.

The glare that flashed in Rhys' eyes and the way his jaw muscles flexed made it clear to everyone looking that he wasn't happy hearing that news—clear to everyone except Lane, that is.

We're trailing 2-3 when we trudge to the locker room for the break before the last third of the game. It's not a position we're used to being in this season. Coach tears us a new one during the break, and when my blades slice back onto the ice for the final third of the game, I'm determined to keep my head clear and focused on hockey.

I'm almost successful. I score an early goal after stealing the puck from an Everwood U defender, a regular opponent of ours from the Portland region in Maine.

But I'm not entirely successful. Towards the end of regulation, I have the perfect opportunity to slam the puck into the net. The goalie is totally out of position, and the puck is rocketing over the ice in my direction off a pass from Sebastian. It's the perfect opportunity to slice a one-timer shot past the goalie's right side.

But just before my stick contacts the puck, I remember Olivia's sarcastic insinuation that we're not even friends. I hit it at the wrong angle, and my shot goes wide, ricocheting off the edge of the goal.

With a score of 3-3 as regulation time expires, we're heading into overtime.

It's a nail-biter, especially on our end. Everwood's offense is skating with a vengeance, peppering Hudson with shots on goal. He's blocking them like a man possessed, though.

It's Carter who bails us out, intercepting a pass between Everwood defenders and then firing off an outrageous shot at distance, sending the puck slamming against the back of the net before the goalie even realizes what's happened.

We eke out the win, and it's the very definition of *eking* out a win.

Normally we're rowdy and pumped-up when we celebrate a win in the locker room, but this time none of us feel like we really earned it.

Coach steps into the locker room, his hands on his hips as he levels us with a stern gaze.

"I almost wish we'd lost out there," he says, "so I could really give you boys the dressing down that performance deserved." He reserves especially cutting glares for me and Rhys.

He spends a couple minutes drilling home how important it is for us to remember that the playoffs are right around the corner, and that they're going to be an entirely new level of competition. Telling us that if we play like that in even a single game during the post-season, we can forget about the Frozen Four championship that everyone here wants so bad they can taste it.

Then, after his spiel, he drops news no one is excited to hear.

"You all know about the NECA gala," he begins. Brumehill is part of the New England College Association, which hosts a fundraising gala every year. "They want a representative of the hockey team there. One of the first line players."

We all groan. All the NECA colleges send students they like to show off to the gala. Some mixture of academic geniuses, students who've started successful businesses or nonprofit organizations, students with compelling backgrounds, and, of course, athletes.

"I know none of you are excited at the prospect and I'm not going to get any volunteers. Trust me, they make me go to the damn thing, too, and it's not exactly a date on my calendar I have circled with a heart. So, we're gonna do this quick and fair."

He holds up his cell phone. "I downloaded an app where I can enter in names, and it'll choose randomly. I put in all your names, so here it goes."

He presses a button on his screen, and we all wait to see which of us is going to be subjected to a night of *mingling* with rich donors and aging academics, wearing a stiff and uncomfortable tuxedo.

"Rhys," Coach announces.

Rhys groans. The rest of us sigh in relief. Then the rest of us start ragging on Rhys about having to go.

"Look on the bright side," Lane says, jabbing him in the arm. Rhys' best friend wears the smile of a man who just dodged a bullet. "Maybe one of those rich donors will be some old widow. You can seduce her and get yourself a sweet place on her will."

"Stop trying to vicariously live your cougar fetish through me," Rhys grumbles.

"Hey, it's not like you had anything better to do on a rare Saturday night when we don't have a game," Carter needles him. Rhys holds up his middle finger.

Rhys may be pissed about having to waste a Friday night at this gala, but as we're trudging home from the arena, I'm pretty sure he isn't the one of us in the worst mood.

The sinking feeling is still in my chest a little later when I walk upstairs while the other guys are hanging out in the living room, drinking beers and playing some videogame.

I fall back onto my bed and hold my phone to my face. I'm looking at my text thread with Olivia. I wish I could send her some stupid joke and know that she's laughing, or at least struggling to hold back a laugh, no matter what she types as a response.

But she's still pissed at me. I don't even totally understand why. Or what I can do about it.

My head drops back against my pillow. I think about that night in the club, when she came on my fingers. I think about that day we drove around town looking for Pretzel M&M's.

And I think about what I can do to get more days and nights like those with Olivia.

18

OLIVIA

"Can you *believe* that it turned out he was the underboss of the Mafia family responsible for her own father's death?"

"I *know*," I respond to Summer, leaning towards her over the middle couch cushion, my eyes wide. "But Nikolai had nothing to do with that!"

Summer tut-tuts, shaking her head after taking a sip of her wine. "Still. I don't know if I could have forgiven him."

"Come on," I say. "After the way he groveled?"

She sighs. "You're right. Of course I'd have forgiven him."

Summer's officially pulled me into the world of smutty romance novels. It's Friday night, and we're spending it with a bottle of wine, on the couch, yapping about a Mafia romance book we just devoured together.

I finished the book when I got home from classes this afternoon. Summer finished it yesterday, and for the past twenty-four hours she's been a ball of impatient energy, eager for me to catch up so we could talk about it. We've been obsessing over it together since I finally did.

The book's been a great distraction from the shitty mood I've been in over Tuck.

In the time I've had to stew on it, I've recognized that maybe I overreacted a little. I mean, I understand from his point of view that he was only doing something nice. Something that was easy for him that would help me.

At the same time, it still doesn't sit right with me. How entitled he felt to involve himself in my business. It's like him taking a big step closer to me than I feel comfortable with.

Granted, maybe it's a little silly to worry about being too close to a guy who I grinded against at a club, who I let pull me into a dim hallway and thrust his hand into my panties, giving me the most incredible orgasm of my life.

A hot blush races up my neck and into my cheeks at the memory.

Summer clearly notices my darkening face and wiggles her eyebrows. "Ah, you must be thinking about the kitchen scene," she says, referring to one of the spiciest chapters in the book.

Thanks for the lifeline, bestie. "Oh, yeah," I say. "Definitely. That scene was so hot."

In terms of believability, my reply certainly doesn't measure up to the standard I hold myself to on stage. But it's enough to keep Summer from suspecting that there's something else making me turn crimson.

Salsa jumps onto the cushion between Summer and me. She rolls onto her back and stretches out, clearly demanding tummy rubs.

Summer and I laugh and oblige, which has Salsa purring with delight. She's a big, fluffy Norwegian Forest Cat. She was a stray, living in an alley in town last semester. Hudson found her and decided to take her home.

But Tuck was allergic, so he had to give her up. This set into motion a series of events which involved Summer taking her in to live with us, in exchange for Hudson pretending to be her boyfriend. Along the way they fell in love for real, and our house has become Salsa's permanent home.

No complaints from me. She's a sweetheart. Hudson says she was vicious when he first found her, but I don't buy it.

After polishing off a generous portion of our wine, we've pretty much exhausted everything there is to talk about when it comes to the book we just read.

Summer takes the opportunity to spring a big topic change on me.

"Still mad at Tuck?" she asks.

I roll my lips. "Yes."

She sighs, sinking back into the couch cushion. "Honestly, I get it. Swiping your keys like that, making such a big gesture when you've only just started to be friendly ..."

"Who says we're friendly?" I interject.

Summer waves my protest away, like she knows even I can't deny that Tuck and I have been on a different footing than we were last semester. "I get how it could come across as sort of a violation of your privacy," she finishes.

I take a sip of my wine. Somehow, the alcohol already flowing through me helps me put into words one major reason I'm upset with Tuck. "I don't like feeling like someone who needs saving."

"I don't think Tuck thinks that about you," Summer says. Ever since I first made my distaste for Tuck McCoy clear—the very first night we met—Summer's chimed in with words of defense for him.

As a roommate of her boyfriend, she knows him better than I do. She likes him and thinks he's a good guy despite the cocky playboy act. I guess she has good reason to. I heard about the way he drove out late at night to help her and Hudson look for a bracelet that she dropped that has a lot of sentimental value to her, when she and Hudson were on a hike in the middle of a forest trail.

"Needing help isn't the same thing as needing saving," Summer continues. "No one who knows you even a little bit could ever dream that *you* need *saving* from anything. But you actually did need help. You know what? You didn't even *need* help. Missing out on those second-round auditions wouldn't have killed you. But why *should* you have missed out on them?"

My eyebrows draw together as I take a thoughtful sip of my wine. Summer is making too much sense. She's making me think I should soften my stance towards Tuck. I'm not sure how I feel about that right now.

After all, I did end up using my car to go to those next auditions in Burlington. I mean, not doing so would have been a level of petty that I haven't quite reached.

And they went well. Great, really. I'm still waiting for them to call me back, but I have a good feeling. Even if I don't land the lead role, just being chosen as an understudy for a role like Lady Macbeth by an organization like the Champlain Theatre Company would be a major feather in my cap at this stage of my career.

"Know what I'm kind of looking forward to?" I say, changing the topic. Summer's given me thoughts to ponder, and right now I just want to move on to a Tuck-free conversation. "That gala in New Hampshire the department asked me to go to."

There's this fancy event that the organization of New England colleges that Brumehill is a part of throws every year. Each school sends a couple of their students each year, and this year Brumehill is really banging the drum about its drama department because an alumnus of ours recently starred in a super successful production run of a play on Broadway that got national attention. They asked me to attend the gala as a student representative of the department.

"Yeah?" Summer replies.

"Mhm. I mean, it's not like a night in Concord, New Hampshire is a weekend in Paris or anything, but I feel like it'll be nice to just, you know ... get away from it all."

"I hear you," my friend says. "Sometimes it's nice to just take a step away for a little while. Recharge your batteries while you have some distance between you and your day-to-day life."

"Exactly. I don't expect the gala will be all that fun, but it's supposed to be fancy, so the catering should be good at least. Have a nice dinner, get a little buzzed on free champagne, maybe order room service dessert when I get back to the hotel room they're paying for. And just be a state away from everything that's been stressing me out." I take another sip of my wine and nod slowly. "Yeah, it sounds pretty nice."

Plus, it's a guaranteed Tuck McCoy-free weekend.

Here, even when I go days without seeing him, the possibility always exists that I'll walk out of a building on campus and see him right there strolling towards me on one of the walkways, or that he'll end up behind me in line at a local store, or sitting at the table next to me at a café.

Next weekend, I'll have the time and the distance to just relax and let my brain slowly work out the knot that's been pulled way too tightly in my mind where Tuck is concerned. I'll come back with a clearer head, recharged.

It's exactly what I need.

19

TUCK

"Whatcha laughin' about?" I ask when I come home after classes to find Summer curled up against Hudson on the couch, laughing at something on her phone.

"Oh, hey, Tuck," Summer says, glancing over the couch towards me, her lips still tilted up in laughter. "Just a TikTok video Olivia sent me. It's an edit about a character in a book we just read together."

"Olivia roped you into reading one of those thousand-page tomes she's into, huh? Was it some Russian novel?" I ask after slinging off my book bag and plopping down on the second couch in the living room.

She giggles. "No, it's a romance."

My brow lifts. "Olivia reads romance books?"

"Mhm," Summer nods, typing something on her phone. "I've made a devotee of her."

"Wow," I say, the exclamation coming out as a breath. "That's really cool."

Hudson chuckles. "Cool?"

"Yeah, it's just ..." I tilt my head, trying to put my finger on why that piece of information impresses me. "Olivia's into artsy and intellectual stuff, right? She's in the drama department. Most of those people can be ... kinda snobby, you know? They'd think they're *above* reading anything except *the classics*. The fact that Olivia isn't like that, that she's as intellectual and artistic as they come but has no qualms enjoying what she likes ... I dunno, just think it's cool is all."

Hudson's quiet for a beat, but then sputters out a laugh. "Dude. If you could see the lovesick look on your face right now."

I blow a raspberry. "Whatever, bestie. You're seein' things."

I push up from the couch and head to the refrigerator for a beer.

Hudson's probably not wrong about the look on my face. Not that I'm in *love* with Olivia or anything. I mean, that would be ridiculous. Despite my best efforts, we hardly really know each other.

But I can't deny that I am in ... fuck, I don't know what it is exactly, but I'm in *something* with her.

The fact that I haven't seen her or talked to her since we got in that argument over me having her car fixed last week hasn't dulled any of my feelings.

I still think about her all the time.

Still hope that every time I turn a corner while walking downtown or step into a building on campus, that chance will put her in my path, that I'll see a glimmer of forgiveness in her eyes, just the slightest invitation to make a stupid joke that has her fighting laughter that she wants to fight less and less each time.

"Oh!" Summer exclaims as I lower myself back on the couch, sipping on my beer. "We think we figured out the book Cindy gave Kazu!"

Now that news has me perking up. Watching the ramen shop owner Kazu and the bookshop owner Cindy awkwardly dance around their obvious feelings for each other has been my, Hudson, and Summer's own personal reality-show-slash-romcom for the last couple months.

"What?" I ask, leaning forward with interest.

"A book called *Days at the Morisaki Bookshop*," Summer says. "We're pretty sure it's the book you guys saw Cindy give him, because get this. Hudson saw him reading the book last week and noticed that he was almost on the last page. I saw him reading the book a couple days ago, and he was definitely just starting it."

My eyes pop. "He's reading the same book over and over. Just because Cindy gave it to him." I jerk my hand up to cover my heart. "It's so adorable I can't take it."

"I *know*!" Summer exclaims, her legs kicking.

"You two," Hudson murmurs, shaking his head.

"Don't you pretend you're not wrapped up in this relationship drama, too," Summer reprimands him, slapping at his chest.

"Yeah," I pile on. "You think it's as adorable as I do. You're kicking your feet on the inside."

Hudson rolls his eyes, but he sure doesn't deny it. Summer and I both know he's a softie on the inside despite his gruff and grumpy exterior.

He unfolds himself from the couch. "Getting a beer myself. You want anything, Summer?"

"No thanks," she answers.

"Tell me this at least," I say to Summer as Hudson walks to the kitchen. "Did Olivia at least use her car to do those next audition rounds in Burlington?"

Summer smiles at my question. "She did. She's feeling pretty optimistic about getting the role, too."

I pump my fist. "Nice!" If she has to be mad at me in exchange for getting an opportunity she totally deserves, well, I'll take that deal all day long.

"The car's working great. So great that she's got no worries about the two-hour drive she has to New Hampshire next weekend."

I quirk an eyebrow. "New Hampshire? Next weekend?"

"Yeah. The drama department asked her to go to this event the college is participating in. It's some kind of gala with other colleges from the region. They booked her a really nice hotel room and are giving her a big gift card for gas money that'll have plenty left over. She's treating it like a miniature vacation."

The NECA gala. Olivia is going to the NECA gala.

The gala Rhys got selected to go to for the team. The gala that Rhys really doesn't want to go to.

Suddenly, I'm starting to feel particularly charitable. I might just do Rhys a solid and tell him I'm willing to take the responsibility off his hands.

"Damn, Rhys. You look like shit."

The burly defenseman turns to me, an eyebrow hitched. "Boy, Tuck, you know how to make a guy feel appreciated."

"Don't get me wrong. You're still sexy as hell. I mean, that bad boy aura you've got with the tattoos and the messy dark hair that falls over your eyes? If I were into guys, I'd be ripping that towel off your waist right now."

"I hate to eavesdrop," Lane says, turning towards us from his locker. "But this is a strange conversation even for *you*, Tuck."

"I'm just saying, Rhys looks tired. Worn out. Like he's

been working too hard, on and off the ice. It's making me sympathetic. So sympathetic that I might ... you know what, Rhys? I'll do it. I'll go to that stupid gala instead of you. You need the rest more than I do."

Rhys folds his arms over his broad, ink-covered chest. "Why?"

"Why? What do you mean why?"

Rhys' brow pinches, his eyes searching me. Geez, is it so hard to believe that I just want to do a solid for a good friend?

"It's because Olivia's gonna be there," Hudson says, appearing suddenly and leaning against our row of lockers.

Damn it, Hudson.

"Huh? Who is? Olivia? Oh. That's interesting." I can hear my own voice well enough to know that I don't share the acting talent of the woman in question. "I didn't even know that." I shrug. "I probably won't even see her there. When I go. Because I'm going instead of Rhys. Because he needs the rest."

Rhys rolls his lips thoughtfully. "You know what? I'm kind of looking forward to it. Nah, I'll go."

He turns around to his locker and steps into a pair of boxers underneath his towel before pulling on where he's tied it to his waist and letting it fall to the ground.

"But ... you don't want to go!"

He shrugs. "Changed my mind."

I know Rhys doesn't want to go. Mingling with a bunch of academics and donors is his version of hell.

I know what he's trying to do.

"You're extorting me, aren't you?" I grouse.

"Extortion? Tuck, do I seem like the type to extort a dear friend of mine?" He turns to me, his wry grin giving himself away.

"Yes." My eyes narrow.

"I'm hurt. All I'm saying is, I'm really looking forward to the gala. I want to go so bad that it would take ... *persuading*, for me to give my spot to someone else."

"How much persuading?"

He pushes his tongue against his cheek and looks up to the ceiling in mock thoughtfulness. "I guess if someone did my laundry for a month ... and took over my house chores for a month ... I might consider it."

"Done."

Rhys laughs. "Wow, that was easy. I need to play poker with you sometime. I'd clean you out."

Rhys can gloat all he wants. A couple extra chores and loads of laundry is a small price to pay for a *miniature vacation* with Olivia Lockley.

20

OLIVIA

Concord, New Hampshire is beautiful. It's got the kind of New England small town vibes that I love so much about Cedar Shade, while being way bigger.

Today's a perfect day to appreciate it. The sun is shining bright in the blue sky, and it's not even that cold.

I roll to a stop in the parking garage of the Baron Hotel right downtown.

The ride over was smooth and relaxing. I just jammed to music and let my head clear. It's early afternoon and the gala doesn't start until five, so I have a couple hours to just lounge in the room that Brumehill booked for me before I have to change into my dress.

I'm kind of looking forward to it, because the dress is *fantastic*. These colleges must really want to make a strong impression at this event, because Brumehill gave me a voucher to rent a gorgeous dress from a high-end boutique in Cedar Shade.

I look incredible in it. Maybe there'll be a hot grad student from another school here to flirt with. I'm not in the mood for a hookup or anything, but I wouldn't mind a cute guy giving me a fluttery feeling or two and an ego boost.

Dragging my small roller suitcase behind me, I cross the walkway that connects the parking garage to the main hotel. There's a line for the check-in desk. Not a surprise, I guess, with so many people coming for this NECA gala.

As I approach the back of the line from behind, my eyes settle on the last figure standing there.

My stomach bottoms out at my initial reaction.

There's something about those broad shoulders stretched across the dark green fleece sweater he's wearing, something about his height ... and as I slowly approach closer, something about the messy, sandy-blonde hair that blossoms from underneath the backwards hat he has on ...

Something about the big, veiny hand that holds the handle of his suitcase ...

I slow to a snail's pace, still several yards behind him.

It can't be.

Then he turns his head. Just a fraction. But it's enough.

I catch the sharp cut of his jaw. The high cheekbones. The dusting of stubble that's darker than his hair. Just the slightest flash of his blue eyes at profile.

My teeth grind. Why the hell didn't my department head tell me that Tuck would be here?

Not that Dr. Werther would have any reason to suspect I'd care that a particular hockey player would be here. Not that she'd even know he was going to be.

Still, I'm going to direct my frustration at her for now, because it needs to be directed at something.

Light as a feather, I pad forward. I try to be so quiet that he doesn't even notice anyone's walked up behind him.

Maybe, just maybe, the universe will do me the incredible, unbelievable, impossible favor of making me so stealthy that Tuck won't notice me at all, not even when I'm standing right behind him.

That hope against hope is decisively dashed in about half a second. He turns around like he's got a chip in his brain that immediately alerts him whenever I'm in his presence.

His bright blue eyes flash. He smirks.

My stomach twists. I notice one very concerning thing. Underneath the annoyance I feel at being right behind the guy I was specifically looking forward to spending time *away* from, is an undercurrent of ... gladness.

A warm, elated feeling at seeing his face after fighting with him for a week. A kind of comfort at his baby blue eyes falling on mine again, at the wry grin on his pert mouth that I'd grown so used to, at the way his brow lifts in excitement at seeing me, making me feel ... special, in a way.

It's like sinking into your own, comfortable bed after a week on vacation where the mattress was way too hard.

But that's just the undercurrent. It's easy to push it down and let the more immediate annoyed feeling wash it away. This weekend was supposed to be easy, uncomplicated, relaxing. But uncomplicated is the last thing I feel in the presence of Tuck.

"Olivia," he exclaims, voice boisterous like he's spotted an old high school friend on a visit back to his hometown. "Fancy seein' you here!"

My brow lowers. "What are the odds?" I deadpan.

"Gotta be pretty small odds, I reckon. Just goes to show how lucky you are," he adds with a wink.

Even when he's needling me, a wink from Tuck is enough to make me feel like wings are flapping in my stomach.

When I was thinking about getting a fluttery feeling from a hot guy minutes ago, this was *not* what I had in mind.

I blow out a huff. "I can't believe Brumehill decided to send you to represent the college."

Tuck tilts his head, eyebrows bouncing. "You're telling me. I'd have chosen Lane." He shrugs. "Not complaining, though."

"Don't worry, I'm complaining enough for the both of us."

He lets out a booming laugh, tossing his head back so that the locks of hair spilling from his cap bob luxuriously. "Glad you haven't lost that sense of humor of yours since we last spoke."

Since we last spoke. He just breezes past a reference to the fight we had—that we're *still* having—without hesitation, without even a twitch in his expression. I wonder if Tuck's even capable of feeling awkward.

Speaking of breezing past our fight without a hitch ...

"Have a good drive up?" he asks. I don't miss the stress he puts on the word *drive*.

I narrow my eyes on him. "A lovely one. I was still under the impression I'd be spending a weekend in a different state than you, so my mood was fantastic."

His utterly unruffled grin only climbs higher. "We never know what the future holds, do we?"

Something flashes in his eyes, a spark of heat in the crisp ocean blue of his irises. It's like he's asking me: *at the beginning of the semester, you wouldn't have guessed the things you've already let me do to you, would you have?*

A shudder rolls up my back as a muscle between my thighs pulls tight.

"By the way," Tuck continues, his tone suddenly a register lower. More serious. "I'm sorry. If I overstepped my bounds. About your car." There's a beat of silence while his apology sinks in, before he continues, "But I'm not sorry that it helped you. I heard you went to that second round of auditions. I bet you fucking killed it." He grins, genuine pride beaming from his smile. "And I don't care if you're still mad at me, I'm coming to watch your opening night in Burlington, because I know you'll be on that stage."

My chest swells with a glad feeling. I can't stop the edges of my mouth from pulling up. Even when I try to flex the muscles into a frown, it's useless, like the sides of my lips are tethered to two birds soaring upward towards the sun.

Then Tuck turns around, and I realize it's already his turn at the check-in desk. The line's been moving along, and I've been so wrapped up in this interaction with him that I didn't even notice my own feet shuffling forward.

He shoots me a wink after the guy behind the counter hands him his keycard. Then, instead of walking to the elevator, he steps to the side of the lobby. Waiting for me.

I wish he wouldn't.

I give my name. The guy behind the counter taps away at his computer. "Oh, you're booked with the gentleman," he says.

My expression pinches. "Excuse me?"

"Olivia Lockley. You're in room 419. That room is also booked to Mr. ..." he hits a couple buttons on his keyboard. "Tuck McCoy. You'll be sharing the room." His brow draws down, clearly noting my displeasure. "At least, that's how it's booked in our system. Is that an issue?"

"Absolutely!" the word pushes from my lips. My shoulders are tense, my stomach tight, and infuriatingly, there's a traitorous tingle between my thighs as those words rattle in my brain—*you'll be sharing the room.*

With a force of will, I banish that feeling. I will *not* be sharing the room with Tuck.

After checking to see if there are any free rooms—there aren't—he suggests I contact Brumehill, as the room bookings were all taken care of by the college administration.

I don't even know who to call. I wander into the lobby, feeling like I'm on one of those terrible reality shows where they play cruel pranks on people just to film their reactions.

Tuck's still there. And he overheard.

"Sharing a room, huh?" I know Tuck isn't the best actor, so the surprised expression on his face keeps me from thinking he's somehow behind this. "Wow. Someone screwed up."

"They sure did," I say through grit teeth and a clenched jaw. I sigh as I reach for my phone. "I don't even know who to call about this."

"Probably not much they can do," Tuck shrugs. His surprise is quickly giving way to amusement.

I gnaw at my cheek as I throw an annoyed glance at him. "I'll be fine taking care of this. You can go to your room now."

"*Our* room." Delight dances in his eyes.

I guess I'll try Dr. Werther. I don't have her saved to my contacts, so I have to search through my email app for a message from her and hope against hope that the phone number in her signature is her personal number and not just her office phone.

Of course, when I call, the voicemail makes it clear it's her office phone. I don't bother to leave a message.

"Could just call the main Brumehill number and talk to the receptionist. Maybe they'll have some idea who to transfer you to," Tuck suggests.

"Good idea," I begrudgingly say. "By the way, why are you still here?"

"Roommates don't abandon each other in their time of need." He's grinning from ear to ear.

"We are *not* roommates."

He chuckles. "Why don't you go ahead and make that call and find out whether or not that's the case?"

About half an hour later I've talked to almost a dozen people, and apparently not a single person responsible for any aspect of booking accommodations for this event can be reached today.

Boy, someone thought this through, didn't they?

Finally, I end the call, defeated.

I've been studiously avoiding glancing at Tuck for the duration of the frustrating phone call. When I finally do, that wide grin is still carved all the way across his face.

"We're roommates, aren't we?" he asks with glee.

With a resigned sigh, I push myself to my feet. "Whatever. Let's go."

"Room four-one-nine," Tuck says in a singsong voice as he walks by my side to the elevators. "That's a lucky number, isn't it?"

"I don't think so."

Right as the elevator dings and the doors slide open for us, he says, "Is now."

21

OLIVIA

"I call the bed closest to the window!" Tuck exclaims as we walk down the narrow hallway on our floor.

"Fine," I grumble.

"Unless it's smaller. If the beds are different sizes, I call the bigger bed."

"You got it."

"Unless the bigger bed is harder. If one mattress is more comfortable than the other, I—"

"Tuck!" I snap at him.

He stops in his tracks, turning his crooked grin on me. "Yes, roomie?"

"Please stop."

He chuckles, and there's just a hint of sympathy in the tone. "Relax, Olivia. You can have whatever bed you want. I know this is unexpected, but it won't be so bad. We were able to share a tutoring room together, and that went just fine, didn't it?"

My core clenches as I remember another enclosed space we shared: that dark hallway at Starlite. Pinpricks of arousal buzz all over me. It feels like someone just cranked the heat up to the max setting.

Tuck inserts the keycard into our door and pushes it open.

We step inside. Take a couple steps down the brief entryway, past the bathroom.

My breath catches in my chest.

I blink my eyes tight. Once. Twice. Several more times. Each time hoping that when I open them, I see something other than what's in front of me.

Each time, I hope I see two beds.

But each time, I only see *one*.

Tuck and I stand there, luggage by our sides, looking at the one, single, solitary bed.

Time ticks by.

Then, Tuck laughs.

Tuck *cracks up*. Deep, booming guffaws trumpeting from his open mouth.

"This isn't funny," I say.

"Oh, come on," he manages through bursts of laughter. "Yes, it is. It's hilarious."

I have half a mind to head back to my car and go home. This isn't what I signed up for. I signed up for a relaxing weekend in a nice hotel room, alone and far away from all the stress in my life.

Instead, I'm sharing a one-bed hotel room with the number one source of that stress.

With a guy whose rugged, masculine scent is already lacing into my nose, diffusing through me and winding me tight, tempting my brain to go down dark, treacherous paths it has no business treading ...

With a guy who knows what I feel like pressed against

him, who felt me shudder as he made me come, who knows how the juices of my arousal taste ...

A hot, tight feeling hums low in my center as my heartbeat leaps into my throat.

"I'll just sleep on the floor," Tuck says. "It's no big deal."

"You can't sleep on the floor," I counter. "Your back hurts, doesn't it?"

Tuck's eyebrows draw together, surprise curling on his face. "How do you know that?" Then, the surprise softens, and that signature grin of his breaks out. "Were you watching my game on Wednesday?"

I may have watched highlights.

"I heard Summer mention it," I fib. "I guess she and Hudson talked about it."

"Mhm," Tuck hums, skeptically.

He took a really bad bodycheck against the dasher boards in the Black Bears' last game on Wednesday. To add insult to injury, it was the first game they lost in a while. He looked like he was in a lot of pain. He had to sit out the rest of the game, which, given Tuck's dedication to hockey, says a lot.

"Well, I'm fine," he says. "The floor's good enough for me. You take the bed. We'll make it work."

There's a reassuring quality to his voice now, after he's gotten all his laughs out. It's like he genuinely doesn't want to make me feel uncomfortable.

"If you need space to get changed or whatever, let me know, and I'll go chill in the lobby or grab a drink at the hotel bar," he says.

"Thanks," I say. Tuck may love needling me, but he can be considerate when it counts. *Can* be. "I may take you up on that." It would suck having to get changed into my dress in the confines of a hotel bathroom.

"In the meantime," he says, a hint of gravel creeping into his voice, "why don't you try out that bed? Let me know what I'm missing out on."

After the last hour I've had, I wouldn't mind lying flat on something soft right now ...

So, I do. I turn around and fall back onto the mattress.

When I lift my head and meet Tuck's gaze, his jaw muscles are flexing, nostrils flaring at the sight of me lying here.

"How is it?" he asks, the gravelly sound thicker now.

"Soft." I scoot back until I can lay my head on the pillow. "Really nice, actually."

"Hm," Tuck hums. I notice the indentation of his tongue as he traces it slowly around his inner lips.

"Much better than the floor, I bet," I quip, dipping my toe into joking around like we did before the car incident.

Tuck's expression grows cloudy, his prominent Adam's apple bobbing on a swallow. "Guess I'll never know."

There's something about the way he says that ...

TUCK LOOKS WAY TOO good in a tuxedo.

Way too good.

I guess I shouldn't be surprised. Tuck's tall frame with his wide shoulders, trim waist, and lean muscles is a tailor's wet dream. He was sure to look good dressed up.

But *this* good?

Women have been ogling him all night. Students from the other colleges, professors, administrators, donors, they're all shamelessly getting an eyeful of Tuck McCoy. His cocky smile, wide and toothy and glimmering, makes it clear he notices, and doesn't mind one bit.

He's so at ease here. I guess growing up rich, he feels comfortable mingling at a glitzy affair where everyone's dressed up with a flute of expensive champagne in their hands.

Me? I feel out of my element. I grew up in a much more bohemian atmosphere with my parents and their actor-slash-artist friends.

After a little while, though, I slide into the mingling groove. I talk with some students from a college in Maine, and they're cool. I meet an art professor from a college in Massachusetts who spent time working in stage production on Broadway, and we have an interesting conversation.

Then comes the disaster of the evening: the dinner.

I assumed that an event like this would have great catering. I was wrong. The meat is chewy. The vegetables bland. The potatoes hard and undercooked.

Not only that, but there's *no dessert*.

Who caters a fancy event and doesn't even offer dessert!? Maybe I shouldn't complain. Judging by the rest of the food, it's not likely the dessert would be good, either. Hard to screw up dessert, but I suspect they'd find a way.

I hardly eat anything on my plate. Afterward, I have to sit through over an hour of monotonous post-dinner speeches by university administrators with a growling stomach.

There's more *mingling* after the speeches. I have a couple more conversations, but quickly I'm starting to feel all mingled out.

I also notice that I haven't seen Tuck around for a little while. I wonder if he ditched and went back to our room.

Our room.

My pulse stutters, chills dancing up and down my back.

Then a pang of guilt tugs at my chest. I've seen Tuck

wince in pain a couple times tonight. He's tried to hide it, but I've noticed. Especially when he lowered himself to sit down at his table for dinner. His hand has shot to the small of his back more than once this evening.

I can't let him sleep on the floor. I'll take the floor myself. He might put up a fight. He probably has some stupid idea of chivalry in that macho brain of his that says he can't let a woman sleep on the floor.

Not that the antics he's known for on campus have chivalry written all over them.

Still, I think he's hurting bad enough that I'll be able to force him to accept it.

Then, I spot him. Through the window panes of the closed French doors on the other side of the room, I see Tuck standing on the balcony. He's got his forearms propped against a railing with his back turned.

When I step outside, I expect to be wrapped in the harsh cold of a New England night, barely able to stand it long enough to ask Tuck what he's doing freezing himself to death out here.

But, instead, I'm greeted by the warmth of bronze-coated patio heaters. It makes this balcony comfortable even in my sleeveless dress, though I can still feel the crisp chill in the air. It's nice.

I sidle next to him, mimicking his position as I lean forward and rest my arms against the stone railing.

"Needed a break?" I ask.

Tuck turns to me, and the smile that carves across his face makes my stomach flutter. His blue eyes light up, like he's glad to see me.

It hits me that his eyes always light up like that. Every time his gaze settles on me. Like he's truly, genuinely *happy* every time he sees me.

"Actually," he drawls, "I just got back from a mission."

I hitch an eyebrow. "Oh?"

"A very important, secret mission."

"I'm afraid to ask." I try to deadpan, but I can't stop from grinning.

"I need a drum roll for this."

I purse my lips, staring at him bemused.

He points to my hands resting on the stone railing. "Drum roll, Lockley," he commands.

I huff a laugh, but I oblige. I pat the flats of my palms against the cold stone, gradually picking up my pace, until ...

"Ta-dah!" Tuck exclaims, pulling two packets of Pretzel M&M's from his pockets.

I gasp, greedily snatching one for myself.

He laughs. "That food really sucked, didn't it?"

"I'll say," I agree. "Where'd you find these?"

"I wandered around the hotel checking vending machines. No luck there. Then I crossed the street and found a convenience store that sold them."

My chest squeezes. He went wandering around in the cold just to buy a snack he knows I like?

"Oh, wait," Tuck suddenly says, as if realizing something. "We have to do this right."

He glances inside through the windows. He holds up his index finger as if to say he'll be right back before dashing in. Then, about twenty seconds later, he returns with two champagne flutes.

He hands me one. We clink them together, and I don't even fight the smile as I stand here on this heated balcony on a crisp winter night, drinking fancy champagne and eating Pretzel M&M's with Tuck McCoy.

"The flavor of the champagne really complements the

pretzel, doesn't it?" Tuck says, holding his glass in front of him and swishing it around like a sommelier.

"Oh, yeah," I laugh. "It's a very complex and sophisticated flavor profile."

It's then that I realize something that *should* worry me—but it doesn't.

I'm glad Tuck is here.

22

TUCK

While Olivia is getting changed and washing her makeup off in the bathroom, I allow myself a taste of this mattress she was raving about.

Fuck, this bed *is* nice. Soft, but not too soft. The comforter is fluffy and luxurious. I let out a groan as I imagine how the hard, carpeted floor is going to feel compared to this.

I'm not looking forward to it, not with how my back's been feeling all day, but there's no alternative.

It's not that I wouldn't love to spend a night in bed with Olivia. Even if nothing happened. Even if we didn't even touch. It's an experience that I'd be fisting my cock to for months to come.

But I'm not even going to hint at it. I know Olivia didn't bargain on sharing a hotel room with me, and she sure as hell didn't bargain on sharing a bed with me. I may enjoy teasing her a little bit from time to time—okay, maybe that's an understatement—but the last thing I want is to make her actually feel uncomfortable.

Fuck, she looked good tonight.

I mean, I knew she would. She always looks good. Knowing she'd be wearing a nice dress, I fully expected her to look so good that my heart would skip three or four beats.

But I didn't expect her to look *that* good.

Shit, nothing could have prepared me for what I saw when she stepped out of the elevator into the lobby where I was waiting for her.

The way that dress tastefully outlined her figure, hugging the curve of her hip not too tight but just enough to make my blood pump extra hard ...

I blow out a breath, shaking my head just thinking about it. My cock thickens in my tuxedo pants.

The water from the sink faucet is still running in the bathroom, so I palm the outline of my length through my pants.

Fuck. Probably not a good idea. Now I'm even harder, the tip of my cock tingling and begging for release. Well, I'm not going to get it tonight.

I pull my hand back and try to think about something else. But it seems like right now my brain can only concentrate on one of two things: how sexy Olivia looked tonight, making my cock unbearably hard; or how much my back hurts, making me dread the fact that I'm going to have to lie on the floor pretty soon.

Still, it was worth coming. I had a great fucking time with Olivia eating Pretzel M&M's and drinking champagne on the patio. We were out there for almost an hour, just talking about whatever. It feels like we've finally moved past her being angry at me.

That was the whole point of this. Having an extra achy back tomorrow is a small price to pay.

I heave myself up into a seated position on the edge of

the mattress. I can't keep tempting myself with comforts I'm not going to have tonight.

With a groan, I stand up and finally get out of this tuxedo. I strip down to my white undershirt and green boxer-briefs. Peeking under the bed, I find an extra comforter in a plastic zip-up bag. At least that'll make the floor somewhat less unpleasant.

I turn around when I hear the bathroom door open—and my heart slams against my chest.

Olivia's standing there, wearing an oversized blue t-shirt. The hem of her shirt drops lower than the shorts I'm sure she's wearing, making her smooth, bare legs look so fucking alluring that my abs clench rock-hard.

I stifle a groan as my gaze rakes down those shapely legs and ends at her bare feet. Shit. She looks so good like this, wearing what she'd be wearing any given school night around her house, that it literally hurts. I'm fucking *aching* looking at her.

Her face is unadorned, and as drop-dead gorgeous as her lips were with the red lipstick she had on for the gala, the vivid pale pink of their natural shade makes my chest pang with even more intensity. Her hair is tied in a ponytail, and it rests over her shoulder, swooping in front of her as she toys with it.

I bend down and gather up the new comforter at my feet, realizing I need something to cover my growing bulge immediately.

"Look!" I say, holding up the blanket so it drapes in front of me. "Found an extra blanket." I fix a stupid smile to my face, hoping she'll think I'm just inordinately excited about a fluffy white comforter instead of desperate to have a shield to hide the outline of my hard dick in my boxers.

"Oh. Uh. Cool?" Olivia replies.

I nod. "Cool. Very cool." I settle down on the floor, draping the blanket over me. "Just toss me a pillow," I say, nodding towards the two of them on the bed.

Olivia's mouth scrunches up. "I think I should sleep on the floor. You take the bed."

My lips flatten. "No."

"Really," she continues, trying to make it sound like no big deal. She walks to the bed to pick up a pillow, but she doesn't hand it to me. Instead, she holds it in front of her, standing at my feet. "I'll take the floor."

I reach up and snatch the pillow from her. "Like hell you will." My voice is growly at the thought of it. I fluff the pillow and then place it on the floor behind me, ready to lay my head on it.

"You can't sleep on the floor, Tuck," she says, her voice tight, like she's annoyed at my stubbornness. "Your back's killing you."

"Let a lady sleep on the floor while I take the bed?" I scoff. "Not while I'm above ground. I don't know how the boys you grew up with did things, but my momma raised me right."

"You're being ridiculous," she protests.

"Night, Olivia. Enjoy the bed. I know I'm going to enjoy this nice, firm floor." When I lie back, I groan in pain as a muscle in my back pinches.

"Yeah, sounds like you're enjoying the hell out of it." After a beat of silence, she sighs loudly. "Look. We'll share the bed."

My brow leaps. I prop myself up on my elbows to look at her. That position has my back aching, too, but I don't care right now. "Really?"

Her eyes flit to the side, like she's taking a second to

reconsider her proposal. Her gaze meets mine again, and she nods. "Yeah. Really."

Heat laces into my bloodstream. Immediately, I can *feel* her body pressing against mine under the covers. I can feel my hand raking against her smooth thigh, traveling up, past the hem of that oversized t-shirt, to find out whether or not she really *is* wearing shorts ...

I clench my teeth, trying to extinguish those thoughts. The last thing I need is to get under those covers with her and be pitching a tent with my cock all night.

"You sure?" I ask.

She rolls her eyes. "Yes, Tuck, I'm sure. It's not a big deal."

I grin. "Oh? Because when we first walked in here and you laid your eyes on that single, solitary bed, it sure *seemed* like a big deal to you."

"Don't make me change my mind."

I wiggle my eyebrows. "Just make sure you keep your hands to yourself underneath the covers, Lockley."

That earns me the second pillow being flung in my face.

"Hey!" I exclaim through laughter, tossing it back on the bed. "I'm an injured man!"

"Keep it up and you'll be more injured," she replies. She's side-eyeing me, but I don't miss the way the edge of her mouth twitches.

Olivia crawls into bed first. When I join her under the covers, it takes every drop of self-control I can summon to hold a raging hard-on at bay. Oh, believe me, my cock sure as hell isn't flaccid. I doubt it'll be all night. But at least it's not throbbing so hard it threatens to tear my boxers off my hips.

"Hey, hand me my book bag," I say, nodding towards her side of the beg. When she does, I take out my laptop. "I brought my computer. Want to watch something before we go to sleep?"

She shrugs. "Sure. How about a long foreign movie with lots of lingering camera shots?"

"Pass," I chuckle.

"Really, though, how about something light? You know what I actually haven't watched yet? The Office."

I hum with interest. "Me neither. I've been meaning to, though. Alright," I say, perky with excitement, "The Office it is."

Olivia quirks an eyebrow at me as I pull it up on one of my streaming subscriptions. "Why are you starting with Season 2?"

"Everyone says Season 2 is when it really starts to get good, and that you're not missing much by skipping the first. I think we should make sure our first night in bed isn't a disappointment and just jump into the second one."

She snorts. "Our *only* night in bed."

I arch an eyebrow and crook the side of my mouth at her just slightly. *We'll see about that*, my expression says, though I keep the thought to myself.

MY EYES FLUTTER OPEN. They're met with darkness. It must be the middle of the night, as there's a sliver of space between the two curtains drawn together over the window, but there's not a hint of light.

I can't see much yet as my eyes adjust. But I do smell something.

It's a citrusy, lavender scent, light and airy. It's so good that I take a deep, strong draw of it through my nostrils. I roll my lips in appreciation as the smell suffuses through me.

Then I realize what my head is lying on. It's not just my pillow. It's softer than my pillow, smoother. And the scent is coming from it.

I realize that Olivia's back is pressed against me. While we slept, her hair must have feathered over my pillow. The side of my face lies against the feathered strands, my nose pressed into a thick, luxurious tuft of hair at the back of her head.

I pull in another breath, savoring the smell. Her back is right against my chest. We're practically spooning. The warmth of her body is spreading through me.

My head swims in the scent and the feeling. This is like a dream. No, better than a dream. Like I've died and gone to heaven.

I can feel something else, too. The softness of her ass pressing right against my cock. At the realization, it thickens in an instant. I'm throbbing against her. My jaw muscles flex, and I suck in a deep breath—but the fact that the breath is laced with her scent only makes me harder.

Olivia lets out a tiny, sleepy moan. That's the last thing I need if I'm going to get this hard-on under control.

Her hips tilt back. The soft, round curve of her ass generates friction against my length.

Fuck. I bite my bottom lip to keep a groan from ripping out of my throat. My heart is pounding in my chest, and I feel every pulse of that heartbeat right at the base of my dick.

She does it again. It's not just a tilt, but a roll this time, creating friction that sends a wave of pleasure rippling through me. It takes everything I have not to grind my hips forward, thrusting back into her softness.

A thought makes a jolt of electricity zip up my spine.

Is she awake? Is she doing this on purpose?

It's ridiculous. I shove the thought away. This isn't *that* good of a dream.

Taking deep breaths, I bring my heart rate back down. After a while, my cock starts to deflate. I keep control of my breathing.

Her smell in my nose and the feeling of her body against mine turns into a mellower, contented kind of bliss.

I wrap my arm around her waist, lightly. The feeling of holding her, cradling her, makes my heart flutter. My chest hums with satisfaction.

Soon, I'm drifting back to sleep, my arm draped over Olivia, her warm body against my chest, her scent dancing in my nostrils.

Just as sleep pulls me back under, I wish that this moment would never end.

23

OLIVIA

A feeling of emptiness claws at me when I wake up. The bed feels cold. Like there's warmth that should be here but isn't.

I'm sleeping on my side, curled up, facing the window. I roll onto my back and spread out my arms. That's when I realize it. Why the bed feels so empty, so cold.

Turning my head to the side, I see that Tuck is gone.

The stupidest thing happens. My stomach drops, a hollow and disappointed feeling panging inside me.

Must be one of those weird tricks your brain or body can play on you when you first wake up. Like sometimes you'll wake up and swear it's Saturday morning for a blissful second, only for the realization to come crashing down on you that it's Wednesday.

My brain's playing a much stranger trick on me this morning. It's fooling me into thinking that I *wanted* to wake up in bed with Tuck next to me.

Much more ridiculous than mixing up what day of the week it is. Surely the realization that what I'm actually feeling is *relief* will hit me at any moment.

I lie still waiting for it to happen. But it doesn't.

I wonder if he decided to check out already? Maybe he's an early riser and didn't feel like waiting around for me to get up.

At that thought, my stomach sinks even lower, a deeper disappointment simmering in my chest.

I haul myself to a sitting position. I stretch, yawning loudly. My head still feels groggy with sleep when I finally fling the cover off and stand up. I shake off the cobwebs—and when my mind clears, a memory rushes back to me.

Last night. Waking up sometime in the dark, early hours of the morning. Tuck pressed against me. Feeling the hard, impossibly huge outline of his length against my ass.

Pressing back into it. Rolling against it.

Heat gathers between my legs, pinpricks of arousal skittering up my back.

A dream, surely?

Somehow, the excuse that I only *dreamt* about Tuck's dick doesn't make me feel much better.

A sigh whooshes from me. I head to the bathroom, rubbing my sleepy eyes.

Maybe if I weren't rubbing them, I'd notice the sliver of brightness underneath the bathroom door, advertising that the light inside is turned on.

Then I wouldn't thoughtlessly push the door open. But that's exactly what I do.

I come face to face with Tuck—completely naked.

He's toweling his hair, arms lifted. His body angles towards me, and I see *everything*.

I freeze. My eyelids snap open.

I might be unable to move, but my eyes don't suffer from that problem. They rake over him.

His body is unreal. Like a renaissance sculpture come to life.

My eyes fall first on his chest. Two slabs of hard, dense muscle. Wide and deep. As my eyes crawl down his torso, it tapers to his trim waist. On the trip down that torso are his abs, starkly defined and deeply cut into his physique. Below them are the carved ridges of his hip muscles, making a crisp V-shape pointing straight to ...

My breath catches in my chest. I'm watching Tuck's cock swell and grow hard in real-time. Each fraction of a second that my gaze is riveted to it, I think it can't possibly get any thicker, any bigger ... but it does.

My mouth is dry, my stomach leaping like I've just crested over the highest peak of a rollercoaster going at max speed.

It bobs up and down in the air, throbbing rhythmically. It's big and thick and veiny. His mushroom head is swollen, pink and smooth.

I've been numb until now, standing here with my head scrambled. But suddenly, I feel something.

Arousal.

Arousal like I've never felt before, white-hot and urgent, roaring through my body. A sharp ache detonates between my legs, and I'm now aware of how wet I am.

My gaze crawls back up his body, past the sharp lines of his muscles. He's still frozen, his hands holding the towel at his hair. The pose makes his shoulder muscles pop, accentuating their width.

Our eyes lock.

Adrenaline buzzes through me, making the pads of my fingers tingle.

Tuck's eyes simmer.

Time ticks by. Neither of us moves, but the smoldering

intensity in Tuck's eyes grows while the tension inside me winds tighter.

"Get on your knees," he finally says. His voice is low and thick.

I obey. I don't even think about it. I take a step back and kneel. My bare knees scratch against the rough fabric of the hotel carpet.

Tuck lets the towel drop behind him.

"Good girl," he rasps.

My heartbeat roars in my ears. My pulse is going crazy. My breath stutters as Tuck starts to walk towards me, slowly, my eyes lined up with his throbbing length.

My eyes pop when he steps close enough for me to see the opening of his swollen head glistening, a bead of precum sitting on it like a jewel.

His smell fills my nose. He's freshly soaped, his scent crisp and clean, but there's a raw, masculine undertone.

"You know what I don't think is fair, Olivia?" he asks, his voice full of gravel. His eyes gleam as he looks down at me. "That I got you off, but you never returned the favor. What do you think? Does that sound fair to you?"

Desire hums through my blood. "No," I answer.

A low, raw sound rumbles from him. "What are you going to do to make it right?"

With tingling palms, I reach out and wrap my hand around Tuck's cock.

I grip the base of his length, lightly and tentatively at first. It's hard, like steel, but hot at the same time. His girth is almost unbelievable. It feels like my hand sizzles where it makes contact. Tendrils of electricity snake up my arm and through my chest.

"Fuck," he groans.

I clench my thighs, the need throbbing between my legs growing more insistent.

I look up at him. His head is thrown back, his sharp features drawn tight. His jaw is clenched hard. From this position, the jagged outlines of his muscles are even more defined.

I drag my grip up his shaft. His muscles tense. It gives me a thrill of power, of control, even though I'm the one on my knees.

Tuck shudders when my grip passes the soft, pink fringe of nerve endings right underneath the head of his cock. I place my other hand on the side of his trim, sleek hip. I can feel the tension coiling in his body.

I take a moment to admire his cock. It's gorgeous. Long, thick, veiny, the swollen mushroom tip exquisitely shaped.

"You felt me last night, didn't you?" There's a tease in Tuck's voice.

I nod, my admiring gaze still tethered to his cock. "Mhm," I hum.

"You liked it," he says, smug masculine pride beaming in his voice.

I smirk, rising to the challenge. "Not as much as you like this."

With the tip of my tongue, I graze his opening, applying light but firm pressure.

A shudder ripples through his body. He moans. His sweet, salty taste spreads through my mouth.

"Fuck, Lockley," he says. His voice is tight, but a chuckle breaks through. "Maybe you're right about that."

"I think when I have your cock in my hand and you're dying for me to wrap my lips around it, I'm right about everything."

Then, I give him what he's dying for. I take his swollen head in my mouth, enveloping it with my lips.

Curses drop from Tuck's mouth, his muscles pulling taut. I drag my hand from where it's splayed on his hips and palm his balls. They're tight with desire.

Tuck's breath goes ragged as I start to work his cock. I swirl my tongue around him, slanting the flat of it against the ridged underside of his head.

His raspy, rugged groans are music to my ears. Satisfaction pulses through me, knowing how much pleasure I'm causing him. All the while, the throbbing between my legs grows. My clit is tight, yearning for contact.

More precum beads on his cock while he's inside my mouth, and I moan appreciatively at the flavor. The sound of my own moans muffled from my lips being wrapped around his shaft turns me on that much more.

"Olivia, fuck," Tuck gasps. "I'm almost there, I'm going to …"

Then I stop. I pull my lips away from his hardness just as he's about to tell me he's going to come.

A disappointed groan rips from his throat. His brows draw tight together as he looks down at me.

"Olivia, are you trying to kill me?"

But it's not that.

A coy smile carves on my mouth. We've already gone this far. After I fell to my knees at his command, there's no point in pretending I don't want what I do want right now.

"I don't want you to finish yet," I say, my voice a teasing husk. "Not until you've been inside me."

24

TUCK

Olivia's words slam into my chest like a sledgehammer.

She wants me inside her. Fuck. I have to clench my muscles to keep from coming on the spot.

If I sink my cock into her pussy right now, that pussy I just know is going to fit me so damn right, I won't last three thrusts. And I plan on lasting a lot more than that when I fuck Olivia for the first time.

Good thing I know just how to buy time to recover from the most incredible blowjob of my life.

"Not until I taste you first," I growl.

Olivia gasps as I dip down and gather her in my arms. Her legs kick, her high-pitched giggles making my chest pang blissfully while I carry her to the bed. To *our* bed.

I lay her down on the bed. The same bed where I fell asleep with my arm draped around her waist. The same bed where she pressed her ass against my cock.

"Fuck, Olivia," I growl, pushing her up the bed so she'll be in perfect position for me to feast on her. "You have no idea how badly I've wanted to taste you."

"I think I have *some* idea," she says on a laugh.

"Maybe you *think* you do," I say, dropping to my knees at the foot of the bed. I look up at her, heat blasting from my eyes. This view, her on her back, our gazes meeting over the swells of her breasts, has my heartbeat hammering in my cock. My balls are so tight they ache. "But you're wrong."

She knows I've wanted her. I sure as fuck didn't make that ambiguous. But there's no way she knows I've wanted her, still want her, so bad that I haven't as much as thought about another woman for over four fucking months.

Sparks burst on my fingertips as they brush against Olivia's smooth skin when I reach up the hem of her shirt to grip the waistband of her flimsy shorts.

My chest pulses when I sink my fingers underneath the waistband, the backs of them brushing against the humid softness of her skin. I pause for a beat, savoring the moment.

Slowly, torturously slowly, I drag her shorts down her legs. My eyes are wide, feasting on every new sliver of exposed skin. I've been waiting for his moment so long, I'm going to draw out every second to treasure.

Olivia has other ideas, though. "Hurry up," she whines, her hips rolling impatiently.

I laugh darkly. "No."

My nostrils flare when I get my first glimpse of her pussy. Fucking hell. It's even more gorgeous than I imagined. So fucking pink. So *wet*.

"You're fucking soaked for me," I rasp. I'm still slow as I slide her shorts down the rest of her legs, my eyes tethered to her slick opening.

She bends her knees, and I pull her shorts down her feet, tossing them behind me with disdain, like I'm glad to be rid of them. I am.

I settle my head between her thighs. I draw in a deep, greedy breath of her scent.

I practically roar with appreciation. She smells so fucking sweet. The smell of her wet arousal makes my mouth water. It takes all my self-control not to dive right in and lap at her, finally indulging in the taste I've spent so damn long imagining, yearning for.

But I hold back. I want to tease her first. I want her to know what she's been doing to me for these long months, denying me something I want so bad that it hurts.

She squirms as I drop hot kisses onto her soft, smooth thighs. Each kiss is accompanied by a growl of appreciation for how her skin feels against my lips. All the while her smell has me lightheaded, and the way she bucks her hips forward, clearly desperate to have my mouth and tongue on her greedy cunt, makes my chest thrum with satisfaction.

"Tuck," she whines, thrashing around on the bed.

"Yes, Olivia?" I ask in a mocking, sing-song voice. She shudders as I run my tongue across her creamy skin.

"Stop teasing me," she begs through tight laughter.

"Why should I?" I lower myself over her opening, close enough for her to go taut with anticipation, but I don't give her the contact she wants.

"Damn it, Tuck," she groans. "I'm too horny to think of any banter right now."

I laugh. Doing this with Olivia isn't just a million times hotter than I've ever experienced with anyone else, it's more fun, too. I've always enjoyed sex, but this is different.

"Take your shirt off," I command.

She obeys.

My chest hitches, finally seeing her totally bare. Her tits are a fucking dream. Round and perky, with the most perfect rosebud nipples coiled into tight, sharp nubs.

Since she was a good girl and did what I said, I decide to give her a reward.

I drag the tip of my tongue up her wet slit. She sucks in a quick gasp, her back arching. My eyes roll back as her taste fills my mouth.

I tasted her juices weeks ago, when I sucked them off my fingers. But tasting her arousal right from her pussy is a totally different experience. The flavor thickens my blood, makes me lose all restraint. I can't tease her anymore, because now I need this as much as she does.

I lap at her with my lips and tongue, loving every drop of the juices she gives me.

Her hands spear into my hair and grab tight handfuls. The burning on my scalp feels so fucking good, knowing it's coming from the pleasure my mouth is giving her.

Her hips start bucking faster. The sweet, soft moans she was making grow louder, more ragged. Like she's losing control.

I really, really like the feeling of making Olivia Lockley lose control.

I swirl my tongue around her clit. She gasps. Her hips push up into the pressure. I keep lavishing the bundle of nerves with attention.

My mouth is soaked, coated with her sticky, sweet wetness, and I fucking love it. I could eat this pussy every single day and there's zero chance I'd *ever* get tired of it.

I can feel how tight she's wound. She's so fucking close. All it would take is …

I slide my finger inside her, crooking it upward. It hits the perfect spot just as my tongue slants over her clit. I can tell from the way that her body pulls taut that it sends her over the edge.

She moans, her breaths short and desperate, her body thrashing with pleasure. Pleasure *I've* given her.

Her hips are bucking, stomach undulating, chest heaving because of *me*.

Pride pulses through me, and I greedily suck up all the juices she's giving me as her orgasm barrels through her.

I pull back, giving her time to recover. An appreciative hum sings from my chest as I drag my tongue over my lips, wanting to taste every single drop I can of Olivia.

"Tuck," she pants, "that was ... fuck ... wow ..."

Watching the soft semi-globes of her tits rise and fall with her heaving chest pulls my attention back to my cock. It's so hard that it hurts. It feels like an electric current is racing from the base to the tip.

I can't wait much longer to finally do what I've been dreaming of for so damn long.

I crawl onto the bed, my body hovering over her. Her eyes are hooded, a sated expression on her face.

"Say it, Olivia."

"What?" she asks.

My gaze bores into her. I smirk. "You know what."

She rolls her eyes. "You want me to tell you that was the most incredible orgasm of my life or something, don't you?"

"Yes," I answer, dead serious.

Her eyes lock with mine again. "It was. It was the best orgasm of my life." There's no trace of sarcasm. "Happy?" There *is* a trace of sarcasm in that question.

"Very," I growl, before pressing my lips to her. She groans against the kiss, loving the taste of her arousal, just like she did last time.

"Shit," she says when our lips part. "Do you have a condom?"

I grin. "Sure do."

I hop off the bed and find the pair of pants I wore to the hotel yesterday, fishing out the condom I slid into my back pocket.

She quirks an eyebrow at me as I crawl back on the bed, amusement and a hint of reproach dancing in her green eyes. "You were optimistic, weren't you?"

I chuckle. "Olivia, I'm always optimistic. Often irrationally so. You know *that* much about me, don't you?"

"Guess I shouldn't complain. It came in handy for once."

I slide the condom down my shaft and position myself between her thighs, lining up at her opening. I draw in a deep breath and let it out on a ragged sigh, savoring the moment while my cock throbs in the air, the tip brushing against her slit, so wet and ready for me.

Then, I finally push into her.

"*Fuuuck,*" I groan. Pleasure rips through me, my whole body feeling on fire in the best way.

I slide into her slowly, giving her time to get used to my size.

"You okay?" I ask, softly.

"Yeah," she whispers.

She angles her hips, urging me to push deeper. Gently, I do, until I'm buried as far as I can go. I hover over her, staying still, feeling her adjusting around me.

She's so damn warm. So wet. She fits me so right. Somehow, I knew she would. I fucking knew it. And I wasn't wrong.

Her legs wrap around me, ankles locking behind the small of my back and tugging me closer to her.

"Fuck me, Tuck." her voice is a husky plea. The words make a bolt of lightning race up and down my spine.

I draw my hips back, pulling out of her. Then I thrust in, this time a bit faster, a bit harder. My jaw muscles clench as the pleasure of sinking into her rattles through me. Every nerve ending in my body is buzzing. Already, a tightness is building at the base of my spine.

"Tuck," she moans. Her pink tongue drags across her upper lip. "Fuck, that's so good."

Her moans make me lose control, and soon I'm rutting into her like a man possessed. The tightness low in my spine grows, heat streaking through me with each thrust. I can't even believe how good this feels.

"Yes, yes, yes," Olivia repeats, her voice the sweetest thing I've ever heard.

"You love this fucking cock, don't you?" I growl.

"Fucking love it," she answers. "So good. So ... *ohhh*."

"So fucking perfect," I grit out. I'm talking about everything. The way her cheeks flush. The hazy look in her eyes. The sounds she's making. Her body. The way her pussy clenches around me.

Our bodies press together, fitting perfectly. Like a key sliding into the only lock that it'll fit into. That might be a stupid analogy to use considering this sure as shit isn't my first time, and I know it isn't hers, either. But that's just what it feels like. Nothing's ever felt this right.

Her fingernails dig into the dense muscles of my back as I pound into her harder, losing all control. Our voices are a cacophony of moans and ragged breaths. The feeling is too intense, too mind-melting for me to even form words. All I can do is breathe and thrust.

"I'm ... I'm going to ..." Olivia moans into my ear, announcing the arrival of her orgasm. When her pussy clenches and spasms around my cock, she pulls me with her.

White-hot pleasure unfurls inside me, radiating through every limb.

My eyes clench as I fall over the edge, wave after wave of ecstasy shooting through me. My muscles are tight and coiled, and after one last thrust, I'm spilling my release into the condom, the eruption so intense that it feels like I'll have nothing left when it's done.

Olivia's arms and legs tighten around me, pressing us so close together that I don't know where my body ends and hers begins.

I'm totally spent when I collapse next to her, panting, dripping with sweat, drained of all energy. I couldn't lift a finger right now.

The next sound either of us makes is when Olivia breathes out, "Wow."

I don't know how long we've been lying here since I pulled out of her. Time's lost all meaning. Twenty seconds? Fifteen minutes? Three hours? Beats the hell out of me.

All I know is, I wish we could stay like this forever. Naked, together, totally spent and satisfied.

That's not reality, though. We need to get back home. And we also need to figure out what the hell this means.

I know what I want it to mean. I want to be with Olivia. Not just a fling. Not just a series of hookups. I want her to be *mine*, and I want to be hers.

But there'll be time to think about that later. Right now, I just want to enjoy this moment for as long as I possibly can.

I curl my arm around Olivia and pull her against my side. She leans into it, nuzzling against me, her hair feathering over my chest and sending notes of the strawberry-citrus scent I savored last night floating up to me.

For a moment, I just let myself imagine that Olivia wants the same thing I do.

25

OLIVIA

I click on the Instagram notification alerting me to a new DM.

At first, when I read it, I don't feel anything. What I'm looking at doesn't register.

For a while, time ticks by as I sit at my computer, looking dumbly at the message. Then, the emotions start.

First is surprise.

Then disbelief. Is this some kind of cat-fishing deal? A prank? But that doesn't make any sense.

Then annoyance. I'm annoyed that he's reached his grubby hand back into my life, which he was supposed to be out of for good.

Then anger—anger that he thought he had the right to do so. Anger that he thought I would even consider agreeing to what he's proposing.

My piece of shit ex-boyfriend Ryan messaged me a couple hours ago, telling me that he and his college hockey team are coming to Cedar Shade to play the Black Bears in a couple weeks, and suggesting that we hang out while he's here.

Hang out.

I grind my teeth. My eyes narrow on his profile picture, as if staring daggers at an arrangement of pixels could do anything.

In a flash of anger, I delete the message and block his profile. The latter I should've done a long time ago. I guess I never expected him to contact me again. The last time we talked, he sure as hell didn't make it seem like reaching out to me would ever be on his to-do list.

Be serious, Olivia, he said, casually, like it was the smallest deal in the world, *you're just one girl and you're two hundred miles away. You* couldn't *think that would be enough for me.*

I'd driven from Cedar Shade to his college in Massachusetts, to surprise him. This was the first semester of freshman year. We'd decided to stay together after leaving high school and going off to different colleges, though I was soon to learn just how different a definition of *together* we'd both had.

I was walking towards his dorm room, when I passed the common area on his floor. And there he was, with a girl sitting on his lap, making out with her.

It's been like this since we've been together, he said, gaslighting me to high heaven, acting like it was absurd I didn't already know this. *Come on, you see how many girls throw themselves at me. Sure, we're dating, but this relationship was always a little bit open.*

A little bit open ...

The anger burning inside me dissolves into a weak sadness.

I've worked hard to never again be the girl I was when I was with him. A girl who actually felt *gratitude* that some handsome, popular guy would pick *her.* A girl who put so much more into a relationship than she got out of it, hoping that maybe if she put in twenty times the effort he did rather than just ten times the effort he did, he'd show her he loved her as much as she wished he would.

A girl who had no defenses around her heart, so it hurt that much more when he stuck a knife in and twisted.

I heave myself up from the chair at my desk. I stand in front of my window and look out to the street in front of our house. It's a grey, cloudy day.

I'm sad now, and that fact alone makes me feel angry. Angry at myself.

Ryan shouldn't still have the power to make me feel like this. It shouldn't matter to me anymore. I know I'm better off without him.

Better off without the guy who never texted or called me, who always sat back and expected me to be the one who ever made any effort. The only thing he'd ever be the one to initiate was sex.

But I know it's not the loss of Ryan I feel sad about. It's the loss of something I had in myself that I don't have anymore. An optimism about love that's been shattered. An eagerness to gather up my hopes and dreams and intertwine them with another person.

I look back, and I'm disgusted by how dependent I was, how easy it was for a man to take advantage of me.

But I'm also envious of how hopeful I was. How unafraid.

As I gaze out on the distinctly uninteresting scene in front of my house, my eyes snag on my car. And then Tuck comes to mind.

Thinking about Ryan and Tuck in such quick succession brings a hot, corrosive feeling to my chest.

I know they're not the same person. Not by a long shot.

Tuck, for all his cocky swagger and playboy bravado, is

actually nice. Caring. Even though he's sometimes insensitive to the fact that his privileged background makes him look at things differently than other people do, he's not inconsiderate.

The bottom line is, he's a good guy.

He's funny. He has an actual personality beyond hot, rich hockey player who people fawn over just *because* he's a hot, rich hockey player.

But when I think about letting my guard down, about opening a door in the walls around my heart for Tuck to step through, every instinct screams at me to pull back.

It's the same feeling I get standing near the edge of a cliff, or near the railing of a balcony high in the air, so close to the sheer drop down—the overwhelming urge to step back, to safety.

We haven't really talked since we slept together at the hotel in New Hampshire.

Mostly because I've been avoiding him.

Okay, entirely because I've been avoiding him.

When we left to go to our cars, I told him that I wanted to keep what happened just between us. That we'd talk when we got back to Cedar Shade.

But instead of that happening, I've been studiously avoiding being anywhere I'm likely to run into him. I've been taking my time responding to his texts, and telling him that I'm busy each time I do.

I'm still not totally sure what he wants between us, anyway. Honestly, I'm kind of scared to find out.

If all he wants is to keep having no-strings-attached hookups, keeping himself open to do the same with any other girl who catches his fancy ... the thought makes me feel like my heart's in a vise.

Even though an emotional connection with Tuck is

exactly what *I've* wanted to avoid. It's a paradoxical, hypocritical reaction—but that doesn't make it any less real.

And if he does want more than that ... a warm feeling pulses through me at the thought.

But as soon as I feel that, fear comes hot on its heels. I go through the carousel of self-doubting questions. How long until he gets bored of me? How long until he remembers he's not a one-woman man? How long until my heart gets broken again?

At least when Ryan broke my heart, I could retreat back here and forget about him. We didn't share a campus. But if Tuck breaks my heart? Not only do we share a campus, but our best friends are dating. He'll always be around.

That last fact reverberates in my mind.

I do want to be able to open up my heart again, eventually. I don't want to give up on relationships.

But if I'm going to dip my toes back into that pool, is there anyone more high-risk than Tuck to do it with?

SUMMER and I sit down with our laptops and the books we've just bought. We're at Last Word bookshop. It's an incredible three-story bookstore in downtown Cedar Shade. The second and third floor are stocked with books, while the first floor is a café.

We both picked up a copy of Jane Austen's *Emma*. After reading a couple of Summer's romance books together, she proposed that I choose a book for us to read together. I thought Emma would be a good pick—it's an all-time classic of English literature, while still being a love story.

With a cup of coffee and a croissant each, we open our laptops and take advantage of being here to catch up on some schoolwork, our copies of *Emma* face-up next to our computers.

"Oh!" A delighted exclamation pulls our attention from our computer screens. "You girls are reading *Emma* together?"

"Hey, Cindy!" Summer beams, turning around in her chair to greet the owner of Last Word.

"Yep," I answer, smiling. "My pick for what book we read together next after Summer pulled me to the dark side and got me into those smutty romance books of hers."

Summer flicks her wrist at me. "You love being on the smutty romance dark side."

I don't protest, because she's not wrong.

Cindy lets out a big laugh. She's such a ball of life and energy, which makes it so funny how Summer is convinced she and the ramen shop owner Kazu have a thing for each other.

She's as social and boisterous as can be while he might as well be the definition of *terse*. Even their appearances contrast, both matching their own personality—Cindy on the curvy side with a soft and inviting face, Kazu thin and wiry with sharp, hard features.

"Going from modern love stories to a classic love story," Cindy nods. "I guess love really is in the air today."

I arch an eyebrow. "Is it?"

"Well, I do have a date tonight…"

Summer's squeal is practically a scream. "Really!?"

Cindy nods. "He's a lawyer who moved here a couple months ago."

Summer's utterly delighted expression freezes, then melts off her face. Her brows drop, the excited smile on her lips fading. Clearly, the guy Cindy's going on a date with isn't the brusque ramen shop owner she was expecting.

"Oh," Summer says, before gathering her energy back up and forcing herself to sound more enthusiastic. "That sounds great! I hope you have a great time!"

If I'm not mistaken, Cindy doesn't look terribly excited about the date either. "I'm sure I will," she answers, though it sounds oddly like she's trying to convince herself.

When Cindy excuses herself to get back to work and walks out of earshot, Summer looks crestfallen.

"What is going *on* between those two?" she demands, clearly meaning Cindy and Kazu.

I shrug. "Maybe they're not into each other. Maybe you and Hudson are reading into something that isn't there."

She shakes her head. "*No* way. They're so smitten with each other. It's just …" she sighs. "They're probably just so different they don't know how to express themselves to each other. Am I a bad person if I hope Cindy has a bad date tonight?"

I laugh. "Probably."

Summer scrunches up her face thoughtfully. Then she shrugs. "Oh, well. I'm a bad person, then. I do hope she has a bad date tonight. Her and this … *lawyer*," she says the word like it brings a bad taste to her mouth, "are not meant for each other."

We settle into our schoolwork for a while, until Summer breaks the silence by saying, "Oh, by the way! I was over at Hudson's place and overheard a conversation among the guys. Apparently, Tuck was also up at that gala in New Hampshire you went to."

A knot tightens in my stomach. Both at feeling caught out, and at memories of how sinfully hot *That Morning* was.

"Oh? That's interesting," I say, doing my best to keep my gaze tethered to my laptop screen, my fingers typing, acting like I'm totally unaffected by what Summer just said.

To my considerable relief, Summer doesn't have anything more to say on the topic.

I feel guilty about not telling her what happened between me and Tuck. We're best friends. We tell each other everything. She even kept me in the loop when she and Hudson started fake dating last semester—I was the only one other than them who knew, because *of course* Summer wouldn't think of trying to fool her best friend.

But it's for the best that I pretend That Morning never happened—because I think I've made up my mind where Tuck McCoy is concerned.

26

TUCK

It's the Thursday after the weekend in New Hampshire, and I haven't seen Olivia all week.

I'm at the ramen shop having lunch with Hudson. I feel like a dick, because I've hardly heard anything he's said for the past twenty minutes. I've just been nodding along and giving non-committal grunts as he's tried to carry a conversation.

Hell must have frozen over if *he's* the chatty one between the two of us.

I just keep thinking about that morning with Olivia. How fucking incredible it was. And how much it would suck if it never happened again.

Which, considering how stingy Olivia's been with replying to my texts, seems like a distinct possibility.

"Tuck, check it out," Hudson says, at a rare moment when my attention's drifted back to my immediate surroundings.

I turn in my seat, towards the back of the restaurant. Kazu is right behind the wooden counter, but he's pouring a clear liquid into a shot glass. Without any change to his normal stoic expression, he throws it back in one gulp.

But as I look at him, I realize maybe his face isn't quite that stoic. I can read something there. Not quite heartbreak, but something close. Maybe I'd miss it if I weren't feeling the same thing right now. But because I am, I sense a kindred spirit in this moment.

"Hey, Kazu," I call over to him. His eyes shift to me. I tilt my head back. "Why don't you bring that liquor over here? I could use a fuckin' drink myself."

We're the only customers here right now, so why not?

Kazu regards me silently for a beat. Then he nods, dipping his chin lower than the normal centimeter he doles out when acknowledging people.

Kazu reaches under the counter and picks up two more shot glasses, then grabs the bottle and walks over to us, taking a seat next to me. He pours himself, Hudson, and me a glass of what I now see is sake, and we all throw it back.

My eyes close as the liquid burns down my throat. Fuck, I needed that.

Kazu sighs. "Women are often inscrutable," he says.

"You fuckin' said it, buddy," I reply.

Hudson shrugs. "They made sense to me."

"She gives me a book," Kazu says, pouring himself more sake, "and then suddenly, she's going on a date with another man." He throws back the shot. "Inscrutable."

Hudson purses his lips, nodding his head in thought. "Well, what did you do after she gave you the book?"

Kazu looks at him blankly. "I read it."

"What did you do for *her* after she gave you the book?" Hudson prods.

Kazu's silent for a beat.

"Did you give *her* a book that you think *she'll* like?"

"No," Kazu answers, drawing out the syllable thoughtfully.

"You can't just let her make a gesture and not return it with one of your own," Hudson says.

"You gotta get her a book, bro," I say, grabbing the sake and taking another shot. "Something that, like, relates to her in some way. Or a book that makes you think of her when you think about it."

He nods slowly, his brain absorbing the idea.

"What about you?" Hudson turns his gaze on me.

My brow furrows. "What about me?"

"What's your easily solvable girl problem?"

I huff a sarcastic laugh. "Easily solvable. Yeah, right."

I haven't told Hudson what happened with Olivia in New Hampshire. Haven't told anyone, because she asked me not to. All I've been able to do is think about it—which I do just about every waking moment.

"Well, it's obviously about Olivia," Hudson says.

"Aren't you a fucking detective all of a sudden," I snark. Who else would it be about? Hudson knows I haven't been with any other girls since I met Olivia months ago. "Well, lay it on me, Sherlock. What's the easy solution?"

Hudson's lips straighten, and for a moment I let hope buoy inside me. Is it possible he actually has some advice to offer that's going help me finally convince Olivia to give me a real shot?

He shrugs. "Guess you're right. It's not so easily solvable. Olivia's got her defenses way up when it comes to you, that's for sure."

I let out a groan.

"Swapping with Rhys to go to that gala wasn't worth it, I take it?" he asks.

Oh, if only he fucking knew. I'd have given my left nut for the morning I had with Olivia. A month of doing Rhys' laundry and chores for that? The trade of a damn lifetime.

"No, we had a great time," I say.

And I'm not even talking about her pussy taking me to another plane of existence.

I'm talking about the night before, when we stood out on the heated patio and ate Pretzel M&M's while drinking expensive champagne. I'm talking about when we spent hours in bed watching The Office, making bets on how long it'll take Jim and Pam to get together.

I've been so in the mood to keep watching the show since I got back, but the thought of watching it while Olivia's giving me the cold shoulder just feels like a thorn pricking my heart.

"But I know she's been intentionally avoiding me ever since we got back," I finish.

"She had a bad experience dating a hockey player in the past," Hudson says. "A rich, cocky hockey player. Just like you."

My eyebrows pinch. "I'm not like him at all."

Hudson chuckles. "How do you know? You don't even know him."

I don't need to. I know I'm nothing like that fucker. Because he hurt Olivia, and I never would.

Kazu stands up. "Finished?" he asks, looking at our empty bowls. We nod, and he clears our table. He suddenly seems to have a plan of action in mind, and when we leave the restaurant, he's right at the door, turning the *Open* sign to *Closed*.

I push out a heavy sigh as we walk back home. I wish showing Olivia that I really, genuinely want to get to know her better and spend more time with her were as easy as buying a damn book.

I know one thing, though: I'm sure as hell not giving up. She's got my heart wrapped around her finger, and I've got no interest in trying to untwirl it.

27

OLIVIA

This week felt fifty days long instead of five.

It's Friday night, and I've never been more ready to take the edge of the week off with a couple drinks. I'm out with a group of my friends from the drama department at Loser's Luck Tavern. It's a classic college bar, informal, cozy, and always packed full and lively on a Friday night.

I'm talking with Ramya, a fellow drama major, about a play written by another student. We're both reading through the script and thinking about whether we want to try out for any roles when it gets produced later this semester.

We're discussing which roles we think each of us would be best for, when her gaze flits over my shoulder and her eyes go wide.

"Kevin's here," she says, her tone hushed.

I smirk. Ramya totally has a thing for Kevin, another drama major who's especially talented at playing comedic roles.

With his thick auburn hair and handsome face, his only

real drawback is the fact that for the past couple weeks, he's been greeting everyone with an exaggerated *Whazzup!?*

I think he's trying to make it, like, *his thing*. We're all just waiting for him to realize it's not going to catch on.

Throwing a glance over my shoulder, I notice Kevin's gaze pointed just to my side, tethered unmistakably to Ramya.

"He's looking at you," I say, encouragingly. "Go talk to him."

"Should I? Can I? Do I look okay?" she stutters with an adorable nervous eagerness.

I giggle. "Answer one, absolutely; answer two, absolutely; and answer three, no—you don't look okay, you look hot as hell, and we both know it. Get over there." I nudge her knee with my own.

A nervous grin curls on her face. She takes a deep breath. "Okay," she says, before taking a fortifying sip of her drink. "Tell me to break a leg."

"Break a leg," I say on a laugh, shooting her a wink as she hops off the high-top chair and weaves through the crowd towards Kevin.

The seat beside me isn't empty for long. Aiden saunters over and takes it. His dark, hazel eyes alight on me. He's another drama major who I've acted with a couple times. We even shared an on-stage kiss last semester.

Ever since then, I've kind of gotten a low-key vibe that he might be into me. The way those hazel eyes are looking at me right now, that vibe is shifting up to high-key.

"Hey, Olivia," he greets me. "Heard about you trying out for that Macbeth production in Burlington."

"Yeah," I answer. "I know it's a long shot, but …"

He shakes his head. "Not a long shot at all. The only

long shot is you remembering the little people like us once you're a Broadway sensation."

His tone is flirty and lightly teasing. I laugh in response, though it feels a little forced. "Don't worry, I'll remember you all when I'm on Broadway. Once I make it to Hollywood, on the other hand ..." I jest with a grin.

He barks out a laugh. "Oh, duh, that goes without saying. I wouldn't even imagine you'd still remember my name at that point."

Yeah, I think we're definitely flirting. Which is ... good, right?

Yes, it's good.

I've been thinking a lot about what happened with Tuck throughout the week. Not just the thing that happened with him That Morning in New Hampshire, but what's *been* happening between us. The way our chemistry's been building.

I've concluded that I do want to finally pull down some of the walls I've built up around my heart, the walls that have kept me from even contemplating finding a new relationship for two years.

But I've also concluded that Tuck is the wrong person to do it with. He's too risky. There are too many ways we could go wrong, too many ways I could get hurt. A guy like Aiden, on the other hand ... he'd be a safe choice.

So, I lean into the flirting.

When he makes another teasing joke, I playfully swat at his chest.

I expect *some* sparks to fly. But there's nothing.

When my knee simply brushed with Tuck's for a fraction of a second in the tutoring room, there was an eruption of electricity, a flash of heat that crawled up my leg and spread through my center.

But my palm pressing against Aiden's chest? Nothing. Not even a tiny flicker of static.

When I tilt my head to the side thinking about a question he asks me, strands of my hair feather across my face. Aiden reaches out and gently sweeps them behind my ear.

The gesture doesn't make my chest feel fuzzy, doesn't make my stomach flip—two sensations I know I'd get if Tuck did the same thing.

But then, something *does* make my stomach flip.

"Hey, pal," Tuck's voice, his drawl casual but with an unfamiliar sharp undertone to it, sounds from beside us. I look over and see his blue eyes fastened on Aiden. "Thanks for keeping my date company while she was waiting for me." His brow lowers. "But I'm here now, and I'm gonna need that seat."

"Oh," Aiden peeps, caught off guard. His gaze bounces between me and Tuck. "Date?"

"That's right," Tuck replies, a bite to his voice. "*My* date. Olivia."

"Uh, okay ..." Aiden says, getting up from his seat. Tuck's low and hard brow, his stormy expression, and the iron in his voice don't make Aiden eager to argue. He shrugs at me. "See you later, Olivia."

"Bye," Tuck says, popping the word like a jab at Aiden as he walks away.

Tuck's jaw is set hard, his neck muscles coiling with tension when I turn to him.

"I'm not your date," I protest.

"After I saw that asshole touching your hair, either I got rid of him by lying, or he was leaving on a fucking stretcher," Tuck says, his voice husky and tense. "I think I made the right choice."

A chill dances up my spine at the jealousy laced in

Tuck's voice. I know I should be angry at him for barging over like a caveman and chasing off a guy I was in the middle of a conversation with. He has no right to dictate who I talk to, or what part of me they touch.

But I'm not angry.

A teasing grin twists on my mouth. "Is Mr. No-Strings-Attached Tuck McCoy actually jealous?" I ask, wryly.

"You're damn right I am," he rasps.

The directness of his answer takes me by surprise. My heartbeat leaps up my throat.

"Why?" I ask.

"*Why?*" he throws the question back at me like it's ridiculous. He places his hand flat on the bar counter next to me, angling his body so that his leg intrudes into the space between my knees as I sit sideways on the barstool. "Olivia, the taste of your juices still tingles on my fucking mouth. I fall asleep every night remembering your moans in my ear. You avoid me all week after that, and the next time I see you, some other guy is touching you? Fuck yes, I'm jealous."

His voice is thick with gravel, and he's dipped his head closer to me so I can feel the brush of his hot breath on the side of my face.

Heat blasts between my thighs. I clench them, but that only draws my knees closer together, and they pinch around Tuck's leg. Feeling the presence of him there reminds me of when it was his hips between them, and the heat ratchets up, my face turning red while sparks skitter across my skin.

"You always get this possessive over girls you hook up with?" I ask sardonically, after recovering some measure of my composure.

"*Hook up*? That's what you think happened between us, a hookup?"

"What else would you call it?"

Tuck shakes his head, blue eyes flashing. "I don't know what to call it. But I've had hookups before, Olivia. They sure as fuck never felt *anything* like *that*."

His words spear through me. I know I've never felt anything even close to what I felt with Tuck. But I didn't let myself imagine that the same would go for him.

I know that Tuck's been wanting to see me since we got back from New Hampshire, but I didn't imagine he'd get so worked up over another guy talking to me that he'd march over and glower at him sharp enough to cut steel.

With heat humming through my body, I think that maybe I should stop being a coward. That I should stop caring so much about what could go wrong with Tuck. Maybe even start to think about what could go right. That I should …

But instinctively, I feel my defenses raising themselves.

I cross my arms and put on my familiar adversarial attitude towards Tuck, like it's a suit of armor.

"Whatever it was, it isn't going to happen again," I say. But I can tell it sounds like I'm reading a line in a script I don't like, playing a role I don't believe in, one I can't summon any enthusiasm for.

Tuck huffs a laugh, his eyes glimmering at the challenge. "Just try to pretend there are any other guys in this place, or on this campus, or in this whole fucking state that could satisfy you after what *I* did to you last weekend."

Then he turns and walks away, confident that I won't be able to shake off the truth of his words. Because he's right. There's no one who can make me feel like he does.

The problem is, I don't think there's anyone who could hurt me like he can, either.

28

TUCK

It's Monday afternoon after class when I get a text from Summer, asking if she can give me a quick call.

She and Hudson are skipping classes today and tomorrow, taking a trip to Montreal since Hudson surprised her with tickets to a concert by her favorite violinist who's performing up there.

I reply in the affirmative, and a moment later I'm swiping open her call.

"What's up?" I answer.

"Do you mind checking in on Olivia?" she asks.

Concern nips at me. "What's wrong with her?"

"She started coming down with a cold last night. She woke up sick this morning. I wanted to stay home to take care of her, but she wouldn't hear of me missing the concert. I told her to take a sick day and text me throughout the day so I know she's alright, but she hasn't responded to my last couple messages."

I'm already pushing my feet into the shoes that I just toed off. "I'll head over now. Is your door locked?"

"Yeah, but if Olivia doesn't answer, there's a lock box

with a spare key on the door." She gives me the code, and I promise to call her back in a couple minutes with an update.

My shoulders are tight and heavy as I drive the couple blocks to her house. My hands grip impatiently around the steering wheel at the two red lights I have to sit at on the way, as I fight the urge to just roll through.

I run up her walkway when I finally get there. I press the doorbell firmly and wait for an answer.

Nothing.

I press it again. After again getting no answer, I knock hard on the door and call out to Olivia.

When I still don't hear any footsteps padding to the door from inside, I use the code Summer texted me to open their key box and let myself in.

Olivia's lying on the couch. One arm straight by her side, the other bent over her stomach. Hair feathered across her face. Chest slowly rising and falling.

My heart clenches at how damn beautiful she looks, but it clenches even harder with worry. She must be out cold to be this close to the door and still sleep through my rings and knocks.

I press the back of my hand to her forehead. She's burning up.

Worry streaks through me. Rationally, I know it's probably just a bad cold. But I need to hear her voice, just for a moment, before I'll be able to slow down my racing heartbeat.

I shake her shoulder gently, calling her name in a firm whisper. It takes a little while, but she stirs.

"Hm?" she makes a weak sound in her throat. "Summer?"

"No, it's Tuck."

"Tuck?" there's a thin surprise in her tone, but she's too weak to react much.

"Mhm," I hum. "Summer asked me to come over and check on you. I'll stay here for today, alright?"

"Oh." She turns her head towards the couch cushion. "Okay." She groans as a shiver races over her. "I'm cold."

"I'll get you a blanket. And a real pillow." I'm so focused on my mission when I go into Olivia's room to grab those things that I don't even take a second to look at her bed, letting my cock twitch thinking about the things I would do to her on it.

Okay, that's a lie. I'm not a saint, am I?

But I don't linger too long thinking about it, eager to get Olivia's head propped with a proper pillow and her shivery body covered.

Back downstairs, I gently lift her head to switch out the throw pillow for one from her bed, then drape the blanket over her.

I go to the kitchen, remembering how important hydration is when you're sick. I pour her a big glass of water from their filtered pitcher in the refrigerator. I gently shake her awake again and hold the glass up to her lips, lightly tilting it so she can take tiny sips.

"You should go, Tuck," she says as I pull the glass away from her and set it on the coffee table. "I'll make you sick. You might miss a game."

"Don't you worry about that. I'm not going anywhere."

She makes another weak, humming noise in her throat. Maybe it's in my head, but it seems like a pleased sound.

Once Olivia's drifted back to sleep, I check the kitchen and decide I need to do a shopping run.

She needs medicine, soup for when she gets hungry, and some Gatorade. About fifteen minutes later, I'm stepping back inside Olivia's house with bags full of medicine, tissues, Gatorade, orange juice, a dozen different kinds of canned soup because I'm not sure what she likes, and cough drops in case she ends up needing them.

I also picked up some allergy medicine for myself. I'm allergic to cats, and sometimes Salsa's fur bothers me. Luckily, the girls keep their place clean. Still, I'll pop a couple, because there's no way I'm letting a runny nose keep me from staying by Olivia's side.

When I step through the door, Olivia's eyes flutter open. My heart squeezes in sympathy at her exhausted gaze.

"You take any medicine yet?" I ask, stepping to the couch.

She just shakes her head.

"Here." I fish the bottle of Tylenol out of its bag. Olivia's so tired she doesn't even hold out her hand for the pill, just opening her mouth for it. I try not to let my cock thicken too much as I place the capsule on her tongue. I twist open a bottle of Gatorade for her to wash it down with.

"You got the blue kind," she whispers thinly. "My favorite."

I chuckle. "Your favorite Gatorade is the same colors as my eyes? Can't be a coincidence."

Her mouth crooks with the wisp of a smile, and then she's back asleep.

There's no way I'm leaving here any time soon. I sit on a chair close to the couch to rest for a second.

It's gotta be ten minutes later when I realize I've been sitting here with my gaze hovering on Olivia while she sleeps. I suddenly feel self-conscious, so I rip it away and look around the room.

Should've brought my laptop. Maybe I could've got some schoolwork done. Oh, well.

I think about turning on the TV, but I don't want to disturb her. Instead, I decide to wander back up to her room to pick out a book from her overstuffed bookshelf.

When I step through the doorway, my eyes settle on a book sitting on the small table next to her bed, bookmark sticking out just a bit more than halfway through. Picking it up, I see it's *Emma* by Jane Austen.

The book she's in the middle of reading right now, I guess. The thought of reading the exact book she's reading, my eyes passing over the literal words on the literal pages that her eyes passed over just days ago, makes my heart go crazy in my chest.

I guess this'll be my first foray into Victorian literature.

Wait, is Jane Austen Victorian? Isn't there a Regency era somewhere in the British timeline, too? And Edwardian? Which one is she? Sebastian would know, but I sure as hell don't.

I shrug. Whatever damn monarch Jane Austen's era is named after, I guess this is the book I'll be perusing for a while.

Keeping Olivia's bookmark in place, I open to the first page and start reading, lounging in the living room chair, Olivia sleeping silently just to my side.

I've never been a classical literature guy, but I get sucked into the book. I don't know if it's because it's just that good, or if it's because I feel like I'm sharing something with Olivia while reading it. Either way, two hours fly by before I glance up from the pages.

When I do, it's because I hear Olivia stirring.

"How you feeling?" I ask when her eyes open and her head flips on the pillow in my direction.

She groans. "A little hungry. Maybe. I don't know."

I know the feeling. When you're sick and your stomach

starts to rumble, but you're not sure if you can handle eating.

"I'll heat you up some chicken noodle soup, see if you can handle the broth."

Her eyes are already closed when she answers, "Okay."

Olivia's able to sip five spoonfuls of hot broth before a groan tells me that's all she can stomach right now. I twist open a new, cold bottle of Gatorade for her to wash it down with. Her long breaths tell me she's back asleep by the time I settle into my chair and pick up *Emma* again.

This time, I'm pretty sure my gaze lingers on her for longer than ten minutes by the time I pull it away and direct it to the next page in the book.

29

OLIVIA

I just had the strangest dream.

Tuck was here. Taking care of me for some reason. Maybe because I slipped and hurt myself? But why wouldn't Summer be here to do that? Maybe she had to travel for a violin competition or something.

Anyway, Tuck was here. Taking care of me. That should sound more like a nightmare, right? But it wasn't. He was caring, and gentle, and sweet. It felt good. He fed me soup. Homemade. His grandma's secret recipe. It was delicious.

Why's it so hard to sit up? Or even to open my eyes?

Am I on the couch? I'm able to crack my eyes open just a bit, and through the narrow slice of vision, I recognize the pattern of my blanket. On the back of my head is the familiar sensation of my pillow. Why would I have taken my blanket and pillow downstairs and slept on the couch?

"Are you up?"

A weak kind of surprise hits me, like I'm somehow not strong enough to feel as much surprise as I should at hearing Tuck's voice.

I know it's not a dream. He's really here? Why?

Then I realize it when I summon my strength to try and sit up. Aches pang all over me, my muscles tired and sore. A shiver rushes through me. I feel a wave of discomfort and weakness, and I give up the thought of trying to move at all.

At least I can open my eyes wider and turn my head to the source of the sound to make sure I'm not hallucinating.

Sure enough, Tuck sits in the chair next to the couch. My eyebrows scrunch when I notice he's holding a copy of *Emma*.

Tuck McCoy in my living room reading Jane Austen while I'm just stirring from being passed out on the couch. Am I sure this isn't still a dream?

Then I realize none of it was. I remember coming down with a cold Sunday night, waking up feeling like death Monday morning. Summer even wanted to stay home from the concert Hudson was going to take her to, but I put my foot down and demanded she go.

Did Summer or Hudson text Tuck to have him come over and take care of me?

And he did it? How long has he been sitting there?

My chest squeezes at the thought, a light and almost giddy feeling humming through me. If I had more strength, I'd clamp down on the feeling and chase it away, because it's not something I should be feeling where Tuck is concerned.

But I don't have the strength to do it, so I let the feeling buoy inside me.

My stomach growls. Maybe some more of Tuck's homemade chicken soup will give me strength. It must be a loud growl, because Tuck's lips curl into a grin and he asks, "Hungry?"

I dip my chin in a shallow nod. "More of your grandma's chicken soup?" I ask.

Tuck tilts his head, an amused expression carving on his

features. Then he just shakes his head and pushes up from the chair. "You got it. Grandma Campbell's recipe coming right up."

I lose a couple minutes sinking back into sleep before Tuck's by my side, nudging me awake and holding a bowl as he kneels next to me. He ladles the soup into my mouth, feeding me. It's an intimate feeling, and now there's another surge of a cozy, comfortable emotion thrumming in my chest.

He feeds me about a third of the bowl before I'm full. I'm summoning the strength to tell him that I'll be okay, that I can take care of myself, that he should go home and do whatever he needs to do instead of wasting his day here with me.

But before I can open my mouth, I'm asleep again.

THE NEXT TIME my eyelids flutter open, it's dark except for the soft light of a lamp on the other side of the living room. Tuck's moved, sitting on the chair closest to the lamp, still reading *Emma*. He's about halfway through.

"What time is it?" My throat feels tight and dry as the words croak out.

Tuck looks up from the book. "Little past eight-thirty."

"You should go home."

"No way." Tuck's response is immediate. His tone tells me there's no point in trying to argue with him, even if I had the energy to do so.

"Where will you sleep?"

He shrugs. "The chair."

I roll my eyes. "You can't sleep on a chair."

"You continue to underestimate me, Lockley," he says,

his drawl wryly playful. "I assure you that sleeping on a chair is well within my skill set. You'll be very impressed."

I huff out as much of a laugh as my strength allows. "I'm sure you're capable of it. I mean I don't want to make you do that. It'll be uncomfortable."

He shakes his head. "Nah. This chair is nice. Trust me, I've slept on much more uncomfortable bus seats during long trips to away games. I'll sleep like a baby in this chair."

I let my eyes fall closed, but I don't feel myself falling asleep. I could probably do with staying awake for a little while. How many hours have I been passed out for, anyway?

I nod to the TV. "Wanna watch something?" I ask Tuck.

"Yeah, if you want to," he answers, a flash of eagerness in his blue eyes.

A smile lifts my mouth. "How about picking up where we left off on The Office?"

I know it's a dangerous game to even hint at anything that happened when we shared that hotel room in New Hampshire. I guess I'm sick enough that my inhibitions have taken a big hit.

And I did really enjoy watching the show with him, the night before That Morning. Since I got back to Cedar Shade, a couple times I've really been in the mood to keep watching it. Even pulled up the next episode that we'd left off on. But each time, I just couldn't click the button to start it.

Remembering watching it lying under the covers with Tuck, laughing together and yapping about it between episodes, and then thinking of watching it alone ... it just made me feel cold, made a hollow feeling pang in my chest.

I curl my legs, freeing a couch cushion for him. Again, probably not a smart move. Inviting Tuck to sit next to me to watch something that's going to remind both of us of that hotel room we shared.

But there's that lowered inhibition again.

Even though my muscles are weak, there's one at the height of my thighs that's strong enough to pull at the feeling of Tuck's weight settling onto the cushion at the other end of the couch.

Tuck grabs the remote. The fact that he instantly remembers the exact episode we left off on makes my chest twinge in a way I can't quite describe.

My laughs might be quiet and short as we're watching thanks to my exhausted state, but I still enjoy it. I'm energized enough to groan and ask, "Are they really going to make us wait the whole damn season for Jim and Pam to happen?" while the credits roll.

Tuck chuckles. "Imagine they make us wait, like, two seasons. Or three. Or more."

I gasp. "They couldn't."

"Wanna watch another?" Tuck asks.

I yawn, but I nod. "Yeah. One more."

During the episode, my eyelids start to feel heavier and heavier. Sleep is tightening its grip around me.

I suddenly realize that at some point, I stretched out my legs, and they're over Tuck's lap. At this point, I don't even have the strength to care. I just accept it. My legs are on Tuck's lap, resting on his muscular thighs. Oh, well.

When the episode ends, I let my eyelids fall shut like they've been wanting to do for the last ten minutes. I don't fall immediately asleep, though. I just relax, letting my mind clear, letting all my muscles slacken, feeling nothing but exhaustion, and enjoying the respite from feeling as shitty as I did earlier.

"Olivia?" Tuck asks, gently. "You awake?"

I am. But I'm too tired to answer.

Tuck waits a couple beats, then tries again. "Olivia? Hey, Olivia, you awake?" His voice is louder, more prodding this time, like he's really checking to see if I'm asleep.

Again, I'm not, but I don't make a peep.

He places his hand on my knee and shakes it gently. The spark that shoots up from where his hand contacts me, racing straight to my center, definitely confirms to *me* that I'm awake—but I still don't make a sound. I'll be asleep in a matter of seconds, anyway, so what's the point?

Tuck lets out a long, heavy sigh. "Olivia." He says my name, but he's not talking to me. He says it like an exhale, like a plea, like a lament. "Shit, I wish you'd give us a chance."

My breath catches in my chest. He thinks I'm asleep. He thinks I can't hear him.

I should stir, cough, do something to let him know I'm awake. Something to keep from overhearing what I'm clearly not supposed to overhear, even if he is talking *about* me.

But I don't.

"I know you think I'm some rich, playboy asshole." He lets out a sarcastic chuckle. "Maybe I am. Or was. Not that I've been with a girl since I fucking met you ..."

He hasn't been with a girl ... since we met?

But that was months ago. With Tuck's reputation, he's not the kind of guy to go even *days* without a hookup.

"I just wish like hell you'd give me the chance to show you that I'm not looking for a hookup. Not looking for a temporary thing. What am I looking for?" There's another heavy sigh. "Fuck if I know. I've never wanted anything from a relationship but a short, good time. But this? This is different. I don't have enough experience even thinking about what I want out of a relationship. But I know I want a hell of a lot more with you than I've ever wanted with anyone else."

Do I still think that that's all Tuck wants? Is that the reason I'm still scared to let anything happen between us? Or is it something else now?

Maybe I'm not afraid that he cares too little anymore. Maybe I'm afraid that he cares too much. Maybe I'm afraid that he can make me care about him that much, too. Maybe I'm afraid that's already happened ...

"Well, what else can I do?" Tuck continues. "Sure as hell can't get you off my mind. Sure as hell don't want to. I'd rather keep waiting for you than be with anyone else."

Tuck's words echo loudly in my head as sleep finally pulls me under.

30

OLIVIA

By Friday, I'm feeling fully recovered.
Tuck stayed with me until Summer came home Tuesday evening.

Throughout all of Tuesday, he kept teasing me about how, in my delirium, I imagined him feeding me gourmet, homemade soup from a recipe his grandmother handed down to him.

"Here's your artisanal water," he'd tell me, handing me a glass. "I've infused it with a secret blend of minerals and vitamins that my great-half-uncle Maurice taught me."

"Here's your toast," he'd say. "The bread was grown from a secret strain of wheat that my grandfather smuggled out of a top-secret agricultural research facility."

"If you thought my Grandma's chicken soup was good," he'd say, handing me a bowl of Campbell's straight from the microwave, "wait until you taste my great-grandmother's ex-husband's cousin's vegetable soup recipe. You don't wanna know how much I had to spend on the rare spices the recipe calls for."

I acted like I hadn't heard anything he said when he

thought I was asleep Monday night. But those words haven't stopped bouncing around in my head for a second since then.

My mind's been marinating in them, every word gliding around the grooves of my brain like rivulets of water crawling down the ridges of Tuck's muscles as he stands under a shower ...

I also increasingly find myself thinking of horny similes involving Tuck ...

On Friday, something clicks. A realization dawns that sends a mixture of fear and excitement roaring through me.

Friday night, Tuck and the rest of the Black Bears have an away game that they stay overnight for. On Saturday, when they get back, Summer tells me she's going to visit Hudson and spend the night.

So, I go on a walk around town. Ostensibly to clear my head, but my head does anything but clear. I'm wondering if I'm about to make the right decision. Or if I'm even actually going to go through with what I think I've made my mind up to do—am I going to chicken out at the last moment?

Then, I look into the window of Last Word as I'm passing by—and I see Tuck.

Sitting at a table by himself, working on something on his laptop.

With a deep breath and a pulsing sensation in my chest, I decide to take it as a sign.

My fingertips are tingling as I wrap my hand around the door and pull it open. I take the seat across from Tuck. He looks up from his computer, and our gazes lock.

A beat of silence stretches out between us. I'm the one to break it.

"Because I was afraid," I say.

Tuck's lips flatten. The square between his eyebrows wrinkles. "What?"

"That's why. Why I wouldn't give us a chance."

Surprise flashes in Tuck's eyes. 'You ..."

I nod. "I heard what you said."

His jaw muscles go tight. He leans forward, into the charged space between us over the table. "Everything?"

My stomach does a somersault as I nod. "Everything."

"I still mean it," he says.

Even through the intensity of the moment, his words make the edges of my lips twitch upward.

"The only guy I really seriously dated was in high school. It ... didn't end well." I don't want to share the whole story with Tuck, so I leave it at that. "You ... reminded me of him. At first. Superficially. I know that's not who you are right now, but ..."

Tuck's nostrils flare. Protective anger flashes in his eyes. "I hate that some piece of shit hurt you."

"But I don't want to think about him anymore," I say, pushing memories of Ryan out of my head, where I wish I could make them stay permanently. "I don't want him to have any power over me anymore. I don't want him to be the reason I do, or don't do, anything."

"Then ...?" Tuck asks.

An electric chill ripples up my back. "I think I'm ready to give us a chance."

Tuck's brow hitches, and then a smile splits on his face. A smile that becomes more devious when I say ...

"And I've got my place to myself tonight."

31

OLIVIA

Tuck's lips feather onto mine the moment my bedroom door shuts.

I'm surprised how softly, how gently his kiss starts. The caress of his lips is slow, leisurely. Instead of hurriedly spearing his tongue into my mouth, he gently coaxes the crease of my lips, and I give him just enough access for the tips of our tongues to glance against each other.

His hand sweeps under my hair, his grip resting possessively on the side of my neck. The rough pad of his thumb rakes against the sensitive sliver of skin between my jaw and my ear. Sparks sizzle over me, radiating from his touch.

Gradually, his tongue pushes further into my mouth, slanting and swiping over mine. His lips caress with more hunger, less restrain, and soon we're deep in the savage, all-consuming kiss I was expecting.

Our noses press together, the rough stubble of his chin and his cheeks rasping against my soft skin. Now his hand is moving, grazing up my body to cup my breast through my shirt.

It feels like fire is racing through my veins. I press into his kiss, swirling my tongue around his, like I'm stepping up to a challenge.

I snag his bottom lip between my teeth. He moans into my mouth. His hand curves around my hip to grip my ass. He pulls my center close to him, so I can feel the throbbing hardness of his cock through our clothes.

"Fuck," he groans when I tug on his lip, still clenched sharply between my teeth.

When I let go, he presses the kiss further, sucking on my tongue. My senses are overwhelmingly full of him, of his touch, his taste, his scent.

He pulls away from the kiss and takes a step back. His gaze is hooded, his brow set low with intensity. The lusty gleam in his eyes spears right through me, filling my whole center with a hot, liquid tension.

"Strip for me," he commands, his voice thick with gravel.

His jaw muscles arc when I pull my light sweater over my head. He does the same, pulling off his shirt and dropping it to the floor. My core clenches at the hard lines and sharp ridges of his physique. My eyes crawl down his torso, to the sharp V shape of his hip muscles that points below the waist of his jeans.

He grips the outline of his hardness through his pants. "Take it all off, baby," he growls. "Slow."

His eyes singe every inch of me as I peel my clothes off. A curse rasps from his mouth when I unclench my bra and let it fall to the floor. My nipples are tight nubs. The intensity of his gaze makes them prickle.

When I grab the hem of my panties, he steps forward and stops me.

"No," he says. "Those, *I* want to take off."

He backs me up to my bed, kicking his jeans off his legs

as I lie down. He slowly pulls my panties down my legs, the backs of his knuckles burning against my skin while his fingers are hooked underneath the waist.

My legs quiver as he presses soft, languid kisses up the length of my thigh.

"I couldn't take my time with you last time," he rasps. "Couldn't appreciate every fucking inch of you the way it deserved to be. I'm going to make up for that now."

"Worried you were never going to be able to?" I tease, even as my breath hitches in my chest from the scorching heat of his lips against my bare skin.

Those lips rumble against my hip as they continue to climb higher up my body. "No way. I knew I'd have you like this one day. I fucking knew it."

His kisses trail up the outline of my ribcage, every touch of his lips making my body writhe.

I'm wound so tightly. Between my legs is a hot, slick mess, my clit taut and throbbing with desire. Tuck's hands seem to know exactly where to touch me to wind me even higher.

His tongue gently circles my nipple, and then he blows a breath over it, tightening it so much that it hurts.

Tuck teases me, giving me ghosts of glances right where I want pressure most, but not nearly enough to satisfy me, not nearly enough to dull the ache that pounds fiercely between my legs.

When his tongue finally slants over my nipple, pinpricks of pleasure skitter all over me. His tongue lavishes one nipple with attention while he tweaks the other with his fingers.

My back arches, whimpers springing from my lips.

It feels so good, but it only makes me want contact between my legs that much more. My slick opening pulses, the ache of need so tight and sharp that it's driving me crazy.

I tilt my hips, searching for any contact—with his leg, his torso, his cock, anything I can get. But Tuck intentionally angles himself away from me, leaving me frustrated.

"Please," I groan, unable to verbalize what I need any better than that whiny plea.

He laughs darkly. "I should give you a taste of your own medicine. It's only fair, isn't it?"

His hand glides down from my breast, gripping the sensitive area just under my rib cage.

"After all, you drove me crazy, absolutely fucking crazy, for so damn long," he says. "Making me wait forever for the thing I wanted more than anything else. Isn't it fair that I get to drive you a fraction as crazy as you drove me?"

His lips trail back down my body, finding every nook of sensitivity that makes me squirm, that makes me buck my hips forward again without finding the contact I'm dying for.

He settles between my legs, but he's still not finished teasing me. His lips are everywhere but where I want them most. I'm a quivering mess, the muscles between my thighs tugging, coiled tight and hot.

Just when I think I can't take any more of his teasing, he slides the tip of his tongue up my slit. Pleasure snakes through me. A moan pushes from my lips.

"Fuck, you taste good," he husks.

Tuck's own restraint snaps, and finally he's giving me exactly what I want. He's lapping and sucking at my wetness, groaning with appreciation. Waves of pleasure crash over me, heightened by the delicious relief I feel after he wound me so tight waiting for it.

I look down. The sight of his hooded gaze as he makes a

meal out of me sends me even higher. I thrust my hands into the thick tuft of his hair, my hips bucking into him as I ride the ecstasy that rattles through my body.

"Tuck, Tuck ..." All I can do is chant his name. His tongue swirls around my clit, and my eyes clench, color bursting behind the lids.

My fists are curled so tightly in his hair that it has to hurt, but I think he likes it. The knot of pleasure in my core is tightening, growing, and it feels like at any moment I could ...

Then, the perfect flick of his tongue sends me tumbling over the edge.

Every muscle pulls taut as my climax unfurls inside me. I fall apart, utterly, the intensity of the sensation melting my brain.

I'm a panting mess as I come down. For a moment, I feel like I won't be able to lift a finger for hours.

But when Tuck crawls over me and presses his lips to mine, and the taste of my own release singes my lips, I come alive again.

When I feel Tuck's length between my legs, his hard shaft resting and pulsing against my wet center, lust shoots through me.

I lift my hips, savoring the outline of his cock against me. I sit up, and Tuck lets me turn and push him onto the mattress.

The first time, he was on top; but this time, I want to be. A jolt of electricity races up my spine at the thought of spearing myself on his cock.

I retrieve a condom and roll it down his shaft, then position myself over him with the tip of his length pressing against my slick opening.

"*Fuuuuck*," he groans as I slowly lower myself onto him.

The sensation of Tuck filling me, inch by inch, is otherworldly. When he bottoms out, all my nerves are buzzing, an intense satisfaction like I've never felt washing over me.

I start to swivel my hips. The look on his face is intoxicating, his eyes hooded and blissed while his jaw is set tight.

I draw myself up, which only makes him push deeper into me. I place my hands on the sweaty planes of his chest while I start to bounce.

"Take it, baby," he rasps, his hips thrusting upward to meet my motions as I impale myself on him. "Take that fucking cock."

"So good," I moan. "This cock feels so fucking good."

Inside me, I feel my orgasm building again. The base of my spine grows tight as pleasure radiates through me, ratcheting up a notch every time I lift my hips and drive them back down to take his length.

I fling my head back as I swivel my hips, chasing a climax that I can tell is going to be even bigger than the one I just had. Tuck urges it on by drawing circles around my clit with his thumb.

"I want to see you come again, baby," he says, his breath ragged. "I want to see you fall apart above me, on my cock."

His dirty words send an erotic rush through me. At the same time, he hits the perfect spot inside me while his thumb circles my clit in just the right way, and I'm undone.

I unravel above him, my walls clenching around his thick length. My mind shatters with pleasure. Through the haze, I can hear a deep, guttural sound rip from Tuck's throat. I feel his own body convulse with orgasm.

After, Tuck and I lie together, both totally undone, exhausted, satisfaction lying heavily over us. It feels like hours pass as I loll my head against his chest with his arm wrapped around my shoulder, his rhythmic breathing lulling me.

It feels good to finally let my guard down with Tuck. Even in the hotel room, it felt like there was a distance between us; the distance born of knowledge that what was happening wasn't supposed to be happening, the distance of being conscious of a mistake.

The tranquil silence is broken by Tuck's laughter.

"I can't stop thinking about what Summer and Hudson's reactions are going to be when they find out," he says.

Anxiety slices through me. The thought of everyone knowing Tuck and I are together makes me feel like the control over my heart I've held so tightly is slipping away too quickly for comfort.

I'm ready to give me and Tuck a chance, but I don't feel ready to let him hold my heart in the palm of his hand for all to see. Not just yet.

"Actually," I begin, my speech tentative. "I was thinking we'd start by ... taking it slow."

"Slow?" he asks.

"Slow and ... quiet. At first."

The excitement that was just so vivid on his features washes away. "Quiet as in ... secret?"

I draw my bottom lip in between my teeth, trying to find a way to put what I'm feeling into words. Trying to find a way to explain my emotions in a way that won't make Tuck feel bad.

"It's just ..." I'm searching for a way to express my own feelings out loud at the same time I'm trying to fully understand them myself. "I've been afraid of getting back into a relationship for a long time. I want to move past that. But ... I feel like it would be easier, more comfortable, to dip my toes back in if there weren't so many eyes on it right away. You know?"

Tuck's eyes are contemplative. I'm not sure if he *does* know what I'm talking about, but I can tell he's trying to understand.

He nods, the motion of his head slow and thoughtful. "Alright," he says. "If that makes you more comfortable."

I can tell he doesn't like it, but I can also tell that he wants to check that feeling to make this easier for me. That just reinforces to me that I haven't made a mistake in trusting him, even if, with this relationship, I want to crawl before I walk, let alone run.

"But you can bet your ass that when we're through keeping it quiet," Tuck says, his grin coming back to his face, "I'm going to make up for it by screaming from the fucking mountaintops that you're mine. When you're ready for that."

32

TUCK

I've got a knack for looking on the bright side.

Yeah, it sucks that Olivia isn't ready to be fully open about us yet. We've been together a couple days now, and I just can't wait until we can have everything out in the open. Can't wait until when I'm talking about her, instead of saying *Olivia*, I can say my *girlfriend*.

The thought makes my chest warm in the best way.

But, until then, like I said, I know how to look on the bright side of any situation. And there's one big bright side to the fact that Olivia doesn't want us to share that we're together with anyone we know for a little while.

Sneaking around is hot as fuck.

The other day, Olivia and I were in her room when Summer came home hours earlier than Olivia expected her. But I'd just pulled her pants down her legs and settled my head between her thighs, and there was no fucking way that I wasn't getting what I was starved for.

She had to bury her face in a pillow to keep from screaming as I lapped her up. Hearing her muffled moans as she struggled to stay as quiet as possible while thrashing with pleasure from my tongue was one of the hottest fucking things I've ever experienced.

She wrapped her legs so tightly around my head that when I pulled away, I saw the soft, creamy insides of her thighs had grown red from brushing against the rough stubble of my cheeks.

The sight made me so fucking horny I *needed* to get off, so then it was my turn to struggle to stay silent as Olivia finished me with her mouth.

Yeah, once I can truly say Olivia is my girlfriend, it's gonna be pretty fucking great. But in the meantime, being her dirty little secret has its perks, too.

My cock pulses in agreement as I look outside the window of the small coffee shop I'm sitting at and see her car pull up. I'm going with her on her drive to Burlington, where she has rehearsals for the Macbeth play.

Yeah, she got the fucking role. Of course she did.

It's a way for us to surreptitiously spend time together.

Yeah, she taught me that word. Of course she did.

When her car pulls up, it feels like my heart is bouncing up and down on a trampoline. I hop out of the store and slide into her car, immediately pressing my lips to hers.

"So secret," I rasp jokingly while I caress her lips with mine, "so forbidden."

She giggles, the sounds vibrating against my lips in the best fucking way.

Shit, if she didn't have a rehearsal schedule to keep, I'd tell her to find a dark, secluded alley to drive into and take her right here in this car.

A jolt of electricity zips from the base of my cock and tingles right at the tip. Car sex is officially on my to-do list now. Sooner than later.

I connect my phone to her car radio. "You know what tunes we're singing along to during this drive," I say.

She rolls her eyes. "Taylor Swift?"

"Who else?" I shoot her a wry grin, and then I'm belting out the lyrics of the first song from the very first word.

She tries to resist, but by the third song, I've coaxed her into joining me in this singalong. As the cold Vermont air whips by our car while we drive down the road, we're warm inside, our three voices—mine, Olivia's, and T. Swift's—bounce around the cabin, and both Olivia and I have the biggest, goofiest grins on our faces for the whole drive.

When we get to the theatre, she introduces me to the rest of the cast and staff there as a friend of hers.

None of the actors or people working at the theatre are connected to Brumehill, so I guess she's comfortable that being seen with me here won't affected us trying to keep things quiet down in Cedar Shade.

There are some more people, friends or relatives or partners of some of the other actors, who are here just to hang out and watch the rehearsal. A couple recognize me as a Black Bears player, and we chat about hockey a bit.

It's pitch-black after rehearsals when Olivia and I step outside the theatre onto the streets of downtown Burlington. It's that early darkness of winter, where the sidewalks are still busy with people walking home from work and the streets are packed with the lights of commuters' cars.

"Hungry?" I ask.

"Very," Olivia nods.

We brave the icy wind for two blocks to head to a diner I noticed on the way here.

Linda's Diner. It's homey, the kind of place a diner scene would be filmed at in a 90's movie. I like it immediately.

When we slide into the booth, my breath stalls in my

throat. This is the first time Olivia and I are having a real sit-down meal together.

The thought makes an intense feeling hum through my chest. I realize with a rush of emotion that I'll always remember this moment. I'll always remember how I feel right now. How Olivia looks sitting across from me, with her brown hair pulled back in a ponytail, her pale freckles standing out more than usual, her bottom lip pulled thoughtfully between her teeth as she browses the menu.

No matter what happens between us, I'll remember this moment. Linda's Diner in Burlington, Vermont will always have a special place in my heart.

I realize I haven't even taken a breath in a while, and when I do, chills skitter down my back as my chest expands on an inhale.

When I open the menu, I have the idea to order something I don't eat very often. I want to order something that I'll specifically associate with this dinner with Olivia at Linda's Diner. Something that'll spark memories of this night every time I bite into it from here on.

I settle on a chicken salad sandwich. It's something I know I like, but I just never order it very often. It's something I don't have any specific memories associated with. Now, for the rest of my life, I will.

While we eat, I ask Olivia all about her upcoming role. I have to admit I don't know shit about the theatre. Or about Shakespeare. I read Romeo and Juliet in high school, and in my freshman English class at Brumehill, I was assigned Othello.

I was such a fucking slacker my freshman year that I didn't read it, but at least I kinda know what it was about.

Well, I know there was a character named Othello at least.

The drive home is another Taylor Swift car concert; but, uncharacteristically, I'm the one to turn the volume down right as the thick trees of the Vermont countryside give way to the snug college town of Cedar Shade.

There's a certain item on my to-do list that I've suddenly got a real bad hankering for scratching off.

When we're at a red light, I inject all the seriousness into my voice that I can when I say, "Olivia, I have a very important question to ask you."

She turns to me, her features pinched in concern from my tone. "What?"

I let two beats pass as my eyes bore into hers with a weighty gaze. "Have you ever had car sex before?"

It takes another beat for my words to register with her, but when they do, crimson floods her cheeks. "No ..."

A devious grin tilts my mouth. "Want to?"

Her lips twitch, heat igniting in her green eyes. "Yes."

I incline my head to our left. "I don't think anyone's gonna be walking down that alleyway any time soon."

She has a feline grin on her face while she rolls down the dim, narrow alley on the outskirts of town. "You sound like you're quite the expert in finding places for car sex," she says, a hint of sarcastic accusation in her voice.

"Believe it or not, you're wrong. Never done it before."

Her brow dances as she pulls to a stop. "So I get to take your car sex virginity?"

Her words catch me off guard, and I laugh. "That's right. You get to defile me."

There's a feral flash in her eyes. "I like the sound of that."

We're already pulling each other's clothes off as we clamber to the backseat.

Checking something off a to-do list never felt so fucking good.

33

OLIVIA

"Snow day!"

Summer's excited squeal wakes me before my alarm has the chance. I sit up in bed, rubbing the sleep from my eyes. Then, my mind absorbs what I just heard.

Snow day.

I throw off my blankets and hurry to my window. I look down on our street coated in fluffy white, with thick clumps of snow still tumbling languidly from the cloudy sky.

My breath catches at how beautiful it is. The snow's already piled up so high that it's just a flat, rolling plane of white, eliminating the distinction between the road and the sidewalks. The skeletal frames of the trees are fringed with pristine white snow. The streetlights are still on, throwing off a soft, golden-amber hue that only makes the scene even more picturesque.

Weather forecasts were predicting maybe an inch or two of snow, but for once it looks like they actually underestimated.

My door flies open, and Summer bounds into my room.

"Snow day!" she exclaims again, girlish excitement animating her. "They just sent out the alert!"

Excitement tugs at my chest. I love the snow, and when the day comes that I don't feel a little childish giddiness at a snow day, then I'll know I've *really* been worn down too much by life.

In the living room, Summer and I make some tea and pull back the curtains of the big living room window, gazing out as the flat level of the snow mounts higher and higher.

We chat, letting the hot tea suffuse us with warmth, mesmerized by the beauty outside our window and feeling the simmering excitement of what we're going to do with today.

Obviously, a snowman is called for at some point.

Once the tea's finished and the streetlights have been switched off, our stomachs start to growl. We decide to bundle up and see which stores in Cedar Shade are open.

I pull on my boots, zip up my jacket, tug on my pink beanie, and wrap a scarf around my neck. Summer and I take a moment in front of the mirror before we step outside, admiring our cute winter outfits.

The weather is great. No wind. No sharp bite to the air. Just a mellow chill that's perfect for walking around bundled up.

Flakes continue to fall from the fat, heavy clouds above us as we trudge through the snow, lifting our knees high with each step and leaving a pair of tracks in our wake.

Lots of other students are out, too. There's a buzzing, jubilant feeling in the air. A group of guys are horsing around, throwing and slamming each other into big piles of snow, excitedly shouting "Snow day!" at everyone passing them by, and getting shouts and cheers back in response.

A little bit further up the street, some girls are making

snowmen, and on the other side of the road, people are riding sleds down the slope of a hill. Through the still, snowy air, the sound of a gaggle of young children squealing and giggling carries from a distance.

The convenience store a couple blocks from our place ends up being open. We buy pancake mix and maple syrup, and two big cups of coffee to sip on to keep warm as we walk back home. After stuffing ourselves on pancakes, we decide to go walk around campus.

Campus is almost as busy as it is during a school day, with people making snow angels, drawing in the snow, building snowmen, or just strolling around with coffees in their hands.

I yelp as I feel something soft smash into the back of my beanie.

Turning around with my brow lowered, I see Tuck in the distance, his face beaming with a roguish grin. "Ten points!" he yells.

My heart bounds against my chest at the sight of him. He's wearing a pair of jeans tucked into loosely-laced boots that give him a rugged look. He's got a hood pulled up from underneath his jacket, his thick, tussled hair spilling out of it as he jogs towards us.

Summer is a blur in my peripheral vision as she rushes past me to Hudson, who's right behind Tuck. A couple paces behind both of them are Rhys and a girl I don't recognize. She's really cute, with beautiful black hair spilling from an olive-green knitted hat and dark-rimmed eyeglasses.

I gather up a snowball from the ground and launch it at Tuck, but he easily ducks it, shooting me a wink.

"You'll have to try harder than that," he says, coming to an abrupt stop right in front of me, clearly exerting effort to keep himself from wrapping his arms around me in front of everyone else.

Disappointment gnaws at my own chest, because I'd love nothing more right now than to press into him as he curls his arms around me, rubbing my face into his neck to warm up my cheeks and nose which are starting to sting from the chill.

Summer and Hudson saunter up to us, her slung under his massive arm.

"Hi, I'm Olivia," I introduce myself to the girl next to Rhys.

She beams a smile at me. "Maddie," she returns the introduction. "I'm Lane's sister. Nice to meet you."

She seems super nice. I don't miss the way Rhys can't keep his gaze from hovering on her, and the way his cheeks color every time their eyes lock.

"Where's Lane?" Summer asks.

Maddie sticks the tip of her tongue out and blows a raspberry. "He wanted to *sleep in*."

"Who could sleep in on a day like this?" Tuck exclaims, flaring his arms at his side and spinning around demonstratively. "That guy's gotta learn to wake up and smell the roses."

Maddie tut-tuts and shakes her head. "That's what I'm always telling him."

Tuck's eyes sparkle with inspiration. "Snowman competition!"

"Huh?" Rhys asks, a bemused tone in his voice that he probably often uses around Tuck.

"We need to have a snowman competition," Tuck says, animatedly. "Two on two on two." He steps next to me and wraps his arm around my shoulders, tugging me close. "I call Olivia on my team."

Summer looks at me with a raised brow. I know she's just waiting for me to protest.

Her head tilts, and a questioning gleam lights in her eyes when I don't.

"How do you have a snowman competition?" Hudson asks.

Tuck looks at him like he's stupid. "Uh, by who builds the best snowman, duh."

"And who decides whose snowman is best?" Rhys asks.

Tuck keeps looking at him the same way. "Uh, me, duh."

Maddie purses her lips at Tuck. "Seems like a conflict of interest."

Tuck's expression pinches. "I don't see how."

Summer rolls her eyes. "Let's just build the best snowmen we can and *then* worry about how we'll decide a winner."

Hudson nuzzles his face into the crown of Summer's head. "Mmm, my girl's so smart."

For some reason, seeing Hudson and Summer all lovey-dovey warms my heart in a way that it just hasn't before. Don't get me wrong, I've always been incredibly happy for my friend, and I've always loved seeing her happy with Hudson. But with things going well with Tuck—even if we're keeping it quiet for now—seeing them affectionate with each other strikes a different chord.

When Summer giggles and turns her head for a kiss, I can't help but let my over-curious gaze flit to Rhys and Maddie. Rhys watches Summer and Hudson before dipping his eyes to Maddie when she isn't looking, and an unmissable longing suffuses through his hazel eyes.

"Alright," Tuck claps his gloved hands, "half-hour time limit! Go!"

We all get busy trying to construct the biggest, best snowmen of our lives.

While we're rolling a giant snowball to serve as the base, Tuck gasps with inspiration. "Our snowman should be a hockey player!" he whispers to me. "You keep working on rolling the balls, I'm going to run back to my place and get some supplies."

Hudson throws a crooked expression at Tuck as he dashes off campus at a full sprint. "Where is he going?" he shouts to me from where he and Summer are constructing their snowman.

I just shrug, a glib look on my face. "Trade secret."

I have three perfectly proportioned spheres of snow stacked on top of each other by the time Tuck comes racing back, his arms loaded with a chest protector, helmet, hockey stick, and skates.

"Hey!" Maddie protests. "I didn't know we were allowed to use props!"

Tuck grins from ear to ear. "Never said we couldn't!"

I lift the head of the snowman for Tuck to position the chest protector. He shapes the top snowball so that the helmet fits over it, then props the hockey stick against the snowman and shoves the skates into the base.

We stand back to survey our competition. Hudson's and Summer's is pretty frumpy and basic. From the way his arms are wrapped around her waist while he's standing behind her and taking a whiff of her hair, I think they spent more time kissing and flirting than constructing their snowman. Fair enough.

Maddie's and Rhys' is definitely a step above, but it lacks the accoutrements of ours.

"Fine, you win," Rhys says as the four of them wander over to our snowman.

"Yes!" Tuck shouts. When he holds up his palm, I don't hesitate to slap it, and when lifts me up and spins me around, I just let out a bouncing laugh, not even pretending to object to how he's manhandling me.

"Let's get a coffee to celebrate," Tuck proposes after setting me down. His arm is still slung over me. "My treat, as the magnanimous victor."

"Thanks," Maddie says, "but me and Rhys are gonna go try to wake Lane up."

"We're in," Summer says, her gaze sizing us up.

I know there's a lot of analysis going on in that brain of hers as she looks at me snug in the crook of Tuck's shoulder without trying to take a step away.

I also know I should be resisting this physical touch, trying to keep up the façade that there's nothing going on between me and Tuck, but I just can't summon the will to resist my urge to be close to him.

As the four of us set off to Last Word to see if it's open, giggles reach us from where we left Maddie and Rhys. I turn around to see them lobbing snowballs at each other.

That certainly seems like something to keep an eye on.

A sudden breeze whips down the street once we step off campus, out of the protection of the huddled buildings. Tuck tugs me closer against his side, and I let him, nuzzling my head against the edge of his chest, seeking his warmth.

That warmth isn't hard to seek. It's like his body heat leaps off his chest and spreads through me. Other things spread through me, too. Feelings.

Feelings I said that I wouldn't let myself catch, at least not this soon.

But the more time I spend with him, the more I realize that trying to keep myself from catching feelings for Tuck is like trying to keep the snow on the ground from piling up while big, heavy flakes are coming down from the sky.

34

OLIVIA

School is back in session the next day. After classes, Tuck and I head to the biggest hill in town and go sledding while Hudson and Summer are at the library working on a project for a class they're taking together.

The hill is packed with sledders. The stark white landscape is dotted with color from sleds, jackets, and young kids' snowsuits.

It's certainly not a stealthy place for me and Tuck to spend time together.

But I'm finding myself less and less careful about keeping what's happening between us hidden. I still don't think I'm quite ready to tell anyone about it. Not even Summer, which makes me feel bad, because she's never hidden anything like this from me. But I just need ... a little more time.

It's like I'm on a visitation deck on a skyscraper. I need to gather my courage before approaching the edge and coming face to face with just *how* far the drop down is.

Because I've never felt higher than I do with Tuck, and

once all of our friends know about us, it's going to be real—so real that there will be no fooling myself about how far I'll go tumbling down if Tuck hurts me like Ryan did.

But as we're spending more time together, that worry has grown from a loud, blaring warning in my head to a tiny, but still insidious, whisper that I'm able to tune out most of the time. But not all the time.

Sitting at the front of the sled between Tuck's legs, my back pressed against his chest, feeling it rumble with laughter as we slide down the steep hill makes me feel like I'm floating.

While we're standing at the top of the hill, I catch him off guard and push him into a big pile of snow. He leaps up and scoops me into his arms, tossing me into it, and this degenerates into a snowball fight as we run across the hill, dodging sleds.

When he catches me, he slings me over his shoulder like a sack of potatoes. He picks up the sled and we walk home like that, me perched on his shoulder.

When he takes the opportunity to plant a possessive slap on my ass, I don't even care who's looking.

"Where are we going?" I ask.

"Summer's still with Hudson in the library, right?"

"Should be," I answer.

"Your place, then. I'm hungry." There's a rasp in his voice.

"We don't really have a lot of food in the place right now."

"Don't worry," he says, that rasp now thick with more gravel. "I don't think I'll have a hard time finding what I'm in the mood for."

My thighs clench, the dense muscle of his forearm feeling hot on the backs of them as he carries me.

"Are you going to put me down now?" I giggle as he walks towards my door.

"No," he says, letting the sled drop onto the snow in front of my house. He stops in front of the door and holds his free hand palm-up behind his back. "Key."

My stomach flips at his firm tone. Still dangling on his shoulder, I fish my key out of my pocket and hand it to him. He doesn't put me down after he's opened and carried me through the door, either. He toes off his shoes, and at his command, I do the same, letting them fall in front of him. He steps over them on his march to the kitchen.

"Where are we going?" I ask.

"I told you," he says. "I'm hungry."

Those last two words are a growl on his voice. Heat streaks through me as his hand slides up the back of my thighs and squeezes my ass. He steps into the kitchen and sets me sitting down on the counter.

"For you," he finishes, his blue eyes flashing.

He crushes his mouth to mine, his kiss rough and insistent. His scent dances in my nose, cinnamon and sandalwood. He's sweating from so much physical activity under all those layers, adding a musky undertone of raw masculinity that makes me feral.

He steps forward, nudging himself between my thighs. I spread them wide, rolling my hips against the front of his pants. His lips vibrate as he groans into our kiss. His hands grip the top of my legs, his right thumb tracing the outline of my hipbone through my jeans.

He drags his lips down, dropping hot kisses around the outline of my jaw before raking them lower. His lips hit just the right spot on my neck to make a sharp pang of want detonate between my thighs, and I tilt my hips into him harder, desperate for all the friction I can find.

He pushes back. Flames pulse through me when I feel his hard outline between my legs.

He unzips my sweater and slides it off me, tossing it away carelessly. His hands wrap behind me and he tugs my ass closer to the edge of the counter before falling to his knees between my legs.

My nipples are sharp points underneath my shirt. A knot of anticipation tightens inside me, heat blasting between my thighs as Tuck reaches up to the waist of my jeans. I feel the hot scrape of his knuckles against my stomach as he undoes my button and slowly slides my zipper down.

I spear my hands into his thick, messy hair.

Anxiety hits me when my eyes flit to the clock on our microwave. It's later than I thought. "Summer should be home soon," I say, though my voice is still thick with want.

Tuck grabs a firm hold of my pants and tugs them down. I wiggle my hips so he can pull them past my butt where I'm seated.

"Is that right?" he asks, utterly unconcerned.

"She could walk in ..." The words send electricity shooting through me. My eyes fasten on the front door. The knowledge that the doorknob could turn with Tuck's face buried between my legs makes my clit tighten with arousal.

"I guess she could," Tuck drawls, shimmying back to pull my pants off my legs. He kisses his way back up my thighs, each hot press of his lips making sparks dance on my flesh.

I suck in a gasp when the tip of his tongue drags up my panties, tracing my slit.

"Fuck," he growls. "You're so fucking wet for me."

He's right. My panties are soaked. My center is a hot, wet mess for him. I'm going crazy as Tuck kisses around my upper thighs, stomach flipping and flopping in torturous anticipation.

"Please, Tuck," I plead.

The rough pads of his thumbs tease around the elastic waist of my panties while his mouth continues to lavish attention between my thighs, but only on the places that make the tension in my body curl tighter, not the one place that would relieve it.

"You're so easy to tease," he rasps. "So easy you'd think it would get less fun. But it hasn't."

Mewling with want, I tilt my hips to press my center close to him, hoping for some contact, some friction, to dull the sharp ache of need that's stabbing into me, but Tuck draws back just enough to frustrate me.

Tension winds tighter inside me when he finally draws back to pull my panties down my legs. Heat swells in my cheeks when I look down and see the gleam of appreciation in Tuck's eyes, his gaze fixed on my wet opening.

A low, rumbly hum of appreciation pulls from his throat.

Finally, the wet scrap of fabric is on the kitchen floor next to where he's kneeling between me, and I'm utterly bare for him.

"Fuck, Olivia," he rasps. "This pussy is so perfect. It's a fucking work of art."

When his tongue drags across me, my body goes taut with pleasure. My hands curl into his messy hair, trying to steady myself. Tuck teases me, licking languidly at his leisure. His growls of satisfaction add a vibration that heightens the pleasure rippling over me.

"More," I pant, bucking my hips, my naked ass pressing into the countertop as Tuck feasts on me.

Tuck's lips delve into my folds, lapping up my juices. My stomach is a tight, hot coil of pressure, expanding and radiating through my body. My lower back tingles, my stomach leaps into my chest, my body going crazy as sheer bliss throttles through me.

When Tuck slants his tongue over my clit, a moan leaps from me.

That's his cue to stop being so leisurely.

The kitchen is full of my moans and yelps as Tuck devours me, his lips lavishing my folds, his tongue curling around my tight nub with the perfect amount of force.

I lock my ankles behind him, clenching my thighs around his face, feeling the rough abrasion of his stubble against my sensitive skin. His fingertips knead into the softness of my hips as he groans and curses in satisfaction between my legs.

When the flat of his tongue passes over my clit at just the right angle, I unravel. My climax detonates inside me, hurtling through me and making my limbs shake. My eyes clench, my fists tightening in Tuck's hair as I ride out my release.

Tuck's on his feet to give me something to lean into after my orgasm wrings me dry. Aftershocks of bliss are still flowing over me when he lifts my chin with the back of his knuckle and presses his lips to mine.

My eyes pop open when I taste myself on his lips. I taste it even more when his tongue presses into my mouth and slides against my own.

Tuck presses his forehead against mine. His hooded eyes have a drugged look; his lips are swollen from our kiss and still glistening with my juices.

"We made it," he says.

"Huh?"

A lopsided grin makes one of his dimples pop. "We finished before Summer got back."

I huff out a shallow laugh. "Right. That's good."

"Would've been quite a way for her to find out about us."

A breath whooshes out of me. "That's for sure."

"Was it worth it?"

"Was what worth it?" Tuck needs to stop talking in riddles when my brain is still scrambled from coming on his face.

His eyes crawl down to my naked bottom half. "Was the orgasm worth the risk?"

I roll my eyes and hit his chest with the palm of my hand. "Stop asking questions you know the answer to just to boost your ego."

Tuck steps aside so I can hop off the counter. He leans against it, arms folded over his chest, eyeing me appreciatively as I get dressed.

"It's a hell of a paradox," he drawls. "You putting more clothes *on* is the opposite of what I want. But seeing you actually getting dressed is sexy as hell."

I shake my head. He's ridiculous. "You'll have to bring up that dilemma in your next philosophy class."

"Don't tempt me. I would."

Once I've zippered and buttoned my jeans, I turn towards him. He takes a big step forward, eating up the space between us, and slides his forefinger through one of my belt loops and gently tugs me closer.

"Hey, Lockley."

"Yeah?" I ask, my stomach flipping at the soft way he's looking at me. Something about this moment is more intimate than when his face was just between my legs.

"I had a great time today. And not just this," he slices his eyes to the spot on the countertop he had me seated on. "All of it."

Warmth bubbles in my chest. "Me, too," I nod. "All of it."

35

TUCK

She's wearing my jersey.

When I skate onto the ice for our home game against Cornell and see Olivia in the crowd with my number on her chest, everything else tumbles out of my head.

For a minute, I forget the entire strategy for this game that Coach just drilled into our heads. I forget who our opponent is. Shit, if you asked me what position I play right at this moment, I might just blurt out *goalie*.

All I can think about is the fact that my girl is wearing my jersey. My number on her chest. My fucking name on her back.

Pride and masculine satisfaction roar through me, my chest humming with something I've never felt before. An intense feeling shoots through me, making my fingertips tingle as my grip tightens around my stick.

I'm in a fucking daze looking at Olivia in my jersey. It's not until one of the Cornell players intentionally bumps into me as he skates past me, shooting me a fiery glare for being on *their* side of the ice, that I snap out of it.

Right before he skates over to face off for the puck drop, I tell Sebastian to pass the puck to me if he wins it. Determination is rattling through me, and with my girl wearing my jersey in the crowd, I feel totally in the zone.

Sebastian wins the puck drop and sends it to me. I pump my legs hard and deke past two Cornell defenders. I'm still a long distance from the goal, but with a clear view of it, I pull the trigger and take a shot.

I lift my stick back and slam it forward, sending the puck careening through the air and right past Cornell's goalie.

The crowd erupts. A score within the first minute of the game, and a damn spectacular one at that. My teammates crowd around me, patting me on the back and the helmet in celebration, but my eyes only go one place: Olivia.

I wish I could say that I stay just that locked-in for the rest of the game, but it would be a lie. There are a couple times when I'm handling the puck, but I get distracted thinking about Olivia, and I make a sloppy move that lets a Cornell player steal it away.

But there are other times when the knowledge of her watching on and cheering for me sends a shockwave through me that drives me to pull off an incredible move, or power through a body check that should stop me in my tracks.

I sink one more goal before the game ends in a 4-2 victory. The Black Bears are like a steaming locomotive speeding towards the Frozen Four, and these Cornell assholes sure as fuck aren't going to be the ones to stop us.

We're going to Loser's Luck Tavern afterward to celebrate. While I'm getting showered and changed, the sight of Olivia in my jersey is the only thing I'm thinking about.

Fuck, I hope she's still wearing it when I see her at the bar in a couple minutes.

Or maybe I should hope the opposite. We're still trying to keep what we're doing quiet. And if I see her in that jersey up close, I really, really don't know if I'm going to be able to control myself.

My answer to that question comes about twenty minutes later when the guys and I step through the door of Loser's. My eyes scan the bar, and then I spot her with Summer, at one of our usual tables towards the back.

She's angled away from me, and the first thing I notice is my name on her back.

My pulse stutters. Sparks are crackling all over my body, heat igniting in my bloodstream.

Carter's in the middle of saying something to me, but I don't hear him. My peripheral vision goes fuzzy as I focus in on the name McCoy printed across Olivia's back, her light chestnut hair swept forward over her shoulder so there's not even a strand obstructing it.

Without even thinking, I'm striding forward, pushing through the crowded bar and headed straight towards Olivia, my gaze burning on her.

She turns around when I arrive, her mouth opening slightly in surprise. My chest clenches at the sight of those slick, red lips, parted just enough for me to get a peek of her soft, pink tongue.

My gaze crawls up to meet hers. If there's one thing I love more than her lips, it's her eyes, kaleidoscopic emeralds with specks of gold and silver dancing in their rich depths.

"You wore my jersey," I say.

A smile hitches on her lips. "I did."

I can't stop my hands from reaching out and landing on her hips. Tendrils of heat shoot from where my fingertips curl into her softness, rocketing up my arms and rippling through me.

Eyes are on us. Summer's. All my teammates', who've by now caught up to us here at the table.

We're supposed to keep this hidden. But I'm only human. I'm supposed to hide a feeling *this* strong? I'm supposed to hide what seeing Olivia Lockley wearing my jersey does to me?

With my grip still fastened to the curve of her hips, I bend my elbows, lightly tugging her to me. She steps into it, towards me, our chests brushing together.

That's all I need. I press my lips to hers, and she kisses back. My heart pounds in my chest as I angle my head to deepen the kiss, sliding my tongue across the crease of Olivia's lips. She moans into my mouth, and I drink it up.

I pull back, my hooded gaze searching Olivia's eyes to read her response. My heart flutters when I see them crinkled with a smile.

My eyes are still on her when she turns her head side to side, sheepishly taking in our stunned audience.

"Uh. We're kind of a thing now," she explains, cheeks reddening as her smile climbs higher.

I pull her even closer, the hard planes of my chest pressing against her perfect tits through my jersey. "No kind of about it."

"I knew it!" Summer exclaims, pushing Olivia's shoulder. "I'm mad at you! And happy for you! I'm happy-mad!" She pulls Olivia away from me and wraps her in a hug, before then stepping away and shoving her in the shoulder again with a pout—I guess that's to express the mad part of her emotions.

I know what it means for Olivia to be comfortable about going public with us. It means she knows, finally really knows, that I care about her too much to hurt her.

Kissing Olivia felt good. Seeing her in my jersey felt good. But knowing that she knows *that*?

Nothing feels better.

36

OLIVIA

Summer's been shooting reproachful glances at me ever since she found out about me and Tuck. Granted, they're often tinged with a smile, but she still does her darnedest to inject *some* reproach into them.

She casts another one at me as we're sitting down at Last Word to catch up on some schoolwork.

"I can't *believe* you didn't tell me," she grumbles.

I shrug. "Well, you know now." At this point, we're just teasing each other.

"I, your best friend, found out at the same time as *everyone else*." She shakes her head at the shameful fact. "I feel betrayed, Olivia. What else are you hiding from me?"

"Other than that I'm secretly a princess of a tiny but rich European country? Not much."

"You know what really bothers me? Tuck knew this secret before I did! How could someone you used to hate know before your best friend?"

That gives me such a belly laugh that I pull my hands

away from my keyboard and wrap my arms around my chest.

"The secret was *about* Tuck, Summer. He couldn't very well have not known he was screwing me."

She turns her head away with a harsh *harrumph*. "Still."

There are still tears of laughter at the corners of my eyes when I try to focus my attention back on the essay I'm banging out.

Salsa purrs as she hops up onto my lap from the floor. Today Cindy's trying out what she hopes will be an annual tradition she's calling *Bring Your Cat to Coffee Day*. She's invited the coffee shop customers to bring their cats, turning Last Word into a one-day cat café.

There are adorable cats all over the place, with tons of people here just to look and take pictures. Salsa hasn't had a lot of experience interacting with other cats, but she's been a sweetheart so far. Still, with the way she's curling in my lap, I think she's had her fill of cat socialization.

"Oh my, how adorable!" The boisterous voice of Cindy exclaims as she passes by the most gorgeous orange Tabby cat. She's whistling an upbeat tune when she passes our table and notices us. "Oh, hello, dears! How is *Emma* treating you?"

"Great!" Summer answers, before wiggling her eyebrows and following up, "And what's treating you so well to have you in such a mood? You're glowing."

Cindy blushes a bit, not a common response from a woman who hardly knows the definition of bashful. "Oh, me? Glowing?"

"I take it things are going well with that lawyer?" Summer says, suggestively.

But that just has Cindy's brow scrunching. "Lawyer? Oh, you mean Ed?" she says his name dismissively, like she's swatting a gnat from in front of her face. "Oh, I'm not seeing Ed anymore."

Then I remember Tuck mentioning the conversation he and Hudson had with Kazu at his restaurant some time ago. "I wonder if someone gave you a particularly good book lately that has you in a good mood," I say, slyly.

That color spreads through her cheeks again. "Could be," she chirps in a coy voice before continuing to stroll around, doting on the cats.

My phone pings, and I see that I have an Instagram notification. A knot of tension swells in my throat.

The other day, Ryan tried to contact me again on a different Instagram account. He made a burner just to get around me blocking him, which is creepy and off-putting.

Not only that, but he even left a comment on one of my posts, the first picture I put up with me and Tuck.

It was nothing but a rolling-eyes emoji. This was the day after I blocked the account he tried to use to message me a second time. Tuck noticed and asked who the weirdo leaving a rude emoji on our picture was. I just shrugged and told him I had no idea.

The last thing I need is for Tuck to know anything about Ryan other than the fact he was a shitty ex of mine who I never want to see or have anything to do with again.

Especially since he and Ryan will be on opposite sides of a hockey rink next week. Not once, but twice.

It's my luck that the Brumehill Black Bears are facing Ryan's Withermore University Falcons on back-to-back nights. Ryan's team will be here in Cedar Shade for two games in a row, Friday and Saturday night.

Since I know Ryan is stalking my Instagram—and made an asshole-ish comment on a picture of me and Tuck—I know he knows who Tuck is. But, hopefully, if Tuck doesn't know who Ryan is, they'll be able to get through the game without any trouble going down between them.

The thought of Tuck and Ryan sharing the ice just fills me with an ominous feeling.

I shake off the thought, though. I'm probably worrying about nothing. I'm sure it'll be fine.

37

TUCK

"Can't win 'em all," I sigh morosely.

We just piled back into the locker room after a 2-3 loss in an away game in upstate New York. We played just about our worst game, and our opponents played just about their best. Hey, it happens.

Hudson groans as he strips off his pads. "I can't believe I let that last fucking shot get through. We could've at least held it to a tie and gotten a chance to win in overtime."

"Don't beat yourself up," Lane says. "I totally blew it covering their center."

"And their winger deked me and got wide open," Rhys continues.

Jamie sighs wistfully, walking by. "Losing is a team effort as much as winning is, Hudson. Not like I played my best, either."

Hudson's gotten a lot better about not beating himself up over a disappointing performance, but it's still a habit he hasn't entirely shaken off.

"Look, guys, Coach is gonna ream us out about everything we did wrong in this game all week," Carter says, leaning against his locker. "No reason to do it to ourselves ahead of his schedule. I've got a much more important issue for us to consider than all of that."

"What?" I ask.

"What's the biggest animal you think you could take in a fight?"

Carter's question is like switching on a lightbulb in a dark room. All the guys are perking up, their brains chewing over the question.

Rhys' face pulls tight with thought. "Would I be delusional to say that I think I could take a crocodile?"

"Yes," Lane answers without missing a beat.

"People do crocodile wrestling, right? It can't be *that* hard."

"What about a giraffe?" I ponder. "I think I could take a giraffe. If I had to. They're so damn cute I wouldn't want to. But, like, if some giraffe with a bad attitude left me no choice."

"Are you kidding?" Hudson counters. "How? Just punching its knees? It would kick you into next week."

"Giraffes are slow, right? I'll run around and tire it out. Then, when he drops his head, I'd take my shot."

"I don't think giraffes are slow," Jamie says. "I don't know where you're getting that from."

When the conversation shifts back to Rhys' chances of taking on a crocodile, Hudson pulls me to the side.

"So," he says, nodding slowly, sizing me up with his gaze. "You and Olivia."

Just hearing her name is enough to bring a big, toothy grin to my face. "Yep. Me and Olivia."

Shit, if hearing Olivia's name is enough to make me smile, I don't have the words to explain what saying *me and Olivia* does to me. My chest is fluttering like the wings of a bird flying off a branch on a warm summer morning. It feels like a fucking dream.

"You better treat her right, Tuck." There's an edge of warning in his voice. "I don't need my friend hurting my girlfriend's friend and making things all fucked up."

My stomach tightens at the idea of anyone thinking I'd hurt Olivia. "I wouldn't. Don't you know that? I'm fucking crazy about her."

His eyes elevator up and down me. "Yeah. I know. I don't think you would. But I had to say it. I like her. She's a nice girl, and she's good to my cat. So, I just had to let you know that you better treat her right."

Hudson's a big softy, so I can't hold this little warning talk against him.

"I have a great idea to show you just *how* right I treat her," I say, feeling a spark of excitement.

Hudson tilts his head skeptically, his eyes narrowing. "Please tell me you don't have some weird sexual thing in mind."

I throw back my head with a guffaw. "Nope. Even better. Double date."

A distinctly unexcited look takes residence on Hudson's face. "Double date." He says the words like he's chewing them—and doesn't like the taste.

"Not just a double date. A *karaoke* double date."

Now Hudson's expression is one of mortification. "Tuck, you know there's no way I'd ever be caught dead on a karaoke stage."

38

OLIVIA

Tuck and Hudson are neck-deep in the absolute worst karaoke duet I've ever heard.

What's truly fascinating is how both of them are terrible singers for very different reasons.

Hudson's actually got a good singing voice. Or, at least, he would, if he weren't so half-hearted and self-conscious about singing with a whole bar of eyes on him. He sings on key, but his timing is totally off.

Tuck, on the other hand, can't carry a tune. His voice might be smooth golden honey when he's talking with his gravelly southern drawl, but his singing is hopelessly off-key. On the other hand, he's totally enthusiastic and his timing is perfect.

If you could somehow combine their relative strengths, you'd have a pretty good singer. What actually happens, though, is their flaws amplify each other's. The result isn't pretty.

But at least it's hysterical. Summer and I are leaning against each other, badly losing the battle to hold back our laughter. This just makes Tuck get into his role more, singing with more energy, while Hudson's even more stilted and off-tempo.

"I'm never letting you talk me into this again," Hudson grumbles to Summer when they finally hop off the stage.

The crowd at the bar is actually giving them a roaring round of applause, but it's really the kind of applause you'd give a stand-up comedian after a hilarious set.

"You say that now," Tuck says to him, "but you know you can't resist the allure of the microphone now that you've had a taste. My mind is bursting with ideas for the next duets we're going to sing."

Hudson opts to take a big swig of his beer instead of replying.

Tuck acts like a hype man for every person or group who steps up to the stage, cheering loudly for them and clapping like a madman after their songs are done. He's got such an infectious, positive energy, it's hard to believe I ever used to think he was a jerk.

But that's what bad experiences in your past will do to you. They keep you from seeing things, people, or potential relationships for what they actually are; instead, you keep looking for similarities and analogies between them and the things that hurt you.

"One more song!" Tuck exclaims after finishing the last of his beer. The team is being run ragged with practices this week, so he and Hudson are just sticking to one beer each tonight.

"Don't put Hudson through that again, Tuck," I say.

A mischievous glare dances in Tuck's eyes as he looks at me. "Oh, don't worry. I'm not."

Before I know what's happening, Tuck's pulled me up to the stage with him. My stomach drops as I take in the crowd looking at us.

It's funny. I never have a problem with nerves on stage, when ten times the number of people or more are looking at me. The thing is, when I'm on stage, I don't feel like myself. I feel like the character I'm playing. So all those people aren't looking at *me*. They aren't reacting to *me*. They aren't judging *me*. Only my role.

Tuck puts on the song *Just The Girl* by The Click Five. As usual, he's one hundred percent into it from the very first lyrics, putting on a performance like everyone in here bought a thousand-dollar ticket just to see him.

He's still utterly off-key, but boy is he enthusiastic about it. And the crowd is into it, cheering him on.

As he's singing about a guy who's smitten with a girl who wants nothing to do with him, he's looking at me with a knowing glimmer in his eyes that makes it impossible for me not to smile and blush as I follow along with the lyrics.

Our little audience erupts with applause when we finish. Tuck immediately gathers me up in his arms, lifting me and spinning me around. I kick my feet as his quick, tight spin makes me dizzy, laughing at the hoots and whistles coming from the rest of the bar.

Tuck's still singing the song as the four of us walk home, his arm slung possessively around my shoulders, pulling me into the firm but comfortable warmth of his side.

Sparks scatter over me when Tuck nuzzles a kiss into the soft, sensitive area between my jaw and my ear.

Those sparks only grow hotter and more electric when he whispers, "How about spending the night at my place?"

39

TUCK

My lips crush to Olivia's when we get to my room.

I kiss her ravenously. I don't gently coax her lips open with languid caresses, drawing it out and advancing minute by minute; I jump right into the deep end, my tongue swirling with hers, both my hands cupping the round apples of her ass, fingertips kneading into the soft, warm flesh.

Olivia tilts her hips, pressing her center into the outline of my cock that's already rock-hard and throbbing behind my jeans. When I groan into her mouth, she pulls my bottom lips between her teeth and bites down.

I growl in response to the thrill of the pain. I tighten my grip on her ass, my fingertips delving hard into her softness. When I bend her over and lift this dress up in just a couple minutes, I want to see ten white marks branding these cheeks.

Her smell floods my senses. Even though we only had one drink in the bar, the floral scent of her hair mixed with the citrusy notes from her body wash ignite a rush of intoxication through my bloodstream more potent than any alcohol.

I skim my hand from her ass down her leg, crawling up the hem of her sexy little black dress. Sparks dance as my palm rakes up her warm flesh until I can skim the outline of her panties with the pad of my thumb.

She whimpers into my mouth. It's a needy sound, and I know exactly what it is she needs.

I slip my hand underneath her panties. I moan against her lips, feeling her blissful warmth, the wetness of her arousal as I drag my knuckle up her slit.

"*Tuck.*" She moans my name. I suck on her tongue while she bucks her hips into the pressure of my hand.

I push my middle finger into her opening. She's so fucking wet that I can hear her juices as my finger enters her. Her muscles clench around it, and arousal rips through me viciously.

I fuck her with my finger while my free hand palms her perfect, pert tit. She throws her head back in pleasure, and I trail kisses along the edge of her jaw, underneath her ear, down her smooth and elegant neck.

Olivia quickly undoes my belt, and I draw my hand away from her center as she sinks to her knees, tugging my pants and underwear down my legs at once. They bunch up around my ankles as I toe my shoes off.

My cock throbs in the air. A curse pulls from my throat when Olivia wraps her hand around the base. The warm softness of her hands, slightly damp, sends electric shocks pulsing through my body, emanating from where she makes contact. She glides her grip up my shaft until she hits the fringe of nerve endings.

She grazes the tip of my head with the pad of her thumb, sending pleasure rocketing through me. She brings her thumb to her mouth, licking off the bead of pre-cum.

The ache between my legs is pounding like a fucking hammer.

Olivia wraps her full, wet lips around my pink mushroom head, and I fucking see stars. Every muscle in my body curls tight. I groan and curse as she slides the flat of her tongue over my swollen head, the most intense sensation unwinding inside me.

She applies gentle suction, sliding her lips up and down my length. Fuck, it feels so good I could pass out. Her lips, her mouth, her tongue, her hand still wrapped around the base of my cock that pulses and throbs with my hammering heartbeat, everything is fucking otherworldly.

When the tip of her tongue flicks against the opening of my cock, the pressure in my balls tells me I'm moments away from erupting.

That's when I know I have to stop her.

I'm not ready to finish yet, not until I've buried myself inside her to the hilt, not until my hips are slapping against her ass with that tiny black dress pulled up around her waist.

I draw my hips back, gripping her shoulders and urging her to her feet. I kick my pants from my ankles, walk her to my bed, and spin her around, bending her over the mattress. She gasps and giggles as I push her dress up over her hips.

"Fuck, baby," I rasp. "You have no fucking clue what seeing you like this does to me." Her ass is the perfect heart shape, and my blood thickens when I see those ten marks of pressure my fingertips left on her.

"I have a feeling you're going to show me," she says, coy as she can be while her voice is so thick with need.

I pull her soaked panties down her legs and toss them over my shoulders. I can't resist delving my face into her wet cunt from behind, flattening my tongue over her folds to drink in her juices.

"So fucking sweet," I growl as I lap at her.

Her ass squirms in my face and I fucking love it. She's still wound tight from being filled with my finger earlier. I can tell from the breathy sounds she makes that she's about to come, so I pull back.

When her orgasm rolls through her and makes her pussy clamp, I want it clamping around my cock.

I retrieve a condom and roll it down my length.

Bliss coils around me when I push into her. "Fuck," I groan, eyes rolling as my cock plunges into her warmth, her muscles clenching around my size.

I'm lost in a frenzy of thrusting, my hips slapping against her ass. Our rough, rugged groans mingle with the rhythmic slapping of our skin and the liquid sound of me thrusting into her wetness.

I can feel her body growing tighter while the knot of pressure at the base of my spine swells and intensifies. We fall into our climax together, the walls of her pussy rippling on my length as I fill the condom with my release.

After I've thrown away the condom, I lie on my bed, tugging her close. I still have my t-shirt on, naked from the waist down. Olivia's pulled her dress back over her hips, but the fact that she isn't wearing panties underneath makes my cock twitch a little despite the utterly draining orgasm I just had minutes ago.

I feel words crawling up my throat. Words I want to utter to express how I feel about Olivia. How I've head over fucking heels fallen for her.

But I know they're not words she's ready to hear yet.

Instead, I nuzzle a kiss onto the crown of her head as she lays her cheek over my chest.

I hope she'll be ready to hear what I want to tell her soon. When she is, I think I'll know.

And when I do, I don't think there will ever have been anything so important that'll be so easy to say.

40

TUCK

This Ryan Wentz douchebag has been up my ass all fucking game.

I don't know what the refs are looking at. This guy's slamming me with late hits, trying to trip up my skates, playing dirty as hell.

When he high sticks me to no reaction from the officials, Coach Torres, who's usually stoic during a game, is shouting bloody murder at the negligent refs.

I hop onto the bench for a shift change. Kiran takes my place, and I drop down next to Jamie.

"The fuck's that guy's problem?" the freshman asks.

I shake my head, trying not to let anger both at the dirty player and shitty refs bite deeper into me. Getting fouled is bad enough, I don't want it to affect my focus, too. I just need to concentrate on what I need to do out there.

"Beats me," I say. I watch Went do the same thing I just did, switching out with a teammate for some rest on the bench.

Guess he only wants to be in the game when he can fuck with me.

The players on the bench rise to our feet as Kiran, with the freshest legs on the ice right now, blazes past the Withermore Falcons defenders and scores a goal, putting us in the lead 2-1.

Minutes later, though, the Falcons get us back. Coach signals for all the first line players to head back onto the ice. Sure enough, moments after my blades connect with the smooth surface of the rink, Ryan Wentz is hopping back out, too.

The play is intense and contentious, both teams eager to step out of the current tie with the one-goal advantage. I end up in a battle for the puck with Wentz behind the Falcons' net. I'm zeroed in on our struggle over the puck, when he says something that slices through my concentration.

"You enjoying my sloppy seconds, McCoy?"

His words stab into my chest. Acid rises in my throat. It's enough to shatter my concentration like a glass crashing onto a hardwood floor. All it takes is a split second of me losing focus for him to take advantage and win possession of the puck.

I shouldn't be concentrating on anything but getting the puck back as I pump my legs to catch up to him while he skates towards our goal. But my head is spinning with thoughts.

Ryan Wentz. Ryan Wentz. Have I overheard the name Ryan at any point, from Olivia, or even from Summer or Hudson?

I know Olivia used to date a hockey player. Anger clogs my throat as the obvious thought grips me.

Is this the fucking piece of shit who hurt Olivia? The guy who had the smartest, most talented, sweetest, most beautiful girl in the damn world and taught her to be afraid of her own feelings?

And did that heap of garbage just fucking dare to call her *sloppy seconds*?

Rage boils in my blood.

But maybe that's not the case. All kinds of trash talk goes down in hockey. Sometimes people say random shit, hoping that by chance they hit a nerve that throws their opponents off their game.

Well, if that's what Wentz was doing, I can't deny that he's succeeded.

I try my best to push thoughts of slamming my fist into Ryan Wentz's face until his nose is above his eyes out of my head. I need to focus on this game. The Frozen Four is right around the corner, and we sure as hell don't want another loss after last weekend.

Lane manages to win the puck back and pass it to me. Sure enough, moments later, Wentz is on me, pressing me against the dasher boards as we struggle again for the puck.

I force myself not to think about what happened last time we were in this position. Force myself to think about nothing but winning the battle for the puck and taking it home to their net.

But then he says something I can't ignore.

"I still got Olivia's number, you know. Might text her my hotel room number after the game. I know I got bored of her and traded up years ago, but she's probably still good for an easy fu—"

My fist smashes into his face before my hockey stick even hits the ice.

I see red. Literally. I always thought that was just an expression, but right now the crisp white ice looks blood red.

I'm in a frenzy, throwing jabs and hooks at Ryan as he tries to cover up. I get in a couple direct hits. The smash of my knuckles against his face is the only thing that brings any relief to the incandescent rage that's burning all over me.

His teammates get to us before any of mine do. I can tell that I'm taking hits myself. Someone's pulled off my helmet, and fists are crashing into my head, my cheek, my shoulders. People are tugging at me.

I don't care.

I can't hear anything over the pounding of my heartbeat and the loud thrumming of my blood flow in my ears.

As the first tsunami of adrenaline ebbs, sounds start to lance through my frenzy. The sharp whistles of the referees. The overwhelming roar of the crowd. The shouts of my team and the Falcons as they jostle to hold me back and pull Ryan away.

I stop swinging my arms when I realize Ryan is out of reach. I regain a measure of control over myself, but the rage doesn't die down. If anything, it becomes sharper and more focused when I take my seat in the Sin Bin.

I don't even watch the game. All I can think of are his words. What he said about Olivia. The scummy look in his eyes. The gleeful, malicious tilt on his lips.

I hope I fucking split those lips.

Part of me wants to take a look at him while he's sitting on his team's bench across from me. See if I did any real damage. But another part of me knows that if I get him in my sights right now, I might not be able to resist hopping over this barricade to get more shots in.

With a major penalty, I'm out for the rest of the game. We end up losing 2-3.

I should feel bad. I let my team down and got myself locked in the penalty box when they needed me on the ice.

But I can't feel bad. If I could do it all over again, I'd still throw every single punch. The only thing I'd change is I'd want to make them more accurate. I wish I'd gotten a straight jab right on his nose and made it crooked for the rest of his miserable life.

"What the hell was that all about?" Lane asks me as I'm tugging off my jersey in the locker room.

My nose scrunches as Wentz's words blare in my memory. "He said something about Olivia. Something he shouldn't have fucking said."

"Olivia?" Hudson steps towards me, his tone laced with protectiveness. "How does he know Olivia?"

I glance at him, brow low, not even able to summon the words to my lips.

"Oh, shit," realization dawns in Hudson's eyes. "Is he ...?"

"Her ex," I spit out, hating the taste of that word on my lips. "The one who treated her like shit. And he ..." I don't finish my sentence. My jaw clenches in anger. But I force myself to repeat what Wentz said to me out there.

Sebastian clasps my shoulder. "Then I only wish I threw a couple punches myself. Fuck the loss tonight. We're in the playoffs anyway. That asshole deserved it."

All my teammates murmur in agreement. Even though I'm still simmering with anger, their support, and the fact that they care about Olivia, is like a soothing lotion over a sunburn.

"Oh, what the fuck," Rhys growls, looking at his phone.

"What?" Lane asks.

Rhys shakes his head with disgust as we gather around to look at his screen.

"Someone from Brumehill sent me this Tweet," he says.

It's a Tweet from Withermore's center forward. It's a laughing emoji followed by the message, *Our boy Ryan had some words of truth for McCoy that he didn't wanna hear.*

It's already been liked and re-tweeted by everyone on the Withermore team.

Rage bubbles so high inside me that it almost spills over. I coil the muscle of my right arm, clenching it close to me, trying to overcome my instinct to ball my hand into a fist and slam it into the wall.

"These fuckers are getting it tomorrow," Rhys says.

Coach storms into the locker room clearly ready to rip me a new asshole for costing us the game. But when the guys speak up for me and explain what happened, including showing him that Tweet, he changes his tune.

"I'd go talk to their coach about the behavior of his players," Coach Torres says. "But Mike Galvin was a dirty player himself in his day. I'm sure he approves of this shit if he thinks it'll give them a psychological edge."

The guys continue to murmur in disgust and anger at the Withermore team.

"One thing, boys," Coach says. "I get that you don't want them to get away with this. And hey, this is hockey after all, not soccer. I came up playing this game and I've thrown some left and rights in my time. Take my advice—get it out of your system early, and then wipe the floor with them."

We're throwing smirks at each other while Coach walks out of the locker room. I'm pretty sure we all got his message loud and clear.

Looks like tomorrow's game is starting with a good old fashioned line brawl. And I know just which Withermore piece of shit I'm lining up with to exchange blows.

41

OLIVIA

Summer and I are waiting on the stoop of Tuck's house when the guys get back from the game. When he sees me, he rushes up and kisses me like he won't be able to breathe if he doesn't.

An awkward smile flits on my lips when he pulls away, his eyes beaming concern at me. Not just concern, but appreciation. He looks at me like he cherishes me, like I'm a precious jewel in his eyes. He always does, but it's sharper and more immediate this time.

"I was hoping we'd be able to get through these two games without you realizing it was … him," I say.

Tuck's jaw muscles pop at just the reference to Ryan. "At least I got to punch him in the face," he says, rubbing the knuckles of his right hand. "Not as many times as he deserved, but still."

I force a shallow smile. "I just don't want to talk about him. Or think about him. Okay?"

Tuck dips his chin. "Yeah. Plenty of better things to talk about. Like what's our least favorite public bathroom in Cedar Shade."

"Definitely the one at Pucelli's," Sebastian chimes in, referring to the run-down old pizza joint that only stays in business because it's open until four in the morning on Fridays and Saturdays to sell overpriced slices to drunk Brumehill students.

"Eh," Rhys ponders, "Pucelli's is the filthiest, no doubt, but at least it's got a lock on the door. The bathroom at Tall Mike's Bar is just a single toilet, and the door doesn't even have a handle. You try to take a leak and people are walking in on you every five seconds."

"Ugh," Summer groans. "You men and your filthy bathrooms."

"You realize you guys have yourselves to blame, right?" I say as Tuck loops his arm around my waist while we walk into their house. "Women would never let their bathrooms descend into such a state."

"The cleanly among us are oppressed by the slobs," Lane says.

"Why do I feel called out by that?" Tuck shoots back.

I nuzzle my head into his side as I laugh. With Tuck's arm around me, tugging me close, it's easy to forget about my ex.

Easy to forget I was ever hurt.

And maybe not quite easy, but at least possible, to begin to dare to let feelings blossom that I promised myself I wouldn't have so soon.

THE ATMOSPHERE in the arena is insane.

The air is thick with energy and anticipation. People are buzzing, talking about the fight between Tuck and Ryan last night that made national news, wondering whether there's going to be a repeat tonight.

Plenty of people are speculating what the fight was about, and every time I pass a conversation where I overhear a theory, my cheeks burn, knowing that *I'm* the reason why.

I was tempted to not come here tonight. Very tempted. But I decided that Ryan just isn't good enough to be a reason for any decision I make.

For years since we broke up, Ryan dictated how I handled my heart, even at a distance. Now, I'm not even going to let him dictate how I spend my Saturday night, even though he's here in the flesh.

Maybe it's silly, but it feels like a win. And you know what? Whenever you feel like you've racked up a win, I think it's good to celebrate it. Silly or not.

"Fuck Withermore!" some guy shouts out a couple rows behind us as Summer and I take our seats, drawing raucous cheers from everyone in our section.

As a group of students wearing Black Bears jerseys take their seats in the row in front of us, I overheard their conversation.

"What do you think made McCoy snap like that last game?" one guy asks. "That dude never starts fights on the ice."

"For real," another guy replies. "Everyone knows Rhys Callahan has a hair-trigger temper, but McCoy's usually mellow."

A girl a couple seats to their right chimes in, "I heard the Falcons player stole McCoy's girl."

A knot rises in my throat. Of course, that's not what happened, but it's too close to the truth for comfort.

I've got no problem on the stage in front of hundreds or thousands of people with every pair of eyes in the building on me. When I'm playing a role, that is. But being the center of attention just as *myself*, just as Olivia Lockley? I hate it.

"Tuck McCoy's *girl*? As in singular?" one of the guys in front of us replies. "Yeah, right. I've taken three classes with that dude. Not to mention been to plenty of parties where he was, too. Trust me, the last guy in this state to have one girl is McCoy."

Now that knot is higher and tighter in my throat, accompanied by a bad taste in my mouth.

Some of the tension twisting in my shoulders dissipates as I feel Summer's hand gently squeezing my arm.

"Rumors are a funny thing, aren't they?" she says with a wink-wink lift in her voice.

I force myself to huff out a laugh. "Right. They sure are."

I just hope there's no repeat of yesterday's drama in this game.

I told Tuck that I don't want to have to even think about Ryan, so I'm hoping that no matter what underhanded tricks my shitty ex pulls, Tuck won't rise to them. I told Tuck that I don't need, or want, to be defended against Ryan's words.

When the players skate onto the ice, my hopes of a drama-free game start to look more and more like wishful thinking. One of the Falcons players "accidentally" bumps into Sebastian while he's stretching, sending him tumbling to the ice. Three Black Bears have to hold Rhys back from going after the offending Withermore player.

I start hearing chatter from people in our section about how there was some confrontation between the teams in the back while they were heading to their respective locker rooms today.

Luckily, at least Tuck and Ryan are keeping their distance on the ice.

Tuck's eyes find mine, and I blow him a kiss. I can't help but notice Ryan looking on in my peripheral vision as I do so; but I pat myself on the back when I successfully keep my gaze from flitting in his direction.

It's time for the game to start, and the teams line up. The crowd is rocking, everyone on their feet as the players square off. Tuck and Ryan face off for the puck, the referee standing next to them holding it aloft.

The atmosphere is electric, the air almost crackling.

The referee drops the puck.

Tuck swats it away.

He drops his hockey stick. Ryan drops his.

Everyone else on the ice does the same.

The arena is deafening as a brawl erupts on the ice.

Every player is squaring off with another from the opposing team. Throwing blows, trying to grab holds of each other, struggling to stay upright. Even Hudson's skated out to tangle with the Falcons' goalie.

Everyone in the crowd is on their feet, screaming themselves hoarse.

Tuck and Ryan are in the very center of the rink, raining blows on each other. I gasp as a right hook from Ryan connects with the side of Tuck's helmet, and the protective gear falls off his head and clatters to the ice. But Tuck ducks the next shot and grabs a firm hold of Ryan's jersey, peppering him with straight jabs that Ryan recoils from, trying to cover up as Tuck's fist keeps hammering him like a piston.

Finally, the refs separate them. The crowd is still roaring like spectators at a gladiator fight in ancient Rome. As Tuck skates to the penalty bench, he angles himself towards me and blows a kiss.

Everyone notices.

I feel hundreds of heads turn towards me, people whispering to the person next to them as they glance in my direction.

Are people putting two and two together? Hearing that the fight between Tuck and Ryan last night was about some girl, and then seeing Tuck blow me a kiss immediately after their second brawl?

I try to stop the blush crawling up my neck from spreading to my cheeks, but the burning I feel in my face lets me know how futile it is.

The fight last night already garnered media attention, and after the wild spectacle that started this game off, this seems almost guaranteed to make the national sports news.

The idea of some journalist desperate for clicks and views digging through social media and talking to Withermore players to find the real story grips me. I just want to forget Ryan and move on, leaving him totally in the past, but suddenly I'm imagining his name and mine mentioned side by side on national TV. The thought makes my stomach churn.

Tuck's beaming from ear to ear as he skates to the Sin Bin, a look of pride on his face like he's just defended my honor.

I don't feel defended. I feel embarrassed. Frustrated. Maybe even a little angry.

A massive team vs. team brawl like that happening right at the puck drop had to be premeditated, and this is after I told Tuck that I don't even want to think about Ryan anymore.

I try to pay attention to the game once it gets going, but it's a struggle. It's a good game for Brumehill, at least, with the first third ending 2-0.

When Summer and I go to get something to drink in

between periods, it seems like even more eyes are pointed in my direction. Even more people are whispering to each other as I walk past.

At the concession stands, there are two lines, and when Summer and I are in the middle of ours, I hear a girl in the line next to us gasp and say, "That's her," her eyes clearly pointing at me.

My stomach feels heavy for the rest of the game. Summer tries to cheer me up and tells me to ignore the gossipers, but as I feel the weight of even more eyes, I start to feel like the whole story's gotten out. I guess I shouldn't be surprised with social media, and how willing the Falcons players were to talk about the fight between Tuck and Ryan on it last night.

I just want to leave, but it feels like that would be admitting defeat. I stay for the whole game, as uncomfortable as I feel and as slowly as time passes.

Luckily, by late in the third period, the Black Bears are leading 6-1 and the crowd is so jubilant and so interested in heckling the Falcons that people start paying less attention to me.

Still, I feel exhausted and embarrassed. I just want to go home.

The buzzer sounds, and the Black Bears rack up a decisive win. All the guys are jubilant while they're celebrating on the ice, none more than Tuck.

I'm glad he's happy. But after he started the game doing the one thing I didn't want him to do, and I spent the game dealing with the results of it, I'm not.

42

TUCK

The only damper on the euphoric atmosphere in the locker room is that we don't have a bottle of champagne to pop.

We're all hyped up about a crushing win, the lopsided W made even sweeter by the fact that we got a couple good swings in on the Withermore assholes beforehand.

They're not going to come into our house and disrespect us like they did again anytime soon. And *no one's* going to disrespect Olivia in front of me and get away with it—I don't care whose fucking house they're in.

We shower quickly, still buzzing and talking about the game. The two goals I scored were almost as sweet as the jab I sliced through Ryan's guard that caught him right on the point of his chin.

When I get back to my locker, I grab my phone and send Olivia a text.

> Meet up at Loser's to celebrate?

I put my phone on the metal shelf inside the locker

while I get dressed. Once I've pulled on a shirt, I check my phone to see Olivia's response.

> OLIVIA
> I'm tired. I'm just going to stay home.

My stomach sinks. Even though it's just a text message, just words on a screen, something feels ... off about it. There's a gnawing sensation right at the base of my neck that something's wrong.

I tell the guys to go ahead without me while I go check on Olivia. When she opens the door of her house for me, the small weight in my stomach grows bigger and pulls it lower.

Something *is* wrong, I can tell immediately.

"What are you doing here?" is the first thing she says to me. Not exactly a greeting that puts my nerves at ease.

Still, I force a smile on my face and the usual smooth drawl into my voice. "Visiting you, what's it look like?"

Her lips don't even twitch a fraction of a centimeter.

She shrugs and steps aside, giving me space to walk in. "Summer's out with Hudson and the team," she says.

"You wore yourself out cheering for me too much to do anything else tonight, huh?" Another failure to elicit any upward movement at the edges of her mouth.

In fact, it earns me the opposite. Her lips tug down and her brow scrunches.

"What's wrong?" I ask.

"Noth—" The word is halfway out of her mouth when her breath stalls for a moment; then she lets out a heavy sigh, shaking her head. "You did exactly what I wanted you not to do tonight."

Ridges of confusion dig into my forehead. "What do you mean?"

Olivia's shoulders sag. "I told you that I didn't want to even have to think about Ryan anymore. But after that stunt you pulled at the beginning of the game? It's all anyone's talking about. You and Ryan fighting is even bigger news than it was after last night, and people wanted to find out the story behind it. Guess what? They did. I had to deal with people gawking at me and whispering about me during the whole game."

My chest tightens. "What? How would anyone even connect you with me and Ryan fighting? That doesn't make sense."

"His teammates talking about it on social media. Someone noticing that his Instagram account left that comment on the picture I uploaded of you and me together. I guess there were enough breadcrumbs out there to follow. I just wanted to forget him, not let him take up any more space in my head for even one day longer, but now I'm connected with him in a story that's already getting national attention!"

The frustration is thick in her voice, and honestly, I get it. I didn't even think about any of this. The only thing I was able to think about was wanting to slam my knuckles into the face of the asshole who dared to talk disrespectfully about Olivia. The asshole who treated her like shit for years.

"Fuck," I groan, running my hand through my hair. "I'm sorry you have to deal with this shit."

Olivia huffs out another heavy sigh. "You should've just ignored him. It doesn't matter what he says."

"Baby, I wish I could do every single thing you'd ever ask me to do," I say. "But ignoring someone talking about you the way he did? I'm sorry, that's one thing I'll never be able to do. Even if you made me promise, that's the one promise I'd have to break."

"Why?" she demands. "What does it matter?"

"*Why?* Because I love you."

Everything goes silent and still. It doesn't even feel like the molecules in the air are moving. Olivia doesn't move a muscle, and neither do I. Beats of time tick by without either of us taking a breath.

In this long, drawn-out moment of silence, I feel a heavy weight that I didn't even know I was carrying slip off my shoulders.

I may have uttered those words totally spur of the moment, without even thinking, not even fully realizing what I was saying as they tumbled out of my mouth. But every single syllable was nothing but the truth.

I love Olivia. Maybe this wasn't the right way to say it for the first time, but I don't regret that I did. If I could turn back time and take those words back, I wouldn't.

"Tuck ..." she says my name like it's a question. "You can't be in love with me."

My brow furrows. "Well, that's an interesting theory you've got there, Olivia. The problem with it is that I *am*."

Her arms fold over her chest, like she's closing herself off. "We hardly know each other. We've only been together for a couple weeks." I can't tell if she's saying those words to me, or to herself.

I shake my head. "I first met you five months ago, Olivia. From that very moment, I haven't thought about another woman. Every single day, I've only thought about *you*. I think five months is long enough to fall in love."

"But that's ..."

I cut her off, because there's a question I can't go another second without asking. "Do you love me?"

Her mouth opens. It stays open as time ticks by. Then it closes. My gaze holds her, our eyes tethered silently.

One fact blares loud in my mind: she didn't say *No*.

"I love you, Olivia," I repeat, because I want to say it again so fucking bad. "I've known you long enough to know that. And that's not going to change any time soon."

Olivia breaks my gaze, turning her head downward and to the side. She shakes her head. "This is too much right now. I need some space."

My chest clenches painfully. I can't say I ever had a specific fantasy of what it would be like the first time I tell Olivia that I love her, but it at least would have included her saying it back.

Still, I take a deep breath and try to push out the negative feelings. I can tell this has been a rough day for Olivia. Her having to see that piece of shit ex of hers. Me doing something that's now made it even harder for her to forget him and move on. And then I come over and drop this bomb on her.

It's a lot to deal with. I get it. If she needs space, I'll give it to her for now. But no matter how much space is between us, I'll still be loving her.

"You need space, fine," I say. "But don't think I didn't mean what I said. Don't think that those were just words I spewed out without knowing what I was saying. I love you, Olivia."

Then I give her the space she asked for, hoping like hell that next time I see her, she's ready to tell me she feels the same way I do.

43

OLIVIA

There's a tinge of unreality hanging over everything when I wake up Sunday morning. Sitting up in my bed, I ask myself, could the last forty-eight hours really have happened the way I remember them?

The thing I'd been dreading finally happened: Tuck and my ex faced off on the ice. They got into a massive fight. Then the next night, they got into a bigger fight, with their whole teams. The entire campus started buzzing with rumors about why, placing myself and my relationship with Ryan right in the middle of a story that's attracting national media attention. Then Tuck told me he loves me—and I told him I need space.

I let myself fall backward into my pillow like I'm tumbling off a cliff. A long, heavy sigh slides out of me. The seconds tick by as I'm flat on my back, staring up at the blank white ceiling of my room.

What a fucking weekend.

Tuck told me he loves me.

The memory of his words laces through me. Instantly, a

bright, warm feeling hums through my veins. But it doesn't last long. It's quickly replaced—by fear.

The emotion grips my chest, its sharp talons digging into my heart.

After Ryan, I promised myself I'd never let another man wrap me around his finger like he had.

Remembering those three words on Tuck's lips, spoken in his honey-infused drawl, while his blue eyes held my own, I know that Tuck could have me wrapped around his fingers. He could hold my heart in the palm of his hand. I could fall for him so much harder than I ever fell for Ryan. Because Tuck is a thousand times the man my ex was or ever will be.

I finally haul myself out of bed. As I walk downstairs and make myself a pot of coffee, there are so many thoughts bouncing around in my head that I can't grab onto any one of them and actually think it through.

I take my cup of coffee to the living room couch and plop down on it. I'm glad Summer spent the night with Hudson, because right now I just need time alone to marinate in all this before I try and talk it out with anyone.

I'm not totally alone, though. Salsa hops onto the couch and curls herself next to me.

"Morning, girl," I say, running my palm down her luxurious coat. "You ever have a guy confess his love for you way, way, *way* sooner than you were ready for it?"

She tilts her little cat head to me. "Meow," is her wise response.

I slouch against the back cushion. "Yeah. Good point."

My gaze crawls to the seat where Tuck sat when he took care of me when I was sick.

My chest squeezes. I realize that I miss Tuck right now.

Missing a guy I just saw *last night* isn't a good sign if I'm trying to convince myself it's too soon to be in love with him.

Is it too soon?

Things with Tuck were going so well, and it was so new. We were having a great time together, not to mention sex so mind-blowing I never would have thought it was possible. Why did things have to suddenly get so damn complicated so soon?

Part of me wishes Tuck wouldn't give me the space I asked for.

Part of me wishes he was knocking on my door right now, demanding to be let in, that he'd tell me he loves me again, his blue gaze boring into my eyes, daring me to tell him that I *don't* love him back.

Would I be able to do it? Would I be able to tell him I don't love him?

I'm pretty sure I know the answer to that question, and it makes my stomach twist into the biggest, tightest knot of anxiety that I've ever felt.

I think back to the last time I was in love—or, what I thought was love. With Ryan. I think about the person it made me: dependent, needy, easy to take advantage of. I promised myself I'd never let another man turn me into that person again.

Ever since then, I've thought of it as a strength, the walls I've put up around my heart to keep anyone from touching it.

But maybe real strength is accepting the possibility of being hurt, but still opening your heart to someone you dare to trust.

Opening yourself up to heartbreak, because the reward, someone who will hold your heart in the palm of their hand

and never dare to crush it, is so great it's worth any of the pain you might feel or mistakes you might make while you're looking for that person.

I spend most of the day watching mindless videos on my laptop. Summer comes back later in the afternoon, and she can tell that I'm not in the mood to talk things out yet. So, she just sits on the couch next to me and we watch mindless videos together, laughing. It's just what I need right now.

Late that evening, Tuck texts me.

> **TUCK**
> Hope you had a good day. Sebastian made us watch a long, boring Russian movie. I bet you'd have liked it. Just couldn't get through the day without texting you. Good night.

On Monday, I have a full day of classes and then rehearsal at the theatre in Burlington. It gives me a good excuse to turn down Tuck when he texts asking if I want to get dinner.

The gears are still turning in my head about what Tuck said to me. I think I know how I feel about it. I think I know what my response is going to be. But I just need more time to marinate. Or maybe what I need more time for is to build up my courage.

On Tuesday, when I'm sitting in my second class waiting for the professor to arrive, a girl who's also in the class approaches me.

"Hey," she says, getting my attention. I look up to see her wearing an amused grin. "That guy asked me to give this to you."

She hands me a folded-up piece of paper and then nods her head towards the door. I look over my shoulder to see

Tuck standing there. My heart leaps into my throat seeing him after a couple days. That scruffy hair, those oceans of blue that are his eyes.

I unfold the note. *Hope this is enough space. Still love you btw.* The message is scrawled in his sloppy handwriting, and he's drawn a big heart on the bottom of the page.

I lift my head to look at him again, and he just waves at me with the biggest grin on his face before walking down the hall.

My chest thrums with warmth for the whole class.

Later, in the afternoon, I'm waiting in line for a coffee at Brumehill Brews, when a guy comes up to me.

"Excuse me," he says. He holds something out to me. "That guy out there asked me to come in and give you this."

Sure enough, when I follow the direction of his nod towards the glass doors of the café, I see Tuck standing on the other side. A boyish grin is carving his dimples deep on his stubble-covered cheeks.

My chest flutters. I unfold the note.

In case you were wondering, I haven't stopped loving you since I wrote that first note this morning. In fact, I love you more. See the drawing below for proof.

This time there are three hearts drawn below the message. The first one has *this morning* written under it. The second heart is bigger and has *now* written under it. The third is even bigger and has *tomorrow* written under it.

Tears prick at the edges of my eyes at the same time as I breathe out a laugh and shake my head. It's so silly, so sincere, so sweet, and so Tuck.

Giving up my spot in line, I walk outside to where Tuck's standing, not even sure what I'm going to say when I get there.

Something sparks inside me when I'm in front of him, looking up into the bright blues of his eyes. It hits me how much I've missed him, even over less than three days, so much that I've been carrying an ache in my chest that I've grown used to.

"Finally had enough of all that *space*?" Tuck asks, his cocky, knowing, teasing drawl filling me with warmth.

I roll my eyes. "Tuck," I say his name as an admonishment, but we both know there's no bite to it. Especially since the edges of my mouth are pulling up.

"Hey, Olivia," Tuck says, a quick, upward lilt to his voice like he just realized something he needs to tell me.

"What?"

He waits a beat. "I love you."

Happiness hums through my blood as he looks down on me with that grin of his. "So I've heard."

"Say it."

I roll my eyes. "Say what?"

He places the tip of his finger at the edge of my jaw, just below my ear. Sparks skitter over me as he lightly drags it across the edge of my jaw, down to my chin, which he captures between his forefinger and his thumb, the tip of that thumb grazing below my bottom lip.

"You know you want to."

The truth of his words spears through me, and I can't even play coy anymore.

"I love you, Tuck."

His eyes flash, like he loved hearing those words even more than he expected to. I know I loved saying them even more than I expected to. Then, his lips are pressed to mine.

I moan with relief into his mouth. His taste, his smell, the gentle firmness of his lips caressing mine—I've missed him so much, and it's only been a couple days.

I relax into his body, leaning against his hard torso as he slants our kiss deeper, so deep that I drown in it, lost in his touch and his smell and his warmth and happy to stay lost there.

It wasn't hard to tell Tuck that I love him. It felt right. It felt safe. And when Tuck wraps his arms around me and pulls me closer, I realize nothing has felt as right, as safe, as this does.

Tuck's crooked grin and warm eyes are beaming at me when we part, both of us breathing heavy from the kiss.

"I have a scandalous proposition," he drawls. The mischievous glimmer dancing in his eyes is just one of the so many things I love about this man.

"Do tell," I say, through giggles.

"How about we skip our next class and go back to my place?"

"I love that idea almost as much as I love you."

Those words fill his eyes with a flash of intensity, and before I know it, he's dipping down to scoop me up in his arms and walking me across campus to his house, all while I'm giggling like a nut and he's kissing me every couple steps.

"I love you," I say again, later, in Tuck's bed, with my head resting on his bare chest, utterly spent and satisfied.

"Love you too, Lockley," he replies, planting a kiss on the top of my head.

A swoony sigh swooshes from my lips. "I don't think I'll ever get tired of hearing that."

His chest rumbles with laughter. "I'll put that to the test, Lockley. Don't tempt me."

I lift my head to look at him. "Hey, Tuck?"

"Yeah?"

"Now I've got a scandalous proposition."

His brow bounces. "I like the sound of this."

"Let's skip our *next* class, too."

I squeal in delight as Tuck flips me onto my back and covers me with his body.

We spend the rest of the day proving just *how* much we love each other.

44

OLIVIA

"This is long overdue," Tuck says.

"Are you sure we can't put it off a little longer?" I ask, my voice warbly with nerves.

"Absolutely, positively sure." He steps backward, placing his skates on the ice. I still stand just at the threshold of the rink, my hands in his.

The last time I tried to rollerblade, which was about eleven years ago, it took me a minute and a half to fall, skin my elbow, and smack my chin right on the asphalt in front of my friend Cassidy's house.

I'm not athletically inclined, okay? And just think of how much harder ice skating must be than rollerblading!

"Come on, Lockley," Tuck says, that signature mixture of teasing and encouragement in his voice. "You can do anything, so you can sure as hell do *this*."

I take a deep breath and place my right skate on the ice.

"Halfway there," Tuck coaxes.

I narrow my eyes on him, and he throws his head back with a laugh. After another long, fortifying breath, I squeeze

Tuck's hands extra tight and set my left skate down on the ice.

"Break a leg," Tuck says with a wink.

"Not funny," I grouse, beaming a scowl at him. Tuck's booming laugh in response, however, says we differ on that point.

"Just hold on," Tuck says. He skates backward, and I bend my knees, trying to keep stabilized as he pulls me along with him. "See? Not so hard."

I straighten my knees a little bit, trying to get my bearings on these thin metal blades. Tuck coaches me on how to push off with one skate and glide forward on the other, and soon enough, I'm tentatively skating forward while he's skating backward, our hands clasped together, both of us moving around the rink as one.

"Fuck, Olivia," Tuck says, his voice suddenly heavy with awe. "Your eyes."

"My eyes?" I ask. I blink. "What about them?"

He turns one of his blades, bringing him to a sudden stop. I keep gliding forward, straight into his chest. He wraps his arms around me and looks down at me, his gaze hooded and boring into my own.

"Did you know that the human eye can see more shades of green than any other color?" he asks.

"No," I shake my head.

"That fact feels like a gift from the universe to me. No matter what color your eyes were, I'd never get tired of looking at them. But the fact that every time I look in your eyes, I'll see more shades, more specks of color, than I would in anyone else's, that just feels like fate winking at me for falling for the right girl."

Tuck's lips close over mine, and I kiss him with the thrill of knowing that we have a lifetime of kisses ahead of us.

EPILOGUE
TUCK

When Olivia takes her bow with the rest of the cast, I'm on my feet, cheering myself hoarse, clapping my hands so hard that my palms sting.

The Champlain Theatre Company just finished its third night of Macbeth, with Olivia in the co-starring role.

The first night, Summer and Hudson were here with me. The second night, just Summer and me. The third night, I'm the last man standing.

That's how it's going to be. I'll always be here in the audience to support Olivia. I know it'll never happen, but if she ever performs in front of an audience of only one, that one person will be me, cheering and clapping loud enough to make up for everyone too stupid to realize what they're missing out on.

Seeing Olivia put on three awe-inspiring performances in a packed Burlington theatre house is just the bright spot that I need right now, because this last month has been rough.

We made it to the finals of the Frozen Four. The Brumehill Black Bears vs. the Minnesota Monarchs. We skated out onto the ice feeling like we were on top of the world, feeling supremely confident after a dominant performance throughout the tournament.

Then, in the middle of the first period, Lane got tripped. He stuck out his right leg to try to keep his balance. The front of his blade snagged on the ice at the worst angle possible, and he broke his leg as he fell.

We had to play the rest of the game without our team captain, none of us able to stop worrying about him as he was transported to the hospital. We lost 1-4.

Our concern for Lane numbed the disappointment of losing the championship we spent all season dreaming of, almost *expecting* to hoist over our heads, like it was the only plausible ending to this season.

That disappointment came later, though.

Lane's leg is still in rough shape. His ability to play next year is in question, and he's taking it ... not too good.

I shake off those thoughts. So much of my mental space recently has been taken up by worry and concern for my teammate and one of my best friends, but right now I just want to be fully present for Olivia.

When I find her backstage after the show, I gather her in my arms and plant a big, firm kiss on her lips with all the excitement and pride I had on opening night.

"Are you really going to come to every single night?" Olivia asks through giggles.

I give her a firm, appreciative pat on her behind. "You bet your sweet ass I am." I know she's rolling her eyes—but also blushing—when I sling my arm over her shoulders and walk her to the parking garage.

We drove to Burlington separately. Just being apart from

her in my car on the drive home sucks, even though she's right behind me.

I wish she were sitting next to me right now so I could serenade her with another Taylor Swift concert. She's even started to join in and sing along with me when we ride together.

Close to Cedar Shade, on the densely forested roads away from the lights of the capital city, I drive up the crest of the hill, and suddenly my breath catches at the most stunning view of the night sky, bright with stars.

I activate my turn signal to pull onto a wide berth on the side of the road that's been carved out of the forest for roadside stops. I roll down my window and signal for Olivia to pull over, too. We come to a stop just at the beginning of the downward slope of the crest. Ahead of us is a stunning view of the night sky over the tree cover.

"What's wrong?" Olivia asks as we both step out of our driver's side doors.

"Nothing," I say. I sweep my hand upward and across, gesturing to the sky. "Look. It's beautiful."

Tonight is the warmest night of the year so far. The air feels soft and mild, the breeze a gentle caress. What makes it even better is that it's still just chilly enough for Olivia to have changed into one of my Brumehill Black Bears hoodies that she's pilfered from my room.

Seeing my girl wearing something of mine is never not going to make my chest pound.

I round to the front of my car and wave for her to join me. We hop onto the hood and shimmy back, leaning against my windshield and gazing up into the star-scattered sky.

She snuggles into the crook of my arm.

"Have you ever been good at spotting constellations?" I ask.

"Nope. Couldn't even tell you where the Big Dipper is."

"Let's make our own, then."

I spread my legs, and she positions herself between them, her back against my chest. I dip down so that our eyes are level, and I take hold of her hand, lifting it with mine so we can trace the stars together.

"See?" I say, tracing out a sloppy outline of a cat in the pinpricks of silver light. "There's Salsa."

She laughs, the vibration of it feeling so good with her flush against me. She twists her hand so now her dainty palm is clasping the back of mine, and now it's her turn to trace.

"And there's you," she says, "sneezing when she jumps onto your lap."

I sling my free arm around her waist, pulling her tight against me as I laugh. "How many stars did it take to make that?"

"Seventeen," she says, pulling a number out of thin air.

I don't know how much time we spend just sitting on the hood of my car, gazing at the sky, cuddling together and laughing as we pretend to trace increasingly intricate and ridiculous shapes in the stars.

Olivia guides my hand through an arcing zigzag that isn't even pretending to follow the stars anymore. "That's you when you're singing Taylor Swift songs in the shower."

I guide her hand, tracing out letters in the stars.

M is first.

Then *I*.

Then *N*.

Then *E*.

Olivia turns to me, her brow crinkled. "*Mine?*"

"Yeah," I say. "That's you. Every damn day for the rest of our lives."

My lips feather onto hers, and I kiss my girlfriend as she wears my hoodie, under the star-lit sky, sitting on the hood of my car by the side of the road on a beautiful early Spring night.

I don't know how things could possibly get better than this. But knowing that I've got a lifetime with Olivia ahead of me, I'm pretty sure I'm going to find out.

∽

Want more of Tuck and Olivia? Click the link below!
Click here to sign up for my newsletter and get a FREE Bonus Scene!

I HOPE you enjoyed getting to know Tuck and Olivia as much as much as I did while I was writing them! Ever since I introduced them and their push-and-pull dynamic in Hudson's and Summer's book, I've been so excited to sink my teeth into their story, and I love how it turned out! More books for the rest of the team are coming soon!

Click the link above to read a BONUS CHAPTER checking in on Tuck and Olivia a couple years into their post-colleges lives. It features both their POVs and two spicy scenes, so don't miss out!

ALSO BY LYSSA LEMIRE

Have you read Hudson's and Summer's story yet? Check out the first book in SIN BIN STORIES!

OFFSIDE PLAY: A Grumpy Sunshine Hockey Romance

Check out Lyssa's first hockey romance series, HOT SHOTS!

FIRST SCORE: An Opposites Attract Sports Romance

How to finally lose my v-card without catching feelings? Choose the one guy I could *never* fall for.

TRICK SHOT: A Best Friends to Lovers Sports Romance

When I need a fake fiancée, my best friend Abby seems like the safe choice. But I should have known there's nothing more dangerous than pretending to love your best friend – after you realize *pretending* isn't enough.

ROUGH PLAY: An Enemies to Lovers Sports Romance

Kissing the guy I hate was a mistake. Falling in love with him will be a catastrophe.

OWN GOAL: A Brother's Best Friend Sports Romance

There's no one more off-limits than my best friend's little sister —and there's no one I want more.

SIN BIN SITUATION: An Enemies to Lovers Sports Romance

He's everything I hate about hockey players. And now he's my new roommate.

PENALTY BOX PROPOSAL: A Coach's Daughter Sports Romance

She's the coach's daughter. Totally off limits. But for her, I'll break any rule.

OVERTIME SCORE: An Enemies to Lovers Sports Romance

He's a cocky hockey player. I'm a bookish figure skater.

We've hated each other for most of our lives—so why did I just wake up in his bed?

∼

Check out Lyssa's debut sports romance series, *Kings of Campus*!

Off Sides: An Enemies to Lovers Sports Romance

Sage Ryker is every girl's fantasy. And my nightmare.

Fake It For Now: A Fake Relationship Sports Romance

My game plan for the last semester of college was simple: stay away from Noah Brighton. So why am I introducing him to my family as the love of my life?

Hate You Still: An Enemies to Lovers Sports Romance

Let's play two truths and a lie.

Knox Delton broke my heart. I hate Knox Delton with every fiber of my being. I never want to see Knox Delton again. *Can you spot the lie?*

ABOUT THE AUTHOR

Lyssa loves telling stories with hunky heroes and spunky heroines, who might be just a little bit flawed, maybe a little bit broken, but whose jagged edges fit each other just right to create a happily ever after.

Lyssa can be contacted by email at:
   LyssaLemire@gmail.com

Printed in Great Britain
by Amazon